DIFFERENT STROKES

'I've never stolen before. I swear it! Only my sister's birthday is next week and I wanted to get her something really special.'

'One of my handstitched belts,' said the man, shaking his head sadly. 'It's only fitting that I try it out on your arse.'

She'd never been beaten before, but the spanking had left her with a not-unpleasant tingling. Maybe a taste of the belt wouldn't hurt too much? Laura held her breath.

'Lie on your tummy, then raise your skirts again,' said the boutique owner, flicking the belt down experimentally on the bed.

This time there were no panties to come down.

'How many?' Laura asked tremulously, once again pushing away her skirt to bare her helpless bottom.

'How many do you think you deserve?'

'Six,' she said, burying her face in her hands.

'Six on the bare – that seems fitting.'

By the same author:

THE TRAINING GROUNDS
SERVING TIME
LINGERING LESSONS

Other Nexus Classics:

AGONY AUNT
THE INSTITUTE
THE HANDMAIDENS
HIS MISTRESS'S VOICE
BOUND TO SERVE
BOUND TO SUBMIT
SISTERHOOD OF THE INSTITUTE
THE PLEASURE PRINCIPLE
CONDUCT UNBECOMING
CITADEL OF SERVITUDE
THE DUNGEONS OF LIDIR
SERVING TIME
THE TRAINING GROUNDS
LINGERING LESSONS   *October*
EDEN UNVEILED   *November*

A NEXUS CLASSIC

DIFFERENT STROKES

Sarah Veitch

This book is a work of fiction.
In real life, make sure you practise safe sex.

First published in 1995 by
Nexus
Thames Wharf Studios
Rainville Road
London W6 9HA

This Nexus Classic edition 2000

Typeset by TW Typesetting, Plymouth, Devon

Printed and bound by Omnia Books Ltd

ISBN 0 352 33531 9

Contents

Versions of some of the following stories originally appeared in *Erotic Stories*, *Forum*, *Cul d'Or* and *Moonglow Courier*.

Work Fulfilment

'So, we want something really sexy for our Spanking Summer Special,' the editor said. 'Susie – maybe you could interview that couple who've set up an adult schoolgirls' gym?'

Susie gulped and nodded. 'Consider it done.'

A freelance journalist, she had recently been interviewing more and more S&M devotees, slowly moving away from the consumer writing with which she was bored. Usually she just faxed her work to various London offices, but now she'd been invited to this launch meeting of *Chastened Rear*.

Susie licked her lips. She'd met lots of magazine staff before, but never those involved in editing a corporal punishment journal! Forcing aside her shyness, she glanced up. 'Do you want me to ask the gym about lesbian spanking, touch your toes correction by a schoolmaster, bare bottom sessions or . . .'

'Yes, yes and yes!' the bearded editor said.

Susie felt Jon, the artist, assessing her. She looked over and saw deep brown eyes and thick dark hair. She studied his nonchalant, tall firmly muscled body, thighs in black cords . . . But she was a married woman, she reminded herself, and a faithful one. She looked away and relaxed as the editor tilted his chair towards the artist.

'Jon – the adult schoolgirls don't want to be photographed, so we'll be using you to illustrate Susie's work. We want something a bit teasing, like a girl bending over a set of climbing bars.'

'Shorts down?' Jon asked.

'Half down,' said the editor after a pause, 'so that the crack of her arse is visible, but the reader wishes he or she could see more.'

'A reddened arse?' asked Jon.

'Very,' the editor said.

There was a heavy silence in the room. Susie held her breath and felt desire rush through her. Already her crotch felt swollen and pulsed lightly. Her breasts tingled at the tips.

'Name your deadline,' said Jon.

Susie couldn't help but like him. Their work was such that they could compliment each other. It felt right.

At last the meeting ended. In the corridor outside it seemed a foregone conclusion that Jon would approach her.

'I'm Jon Elsdon.'

'Susie Simmons.'

His grip was measured yet strong.

'As I'm to illustrate your work,' he added, letting go of each finger with obvious reluctance, 'we should arrange to meet.'

She nodded, forcing herself to make eye contact.

'I'm . . . really flexible.'

A mischievous smile flitted over his face. His eyes said 'Oh?' but his voice spoke of his diary; of other business obligations.

Susie got her own engagements book out, and a few moments later they fixed a date.

'That's the when. Now for the where,' said Jon.

'Not my place. My husband works from home too,' said Susie quickly. 'Not that I won't tell him about this, of course – but it's easier to talk with no one else around.'

'Make it my studio then,' Jon murmured. 'It's attached to our house, but my wife's out during the day.'

No wife. No husband. No editor or secretary to take minutes. As Susie entered Jon's studio ten days later she was hugely aware that they were tantalisingly, forbiddingly alone. Her husband, Sheldon, liked her to meet male colleagues at local restaurants. She'd given him the impression

2

she was meeting Jon for lunch. So what? It was a small lie. A safe lie. They wouldn't actually do anything wrong . . .

'Can I get you anything? Tea? Coffee? Mineral water?' asked Jon, showing her round the large sunlit studio. It held a long low couch, a canvas-filled easel and a mahogany desk. Susie shook her head.

'Business beckons!' She took a deep breath. 'You got the manuscript I sent you?'

Jon nodded, then inclined his thumb towards the easel. 'The results are over there.'

Wincing at the uneven tap, tap, tap of her heels on the lino, Susie walked round to the front of the canvas, then felt her tummy turn over as she saw the lust and torment competing for supremacy on the girl's face.

And her body! The way the hips jutted out as she was held across the padded gym horse! The way he'd got the parallel marks left by a stick or a cane. Throughout their marriage, her own husband had only ever spanked her with his hand, so she couldn't be sure how other implements looked and felt. But as a turn-on this picture was just right.

'I don't think I've got the curve of her belly against the bolster exactly as it should be,' Jon murmured, coming to stand behind her. 'My wife Josephine usually poses, but as we've been arguing a lot . . .'

'Oh, I'm sorry to hear that,' said Susie, realising she wasn't at all sorry really. 'As she'd be struggling to rise, maybe her stomach should be a bit more arched.'

'Like . . .?' Jon walked over to the desk and laid his top half across it, then attempted to pull back. 'My physique's too male, alas. Perhaps you'd . . .?'

Susie took a step back.

'Oh! I don't think . . .'

'I could return the compliment,' said Jon. 'You know, show you how to improve the physiological aspects of your work.'

'Such as?' Susie recognised she was playing for time.

'Such as my illustrating how high you can handcuff someone's wrists behind their back without exerting undue pull on the upper arms.'

3

'That would be useful,' Susie admitted. 'I've tried gagging myself and tying myself up for research purposes, but there are limits to figuring exactly how the interviewee felt.' She paused and managed a short shrill laugh. 'Oh, what the hell! I'll try anything once. After all, we're a team.'

'A *Chastened Rear* team,' Jon said quietly as she lowered herself over the desk, and Susie's mons almost moaned.

On their next meeting he showed her his painting of a seventeenth-century maid, forced to raise her skirts for a birching.

'You were great on the painter's motivation, but you didn't describe the actual birch very well, Susie,' he said.

Susie sucked in her breath. 'The fantasy artist I interviewed was still painting the birch into his picture when I called. I've . . . I've never actually seen one up close.'

'Really? Then your education is sorely lacking. We can soon remedy that,' Jon said in a light clear tone. She looked at his slightly pursed lips. They were ironic, faintly mocking. But his pupils were dilated with desire.

Leaving her by the easel, he walked over to the desk and pulled something from a lower drawer. Susie felt the blood rush to her sex lips, felt her clitoris shudder with pleasure and sudden need. A birch! He was bringing over a birch! A birch that could be used on a recalcitrant arse the way that it had been used on the girl in the picture. A birch to make her beg and make her wet and make her want to come.

'The artist said that a real girl would cry out from the first stroke,' Susie said. 'Do you think that's realistic?'

'We could put it to the test,' Jon replied.

Susie half shook her head.

'I can't see how . . .'

'I think you owe it to your writing. I mean, if you were shy I could just birch you over your pants.'

'I suppose . . . I suppose it would be a form of investigative journalism,' she murmured hesitantly, hearing the lie but ignoring it.

'Very investigative,' echoed Jon, leading her over to the desk and lifting her skirts to expose her brief-clad arse.

They weren't doing anything wrong, Susie told herself

4

afterwards, going home with her birched bum to fuck Sheldon until her crotch was crimson. She was sure their work sessions made Jon shaft Josephine with equal fervour, so that was all right.

For the next four months they met fortnightly, and she showed him how a girl looked draped over a chair, on her hands and knees, stretched up on tiptoe. And he told or showed her how to write realistically about the clink of the cuffs or the swish of the cane.

Then another magazine, *Disciplined!*, commissioned some work from Susie, and for the first time she got behind with a *Chastened Rear* interview piece.

'I've been watching the post for days,' Jon grumbled to her on the phone when her usual manuscript failed to appear. 'Well, just bring along what you've done next week.'

'Sure. Yeah. I'll be organised by then,' said Susie, anxious to get back to her *Disciplined!* feature. 'It'll be worth the wait.'

The day arrived, and she left her word processor at the last moment and flagged down a taxi to take her to Jon's studio.

'Let's see it,' he said, as she rushed in through the door. He looked angry, edgy. Walking up to the easel she saw that it was blank.

'Aren't you working on anything?'

'Like what?'

'Well, for some other magazine?'

'Any suggestions?' Jon asked coolly.

'I've been doing masses of stuff for *Disciplined!*,' Susie said.

There was a pause. A rather long pause.

'How did you swing *that*? I sent them my portfolio months ago,' Jon muttered.

'*They* contacted *me*,' Susie said.

'And you didn't think to mention me?'

'I didn't know that you needed the extra work,' Susie returned defensively.

'Well, you know I need *this* work 'cos I phoned you. Let's see it!' Jon said.

Susie gulped. 'Well ... uh, *Disciplined!* wanted a third major feature, and they pay double what *Chastened Rear* does, so I gave them priority.'

'What *have* you got for me?' Jon asked. He grabbed the clipboard from her. 'Is this it?'

In pen Susie had scrawled the words: *Find S/M Club with Role Playing evening. Illustration – slave girl over her master's knee?*

'Call this team-work?' asked Jon. 'You're just not trying!'

'I thought you could use your imagination,' Susie quipped. She smiled up at him, but his eyes were fixed, ungiving.

'Oh, I intend to, my dear,' he said.

He took both of her slender wrists in one large firm hand.

'What are you doing?' Susie muttered. It came out sounding faint, apologetic, scared.

'What does it look like?' Jon asked coldly.

She shook her head and said nothing. She felt weak. She stared at the floor, not really seeing it, and let him lead her silently over to the chair.

He sat down, still holding her in front of him.

'I'm about to teach you a lesson.'

Susie opened her mouth, then closed it again. Her legs shook.

'The slave goes over her master's knee,' Jon added, pulling her over, over, over, transferring both her wrists to one hand whilst he used the other to put pressure on the small of her back.

'Research!' yelped Susie with a breathless giggle.

'Oh no,' said Jon grimly. 'You've earned a damn good thrashing for screwing me about so much. This is for real.'

Holding her down with his left hand, he used the right to push up her skirt and pull down her pants, exposing her defenceless bottom.

Susie closed her eyes and tensed her buttocks. Jon's hand slapped down.

'Ouch! That really hurt!'

6

She was still half-expecting him to stop, to go back to their project. Instead his palm lashed her other bottom cheek.

Susie drummed the toes of her high-heeled shoes on the ground, realising that a straight-legged spanking was much more painful than the ones her husband gave her whilst she lay face down on the mattress. Like this she felt humiliated. Jon was examining her blushing buttocks and noting the way they warmed and flinched.

She whimpered and writhed as the spanking continued; she tried to scrabble from his lap but he held her in place and slapped harder. She could feel his hard promise digging into her belly and knew that her passion passage was wet, wet, wet.

'Such a bad little slave, disobeying her master's orders,' murmured Jon, stopping to palm her glowing posterior. 'So wilful.'

'I could phone you tomorrow with the details you need!' Susie said.

'Tomorrow? Oh, I don't think you'll be able to sit down to dial by tomorrow.'

'Today, then. Now! I could phone that couple I interviewed last time. They'll know of a dungeon-style club! They'll get me in!'

'I'll think about it,' said Jon, stroking her wriggling rear. 'You still have to be punished, though.'

'Not like this,' whispered Susie. 'Please.'

'Why not like this?'

'I . . . I feel so silly!'

'But you *are* silly. Silly and wicked and in need of the kind of spanking that'll make you beg.'

He lifted his hand and brought it down full-force again. It stung even more after the much-needed hiatus. Susie yelled. She hoped Jon's studio was soundproofed. She hoped Josephine wouldn't return.

'What if your wife . . .?' she gasped.

'She's in Birmingham for the day. A conference.' He paused. 'As for your husband . . . I wonder what Sheldon will say when he sees this chastised little rear end?'

7

'He – I can keep it hidden from him,' muttered Susie. She moaned as Jon ran an exploratory finger over the crease where arse met thigh. 'He works long hours. We usually make love late at night in the dark. He'll never know.'

'Unless I tell him,' whispered Jon. 'Unless I send him a drawing of you bent over my knee with your reddened rump raised for my inspection.'

'You wouldn't!' Susie breathed.

'Why wouldn't I? Ask nicely for twenty more spanks and I'll consider being merciful,' Jon said.

'Please give me twenty more spanks,' Susie repeated tonelessly.

'Please, *Master*, give me twenty more hard spanks on my unruly little posterior,' Jon corrected. Susie echoed his words. She let her head hang nearer to the floor as shame and desire swelled through her, sweeping through her lower belly and her lust-streaked thighs.

After ten more spanks she was promising him anything. After twenty she meant it. He pushed her from his knees and on to hers.

'Make amends,' he said.

'Yes, Master.'

Flushing further, Susie unzipped him, eased his trousers down, took his thick hard cock from its prison and licked the tip. Jon closed his eyes. Susie opened her mouth and fed the first two inches in.

'Christ – you give great head!' muttered Jon.

Susie sucked harder at his shaft, then brought her lips up over the top before tonguing down to the root then back again.

'I want to be inside you,' Jon moaned.

'I want you inside me,' Susie said.

'Bend over the desk,' he muttered.

Susie stook up shakily, and started to smooth her skirt down. 'No, hold it up round your waist. Keep your knickers at your ankles.' He watched as she shuffled to the desk. 'Now bend right over. That's it, backside up. Grip the drawer handles at the other side.'

Susie did so, too far gone to care how she looked. Correction: *excited* by how she looked and how she felt.

'Such a pretty picture,' Jon said mockingly.

Susie closed her eyes, her sex lips saturated with shame.

'Ask nicely for my cock,' he instructed, approaching her and putting his helmet at the entrance to her hat box.

'Please . . .' Susie said.

'Please what?'

'Please put it in me now.'

'Please put your cock in my greedy little fanny, Master,' Jon corrected, with a sneer in his voice.

'Damn you! I won't say it!' Susie muttered, a little of her former spirit re-asserting itself.

'Oh, you wish to damn me, do you?'

Jon's fingers slid between her parted thighs to find her contact-craving clitoris.

'Yes! No! Oh God, that's too much . . . Don't stop. Aaah! Please!'

Jon took his hands from the hungry bud, played around near the hood, slicked a finger down her inner lips.

'Say sorry, little slave girl.'

'Sorry. Really sorry. Please, Master, please!'

'Please what?'

'Please fuck me!'

'Why should I fuck you?'

'Let me come!'

'My dear girl, this act is for *my* pleasure – not for yours.'

'I know! I . . . I'll be so tight for you. I'll suck my juices from you afterwards. I'll swallow all your come.'

'I suppose I may as well fuck you now that you're here,' said Jon coolly, pushing forward into her aching quim.

Susie gasped as he filled her up, as he probed her depths and pumped her breasts, and told her what he was going to do to her. Told her what she deserved, words intended to ignite.

'Ask nicely for each thrust,' he grunted, moving his hard hips skilfully.

'Oh, please!' Susie whimpered, aware that her normally large vocabulary had shrunk to this one pleading word.

Her tummy and her more tender bits were rubbing against the desk top. Her arse was being slapped by the insistent surge of his taut belly, his right hand still gently caressing her throbbing clit.

'Beg for it,' he murmured throatily.

'I can't . . .'

'I think I'll stop. I think I'm bored with fucking you.'

He stopped shafting her and partially withdrew, circling his body lightly so that the tip of his cock still teased.

'Please let me come,' Susie begged.

He rammed forward another ten or twelve times and she forced her arse further back against him as the waves of shrieking satiating pleasure coursed through.

He kept thrusting, kept talking dirty. She came again, fingers convulsively closing on the drawer handles, crying out into the polished wood. Then Jon groaned loudly and called out her name and strained into her and they lay over the desk, breathing hard.

'I'm going to have to discipline you next week for not being respectful enough,' he murmured, sliding a sweat-slicked hand down to her still-heated buttocks. 'I may have to use my belt.'

'. . . If anyone will be using their belt, it's me!' Sheldon snapped as the tape came to an end. Josephine switched it off, and gazed angrily around Jon's empty studio.

'But surely she'd enjoy it?'

'Not if she didn't get to come at the end,' Sheldon said.

'In that case I think I know how to teach her a lesson,' murmured Josephine slowly, the focused look that signifies revenge entering her eyes.

The following week Susie let herself into Jon's house as usual.

'Down to work!' she giggled, hurrying through the partly open studio doorway. She stopped when she saw the woman. 'Oh! You must be Josephine. I've . . . er . . . got this manuscript to give to Jon.'

'I know what you've been giving Jon,' Josephine said evenly. She started to unbuckle the belt from her waist. 'Bend over the desk. I believe you enjoy it.'

'Don't be ridiculous! I . . . I won't. You can't make me!' Susie said, disbelief and panic fighting for supremacy as she backed away.

She turned to go, but found her husband blocking the door.

'How on earth . . .?' she asked faintly.

'Josephine knows Jon tends to stray. She's left her tape recorder running throughout your every meeting,' Sheldon said. He sighed. 'She contacted me after your first, uh, research session, but we let it go on till last week when you were completely unfaithful to us both.'

Put like that it sounded dreadful. Susie's legs, in their polished stilettos, felt suddenly weak. She walked towards the chair, but Josephine pulled it away and started to lead her firmly towards the desk.

'You can't! I haven't agreed to this!' Susie shouted.

'If you don't agree I'm going to send copies of this tape to every magazine you've ever worked for,' Josephine said.

Oh God, thought Susie, *anything but that.* Susie let herself be bent over the desk, felt her jeans being unzipped and pushed to her ankles, felt the other woman's hand on her briefs, edging them down till her arse was completely bare.

'What about Jon?' she asked.

'Bring him in,' Josephine told Sheldon.

Sheldon went next door and came back a moment later with Jon who was naked save for an effective-looking chastity belt around his cock.

Susie stared at him over her shoulder.

'Josephine's going to punish you once a week for a month whilst I watch,' he said wearily. 'I've to wear this bloody restrainer. It means I can't come.'

'Call the cops!' Susie said.

'And have them and the rest of the world hear me playing my Master and Slave games? You've got to be joking!' Jon sighed.

'This isn't fair,' Susie said.

She trembled as Josephine stroked her bottom, sensed that the woman had stepped back, heard the strap whizzing down.

11

'Please stop,' she yelled, knowing that her pride was hurt most by having a woman do this to her. 'I can't bear it!' she cried.

She looked to Jon for support, but he was staring from her striped sore arse to his shaft as it pulsed impotently inside the taunting restrainer.

'Nor,' he wailed, 'can I.'

Medical Intervention

He'd whipped her in a basement room. He'd been faceless, nameless. She'd stood on tiptoe, tethered to the wall, and orgasmed behind her gag. She had pulled down on the cuffs as her body convulsed with pleasure. She had heard him groan, felt his semen slick the back of her thighs. Then, footsteps faded away. A door was closing. Someone had unchained her. She'd untied the blindfold with numb fingers. She had rubbed her lids, her limbs, cupped her liquid-leaking labia, and by the time her sight adjusted to the darkness he had gone.

And she'd gone back to the daily grind first thing this morning. The daily grind! God, she had to stop thinking about pushing her still sexed-up quim against a cock. She had to cross this road – she looked at her street map for reassurance – then find the recruitment agency where she was to temp.

No cars or bikes. Shelley stepped carefully off the kerb, and took a step forward. She felt an explosion of pain at her calves and feet.

'What the . . .?'

She was thrown forward on her hands and knees into the road, her shoulder bag sent flying. Had she been mugged? She heard a female passerby's voice.

'These bloody skateboarders!'

She focused, and saw the boy lying a few yards away.

He jumped up. He sped off. She watched him through a blur of tears, pain and confusion: this wasn't the exciting asked-for pleasure-pain of last night, but an unplanned bruising ache.

'Are you all right?' Shelley could make out the outline of a woman: all shopping bag and floral head scarf. 'Lucky that there's a doctor's surgery along the way.'

A yellow stone building. A nameplate with three doctors listed. She gave the receptionist her name and explained.

'I'll leave you to it, then.'

Shelley's Good Samaritan backed off into the outside world as a surgery door swung open.

'Thanks,' Shelley smiled. 'I don't know how I would have managed without you. You've been great!'

She looked over at the doctor who was fast approaching. He had on an unbuttoned white coat, a black shirt, pressed black trousers with a thick brown belt. He stared at the long, long run in her tights.

'You've been in the wars, my dear.'

Shelley took a deep breath. 'You should see the other guy!' she quipped.

'I'll settle for examining you.'

He obviously wasn't the joking kind. She followed him into his surgery, and saw the name Dr Pearce on the door.

'Please lie flat on the couch.'

She stretched out on her back as he'd ordered, and felt his strong fingers probe the small cut in her knee.

'You'll have to take your tights off, I'm afraid.'

'Oh. Right.'

His unwavering dark eyes and neatly trimmed black hair were making it hard for her to concentrate. She sat up and edged the tan nylon down over her panties. Blood had made the material stick to her calf.

'We'll soon get you cleaned up.'

She nodded, tossed the torn ball of nylon on to the surgery floor, and laced her hands awkwardly in her lap.

Dr Pearce brought over a soaking swab and stroked her leg with it. She grimaced.

'You're not a masochist, I see!'

It was a harmless remark. Shelley shifted awkwardly. The movement sent a ripple of protest through her right thigh.

'Ouch, I think I've strained something!'

14

She rubbed beneath her skirt. The doctor pulled her hand away. 'Let me.'

She wanted to let him – God, she wanted to let him! Since last night she'd been permanently on heat. Her pubis pulsed, reliving the way the shadowy Master had held her wrists before he clipped the cuffs round them. The way he'd told her what he was going to do next . . .

'Stand up. Take your skirt off.' The doctor stood back to watch her progress. 'Put your weight on that leg. Careful! How does that feel?'

'Fine,' said Shelley, hesitantly. She felt silly standing there in just her blouse and pants.

'There should really be a female nurse present, but I wasn't planning on examining any women till later,' the GP added.

'I don't mind,' said Shelley and she closed her eyes as he put all ten fingers on her nearest thigh, probing, seeking. He had such strong firm hands . . .

'I'm checking to see if there's any sign of swelling,' he said rather obviously. Shelley looked down at him and stared in gratified surprise at the increasingly obvious swelling between his legs.

So much for medical men being neutral. Still, nothing could come of it.

'All present and correct,' he said. 'Nothing that a hot bath can't put right.'

Or a tension-killing come, Shelley thought shakily, walking past him. She'd sneak off to the Ladies after this and administer some first aid to her clit.

She bent down to retrieve her tights, belatedly aware of how her raised rump must look to him in her briefest of silk briefs.

'Oh. You're marked,' he said.

'Wh . . . where?' Even as she stammered the word, she knew the answer.

'On your ar . . . on your buttocks, my dear.'

She felt the flush start, knew her face was glowing more fully than her rear end, and concentrated on putting her torn tights into her shoulder bag.

'I must have skidded along the pavement after the skateboard hit me,' she fibbed.

'We'd better lie you on your tummy, have a look at it.'

'I don't think . . .'

'Doctor's orders.'

Her legs weakening, Shelley clambered awkwardly back on to the couch and lowered herself down till the cool leather was against her belly.

'Remove your pants for me, please.'

So cold. So clinical. She felt so hot, so wet.

'Bloody skateboarders,' she muttered, remembering the other woman's words. She screwed her eyes shut and pulled her pants down. She felt his fingers trace along the still-tingling welts.

'A little healing ointment won't hurt.'

She turned her head sideways on her folded arms and watched as he crossed the room. He was walking carefully, brick hard beneath black cotton. She wanted to touch him. Wanted him to touch her deep inside.

'Just relax.'

She tensed as his palms slid over her bum, oiling the contours. *Please*, her flesh was whispering, *slide down, slide in – just let me come!*

'Treatment complete!' said the doctor, taking his hands from her posterior. She felt a strong sense of loss.

'Now what?' She remained lying still.

'You can go to work. Just be careful. If those weals itch you can try some calamine.'

He'd been using a lubricant on her just now – wasn't calamine's effect the opposite; horribly drying? 'Correct me if I'm wrong . . .' she started.

'I'd love to,' Dr Pearce said.

Desire rushed through her and she whimpered, buffed her swelling bud against the couch and pushed her thighs together. His words had created an electric band around her aching vulval rim. He had the cure, but he was a doctor – even if he wasn't *her* doctor. He might be breaking some law if he made the first move.

Shelley sat up shakily and swung herself into a sitting

16

position. Taking a deep breath, she reached for the truncheon in his trousers and held on tight.

'Is that a probe for examining me, Dr Pearce?'

She felt the long thick tube of his tumescence. The oath he muttered was not the Hippocratic one.

'We certainly have to investigate the situation,' he said thickly, hesitantly. She put her hands on his shoulders, eyes and lips daring him to do the rest.

'Can you kiss it better, Doctor?'

'Oh, you're too big a girl for niceties like that!'

Holding her against him, he gripped her waist and lifted her down from the surgical couch. Grimly, he steered her towards the desk, bent her over it. His right hand palmed both cheeks.

'I'm a medical man who understands female flesh – these marks weren't made this morning. And they weren't caused by a fall.'

Shelley gulped. Her tits were bulging forward against her blouse. Her anus felt totally exposed to him. She wriggled against the hard wood and flexed her toes.

'What caused them, my dear?'

She shook her head. She couldn't say it.

'Where were you, then? Let's try a different tack.'

She stared at the desk. He obviously had a fair idea.

'At the Correction Club. A friend wanted to go. I . . . was curious.'

'And she whipped you?'

'No. It was a stranger – a man.'

'A stranger,' said Dr Pearce. 'Little Shelley, would you lie to a stranger?'

'No, of course not.'

'Yet you'd lie to a doctor who gives up his coffee break to help you out!'

Shelley closed her eyes.

'I'm sorry, Doctor. I was ashamed to admit what I'd been up to.'

'I'm going to *make* you sorry. I'm going to teach you not to waste a professional's time.'

Her bum was still wet with the balm – and still sore from

the previous night's lambasting. She yelled as his palm slapped one buttock, and he turned his painful attention to its twin. 'So noisy. Such a quarrelsome convalescent. Stay there or you'll get it twice as hard.'

She heard him walk away, return, felt a bandage or similar soft bond being used to bind her wrists behind her back in a praying position.

'There. Now I can concentrate on correcting your arse!'

His were not so much healing hands as wealing hands. He lashed a hard palm into her soft posterior again and again.

'We must show our respect to the doctor. We must tell him the truth at all times.'

He punctuated each half-sentence with a spank that covered alternate buttocks. Shelley squealed and thrust her sore seat forward, waiting for the moment when she could thrust her sex lips back.

'Please Doctor, I need an internal really badly,' she begged.

'You've been such a bad girl. Maybe I should give you an enema?'

Shelley swallowed.

'Maybe I should tie you up in the waiting room afterwards and warn you not to void?' He ran a thumb around her entrance. And then he stopped.

'I'll take the enema, Dr Pearce, I promise!'

'And ask me to hold you out over a potty whilst the other patients stare?'

She cried out at the thought. Not that! Oh God, but he was using his thumb to tease her clit again.

'Yes, Doctor, whatever you say!'

'Have me put diapers on you, and rubber pants, because you're behaving like a baby?'

'Yes, Doctor, yes!'

The strokes to her sex lips were making her desperate and shameless. She would say – and do – anything he asked.

'Just stick your probe up me,' she begged. 'I want it hard.'

'How hard?'

'Right up to the hilt, please.'

She wished that she wasn't tethered, and could nurse his balls with her hand.

'The patient requested a thorough going-over.' With a smile in his voice, he entered her roughly. She sighed with pleasure. Even without his stethoscope he must hear her heart hammering like mad. 'The patient squirmed a lot,' he added, sliding fingers between her drenched dusky lips, 'and had to be restrained for her own safety.'

The patient moaned with lust and bore down on his taunting hard-on and helping hand. She wanted his soft fingers, his hard cock. She wanted everything!

'The woman is in her twenties. She insisted every avenue be thoroughly explored.'

He thrust in and out as he spoke, his voice heightening when her quim gripped him especially tightly.

'I had to bring in a nurse to hold her down.'

'No. Not that!' Shelley closed her thighs tight, squeezing more pleasure from his prick with her lust-crazed contours.

'A woman to watch you taking your medicine.'

She couldn't see, couldn't think. Everything centred on her desire-distending quim.

'These panties were all wrong for a patient. We'll have to parade you in reception dressed in one of those surgical gowns.'

'But they're all open at the back!' she gasped.

'Exactly! Let the others see your chastised young cheeks, the way they glow when they've been punished.'

'They'll stare.'

'Of course they'll stare. They may even touch you. May have a few home remedies of their own.'

'I'll let them feel me, if that's what you want,' she gasped-ed, her intensity peaking. 'I'll invite them to examine my arse, my cunt, my tits!'

He pushed further in and she cried out. She came against his cock, against the desk, her enlarged tits scraping the wood as she moaned each rush of pleasure.

'The patient is wicked, immoral,' he whispered, thrusting

extra hard for long, long minutes. Her slit was too sensitive now. She tried to squirm away, but he held her in place.

Shelley writhed. She heard him gasp and felt his thrusting hard-on; helmet against soft wet cervix.

'The patient requests oral surgery,' she murmured, and he came.

She felt him pull out, pull away. She pushed back from the desk, her arms still lashed behind her back. He untied her.

'Leave your address,' he said. 'I'll have to make a house call tomorrow night.'

Tearing a page from the pad, she wrote her details down in tremulous large letters.

'What further help will I need?'

'I reckon you'll require a repeat prescription, maybe a double dose to warm the extremities.'

He touched his belt.

'So if I'm still limping when I answer the door to you . . .?'

'I'll know you've not been resting, not been trying to get better.'

'And?'

'And I'll have to correct your behaviour until you're on the mend.'

The patient nodded. Her legs were quivering as she left the surgery, the swamp between them making walking hard. As she reached the road she tensed her carnal canal inwards. It was not enough to stop a river of lust tracing its way down one stiffening inner thigh. Shelley sighed contentedly. She had a feeling that she'd still be walking badly when he called tomorrow, and that afterwards she'd find her legs spread apart for quite some time.

Neighbourhood Watch

Rap music! He'd give her rap music! As the dull insistent beat began to throb through the ceiling, Paul Reeves sat up in bed. This was the third time that the girl upstairs had woken him. Flexing his fingers in frustration, he wondered what her arse would feel like beneath his palm. He'd like to spank her till she wept, till her bottom was blazing. He'd got nowhere by simply asking her to tone down her nocturnal noise.

The following teatime he waited for her to come home. 'Miss Marrant?'

Blonde bob-cut hair, pink lipstick, purple-stained lids. A cute face – but an impudent one. One that stilled into uncertainty when it saw him standing at his open door.

'Uh huh?' Her eyes flickered over him, past him. Her moving jawline showed that she was chewing gum.

'I've had enough of your music waking me up at night.'

She kept walking, her bottom outlined in clingy cycle shorts, her shapely calves in dove-grey tights. 'I wasn't playing it that loudly!'

'Loud enough.'

She half shrugged. 'Right. I'll try to remember to –'

'I'm going to *make* you remember.'

She looked back at him blankly, and hesitated mid-stair.

'I've got the address of your landlord. Seems he hates awkward tenants! I think we should discuss the situation, don't you?'

Her eyes opened wider: 'I guess you could come up to the flat, or . . .'

'No.' He wanted to be on home territory. 'Be at mine for nine p.m.'

Letting himself into his bachelor pad, Paul immediately went to the large black suitcase he kept under the bed, and took out a flat-soled slipper. Then he transferred it to his study, a room in which there was lots of space to spank. Smiling grimly, he phoned his downstairs neighbour and one-time lover, Stella: 'Our naughty young friend will be here at nine.' He paused and smiled to himself. 'I'll probably need you about an hour or so later. No, I'll phone and confirm. Oh, believe me, I've got everything I require!'

9 p.m. 9.05 p.m. 9.10 p.m. . . . At a quarter past nine the doorbell rang, and Cindy Marrant stood there.

'You're late.'

She shrugged, deliberately vacant. 'It's not as if we're going out.'

'Oh, believe me, my dear – we're staying in for several hours. Though you might not be sitting down . . .'

He walked behind her as she sashayed up the hall and steered her towards his study. 'Stand there.'

He took a seat behind the desk.

'What're you reading about, Mr Reeves?' She seemed more nervous now, anxious to talk.

'*Writing* about?' He pushed the folder of stills and stats over. 'About homelessness.'

'You're a journalist?'

'Chief reporter on *The Standard*.'

'Uh huh.'

'And you? What are you, Miss Marrant?'

'Dietetics student.'

'You'll know, then, how quickly people become demoralised and undernourished when they don't have access to hot food.'

Cindy rubbed one wedge-heeled shoe behind the other. 'I guess so, but –'

'If I tell your landlord that you are committing a breach of the peace day and night, that you're rude and uncooperative, he'll throw you out.'

Cindy looked down at the rug. 'Christ! Don't!' Her eyes showed alarm, then acceptance. 'I'll be better! I'll never play my music loudly again!'

'Glad to hear it.' Paul looked more closely at the vanquished girl. 'But you have to be punished for the times you *did* play it loudly enough to disturb me. How many was that? Three in all?' He shook his head. 'What are we going to do with you, you wicked young whippersnapper?'

Cindy gulped and shrugged.

'Spank you over your pants for starters,' Paul said consideringly.

'You what?'

'You heard. Bend over my desk and count the slaps.' He kept staring at her flushed face. 'I think twelve will cover the first misdemeanour, and make you learn.'

'You must be . . .'

'I never joke. It's a good thrashing or . . .' He pushed the photographs of people in cardboard boxes across the desk at her.

'All right,' Cindy muttered. 'Get it over with.'

'Oh, I like to take my time,' corrected Paul. 'I like a naughty girl to feel each spank, to have a few seconds to think about the next one. She tenses up more that way, you see – it really hurts.'

Cindy was blushing furiously now, biting her lip rather than chewing gum. Waiting.

'Over the desk,' he said again, coming to stand behind her and putting a guiding hand on the small of her back to help her over. 'Push your backside out.'

She did as he ordered, her small bottom now encased in a gold-hemmed black lycra mini that clung even more closely than the cycle shorts.

'Lift your skirt up.'

'Do I have to . . .?'

'Lose your home? It's up to you.'

He heard her sigh and saw her fingers reach back, edging the material up centimetre by centimetre. Her briefs were full, white, completely encasing each small pert buttock. But the glossy lace-edged material was encouragingly thin.

'Good girl,' he said, when she'd revealed her entire backside in full-pantied perfection. 'Now grip the other side of the desk. Keep your hands there. You get an extra thrashing each time you bring them back.'

He had a feeling she'd never been spanked before, and a girl who was new to spanking often tried to cover her bum at the first brutal slapping, as the shock of the heat radiated across her tender untouched cheeks. 'Count,' he reminded, stepping close to her before flexing his arm back, letting the strength flow in before bringing the palm smartly down.

'Ouch!' Cindy jumped. 'That hurt!'

'It wasn't supposed to tickle. Keep your belly flat against the desk. Stick your arse out further, that's a good girl. You forgot to count, so you get that slap again.'

He repeated the spank. She grunted: 'One!'

He warmed the other cheek.

'Two! Three! Four!'

She jerked each time his hard hand crashed down on her soft rump, but got back into position across the desk.

'Five!'

He put the sixth slap on top of the fifth and she gave a little half-whimpering gasp, then said, 'Six!'

He treated her neighbouring buttock to the seventh.

'Seven . . . Eight . . .'

He was dishing them out more slowly, but much harder now. 'Nine . . . Oh please! Ten.'

He fancied he could see a pink glow through her thin white knickers. Her thighs were marked where his straying fingers had caught the delicate flesh of the sulcal crease. Her pants were riding up her legs as she strained against the wooden surface, the material clinging more strongly to the valley between her cheeks.

He laid the last two on with lightening speed, just in case she got complacent about his rhythm – about anything.

'Uh,' she grunted, then, belatedly, 'Eleven! Twelve!'

'Too slow – disobedient,' Paul murmured sadly, moving closer to her punished raised posterior. 'I've got a good mind to repeat the last two extra hard, and perhaps double them.'

'No! I did count, sir!' Her voice was thin and high-pitched.

'I suppose you did.'

He stared down at her backside, which she was obviously trying to make a less inviting target by pushing her tummy even more firmly against the ungiving desk. He flexed his fingers, planning how to make her sore. 'Oh, well, I'll be merciful this time. You've enough further punishment coming to you as it is.'

The girl twisted the top half of her body round with obvious effort, and looked nervously back at him.

'What further punishment?'

'For the other two episodes when you played your music loudly. For being rude to me when I complained. For not being respectful enough earlier this evening on the stair.'

Cindy slumped back against the wood.

'You can get up, my dear.'

She did so, hope evident in her eyes.

'You mean you're not going to . . .?'

'Oh, I am. I am! You're going over my knee, that's all.' Smiling at her red-faced shuffling figure, he pulled out the big chair without arms that he'd bought from the antique shop for prolonged sore sessions such as this.

'But I'm eighteen!' She looked longingly towards the door. 'I'm not a baby!'

'You've behaved like one, so you must be treated like one.' He patted his lap.

'Can I keep my pants on?'

'For now. But keep your skirt around your waist, my dear.' His groin thrilled at the thought of unveiling her posterior, or of adding to her humiliation by making her bare it herself.

Licking her lips, her panties still partially embedded in the generous crease, Cindy walked slowly over to him and, turning sideways, lowered herself and positioned her soft tummy across his knees. She kept the front half of her torso stiff, staring at some unseen landmark, till he gently pushed her downwards so that her head and shoulders were hanging towards the ground.

'Ten more spanks for your second breach of the peace,' he said quietly. 'In the past, the police would have birched you on the bare, you know. You're getting off lightly.'

'Huh!' Cindy muttered through gritted teeth.

'Did you say something, my dear? As chief reporter I'm well used to disciplining cheeky junior staff.'

'No – nothing!' Cindy muttered.

'Say "No, sir".'

She said it, though her voice was so strained it sounded like a ventriloquist's dummy.

'Such false pride,' murmured Paul. 'I'll have more respect, if you please.'

He flexed his arm, his wrist, his fingers. Then he toasted her helpless backside ten times.

Cindy had started to count, but the shock of the spanks seemed to overwhelm her. 'Aaah! Uh. Ah!' she grunted, her belly writhing against him, her rump moving convulsively under his slapping palm. Her pantied curves kept moving after the tenth spank, as if the chastisement was still going on.

'Please . . .' she whimpered.

'Please what? Please spank me harder, sir?' Paul mocked.

'Please be gentle.'

'Were you gentle with my eardrums the first two times you disturbed me?'

'No, sir.'

'No, you weren't.' He ran a considering finger along her tender thigh tops. 'So I have no option but to punish you for your third offence.'

He fondled her curves through the scant protection of her panties.

'But we don't get to keep these on, do we, my sweet?'

Cindy seemed to expel two lungfuls of breath in one drawn-out sigh. 'Please don't pull my pants down, sir!'

He felt her tense.

'Take your knickers off yourself – very slowly. You'll get a taste of the slipper if you don't do what you're told.'

Cindy tensed some more, hung her head lower still. He stroked her pantied bottom.

'Please – not the slipper!'

'Pull them down now, then – there's a good girl.'

For a few seconds her hands strayed back towards her

arse, stilled at the waistband, and some inner battle seemed to go on. Then she swallowed hard and her slim fingers sluggishly pushed the material away, revealing centimetre after centimetre of glowing red flesh.

Did it feel as hot as it looked? He stroked an enquiring finger over first one heated buttock then the other. She wriggled helplessly beneath his exploring digits, her own hands flat against the carpet to keep her balance, her legs staying quiveringly in place. Her bottom was small and firm, yet soft to touch. Pertly beautiful. Each hemisphere seemed to have taken on a life of its own as it puckered and relaxed. He cupped an enquiring palm across one buttock and felt it tremble ever so slightly. Ran a finger down the crack of her arse, and watched both sore cheeks close together as if to protect her most intimate crease.

Not that she was going to be protecting anything for the next couple of hours! She was his to humiliate, punish and pleasure. 'This is for the third time you disturbed my sleep,' he reminded her, stroking her waiting extremities. 'Are you sorry?'

'Oh, Mr Reeves – yes!'

'I don't suppose you've been spanked as a grown-up before?'

'No, sir.'

'Maybe just a few playful slaps on your rump to celebrate your birthday?'

'Not even that, sir.'

Cindy slithered about on his lap until he hoisted her backside further in the air and held her more firmly across his knees. 'Stop moving, my embarrassed little dear. Submit to a lengthy punishment. You're not going anywhere until you've been soundly thrashed.'

He contemplated his target.

'Is it already a sore bum?'

'Oh yes, sir!'

'A hot bum?'

'*Very* hot, sir.'

She said each sentence through clenched teeth, head hanging, no longer the opinionated teenager who'd dismissed him the day before.

27

'Can you imagine how much hotter it'll get when it feels my palm on bare flesh?'

Cindy shuddered.

'Oh, please, sir! I'll never play my music loud again, sir.'

Paul stroked her helpless bottom for moment after moment, letting the thought of her punishment sink through, knowing she was imagining the onslaught against her buttocks, how much they'd sting.

'Your arse is about to get a serious roasting. You'll think twice before being a bad girl after this.'

He smiled to himself. He was going to give her the type of spanking that would remain in her memory for ever. She'd never be able to look at another male lap without remembering what it was like to be over one, knickers at her feet. She'd never be able to see a raised palm or perhaps a slipper without picturing it crashing down on her bare backside.

'Twenty spanks coming up,' he said. Saw her head jerk up slightly. Felt her tremble. 'I'll not make you count – you'll be too busy catching your breath.'

He treated her to the first whack. She grunted low. He watched as his palm's shape imprinted itself upon the existing uniform redness. Made the neighbouring buttock equal. Fondled her fiery flesh.

It looked sore, wriggled hard.

'Just think – eighteen more to go,' he whispered, caressing her.

'I'll be such a good girl . . .'

'If only you'd been good before.'

He brought down his hand another four times over the fleshiest part of each raised cheek, enjoying the noise of the contact and her little breathless squeals.

'I hope you're not going to be noisy.'

'No, sir.'

'For I may decide to punish you for each whine if it annoys me.' He meted out spanks seven and eight further down, nearer her soft slim thighs. She pushed her pubis closer to his trousered groin and his body convulsed with pleasure. He laid on the next two wallops with increasing zeal, in case she was trying to tempt him away from each well-deserved spank.

'Ten to go,' he said, as she twitched and squeaked. 'But I've got to make a phone call first. I want to look at your punished bottom as I do so. Stand up and point that red arse in the direction of the phone.'

She scrabbled quickly from his lap, turned around so that her back was to the little telephone table.

'Now bend over and grasp your ankles,' Paul instructed.

He walked over to the telephone seat and sat down, looked gloatingly at her taut bared arse.

Stella answered on the second ring – she'd obviously been eagerly anticipating this moment.

'I'm staring at a well-spanked posterior,' Paul said. 'It's been disciplined for breach of the peace, has got ten whacks still to go. After that it needs to be disciplined for insolence. I thought perhaps a woman's touch?' He listened, smiling for a moment. 'See you in ten minutes, Stella. I'll have finished correcting her by then.'

All the time he'd been talking, Cindy had kept her naked backside still. Now, obviously hearing him stand up, she moved her calves a little and both scarlet buttocks seemed to give an involuntary twitch.

'Where were we?' murmured Paul. 'Ah yes, I had a pert bottom over my knee and I was teaching it manners.'

'I'll be polite, sir!' whispered Cindy.

'After another ten spanks you will.'

He walked in front of her, took his place in the big armless chair. She shuddered.

'Over you go,' he said easily. He smiled as she let go of her ankles, turned sideways and draped her half-nude torso over his knees.

'We'll have to tuck this skirt further up, I think,' he added, noting that the clingy material had edged down a little. He pushed the garment well up over her waist to give him unrestricted access to her bare bottom. Then he delivered the ten spanks quickly but forcefully, knowing that he wanted to give her a few moments to recover before Stella arrived.

'Go stand in the corner,' he said.

'What's going to . . .?'

He gave her an extra spank low down on each thigh.

'Just do what you're told immediately, you wicked girl! Do you want me to start all over again?'

Cindy pushed herself awkwardly free of his lap, and shuffled to the top of the room facing the wall. As Paul stared, he saw her hands reach round as if of their own volition to cup her fiery little rump.

'Hands away!' he ordered. 'Did I tell you to touch yourself? Your Auntie Stella wouldn't be at all pleased if she saw you protecting your disobedient little bum.'

'Who's Stella?' whispered the girl.

'You know – Ms Wellings from downstairs, in the middle flat. She's a probation officer who's edited a report on Borstal practice. She has a special interest in wayward girls.'

He looked at Cindy's uncovered arse as she faced the wall, wished he could see her anguished expression. How would she feel when a second neighbour arrived to discipline her most tender parts?

'Stella has a woman's intuition about these things,' he continued gloatingly. 'Knows how to torment a wicked rear without being too heavy-handed.'

Cindy looked at him pleadingly over her shoulder.

'Sir – I'm so sorry, so very sorry. I can't bear for a woman to see me like this!'

'You can leave now, keep your pride,' Paul said. 'Lose your home, of course. Better a hot bum in here than a cold bum outside, I should think.'

Cindy's shoulders slumped in defeat.

'I'll do what I'm told, sir,' she whispered acquiescently.

'Say "I deserve a thrashing from my Auntie Stella for being rude to Uncle Paul on the stair tonight",' Paul said.

Cindy muttered the words.

'Louder! I can't hear.'

'I deserve a thrash–'

The doorbell pealed through the house.

'You're about to get one,' said Paul. 'Looks like Stella has arrived.'

He let her in. In tandem they walked to the study. Cindy was still facing the wall, her bum tense, her head bowed forward slightly.

'I believe you've been a naughty neighbour,' said Stella. 'No – keep facing the wall.'

'Yes, ma'am. Whatever you say, ma'am,' whispered Cindy.

'And what do we do with naughty girls?'

'We spank them,' muttered Cindy through clenched teeth.

'But you've already *been* spanked. I think you need something stronger than a palm to teach you to obey, to really warm your bottom.'

Cindy groaned.

'Like a slipper,' Stella continued, picking up one of the pair which Paul had bought for such occasions. 'Do you have a boyfriend, Cindy? Only he's bound to notice the tell-tale marks.'

'No,' Cindy muttered.

'Pity. He might have got a taste for spanking you himself. Paul – get one of the wooden stools from the kitchen, will you?'

Cindy twisted her head round. 'What are you going to . . .?'

'I'm going to bend you over the stool and slipper your arse.'

'How many times, ma'am?'

'I haven't decided yet.'

Cindy looked at the ground as Paul came back into the room carrying the stool.

'If you could put it in the centre there,' said Stella gratefully. 'I need space to pull my arm back.'

'There's a table tennis bat as well if she gives you any cheek.'

'The only cheek she's going to give me are her little backside cheeks,' Stella said as Cindy followed her orders to lower her belly over the kitchen stool. 'And they're prettily heated little things, aren't they, my dear? Now, now, settle down, girl. Don't wriggle about when Auntie Stella's kind enough to fondle your wicked bum.'

31

'No, ma'am,' Cindy gasped, obviously wriggling despite herself.

'A slipper hurts more than a palm,' Stella added conversationally. 'Leaves a more lasting impression on a girl's susceptible flesh.'

She placed the slipper first on one cheek then the other as if sizing up her target. Flicked the toe of the hard sole against the backs of Cindy's thighs till she squealed.

'Just warming up my arm muscles so that I can have a good whack at you in a moment. Here goes. One for being rude!'

'I'll tell!' Cindy half-sobbed, putting her small hands over her burning bum.

'Tell who?'

The girl was silent.

'Tell the authorities?' Stella persisted.

Cindy shifted about awkwardly over the stool.

'No ... don't involve the police.'

Stella heard the note of panic in her victim's voice.

'You've got a record already,' she stated, bluffing.

Cindy's thighs and bum tensed further.

'God, you really have checked me out!' She looked back, licking her lips. 'I was only seventeen – a friend gave me it. I only smoked half!'

Stella stood back, contemplating the waiting arse. Knowing that that selfsame arse was contemplating the correction it had coming to it.

'Drug possession as well as breach of the peace and general insubordination. No wonder Mr Reeves had to call me in!'

'I'll make amends!' Cindy gasped.

'I'll make you ask nicely for your slippering,' Stella said.

She sat down in the armchair and patted her lap. 'Get over my knee.'

Cindy's look said *not again*, but she obeyed without question.

'Spread your legs wider for me, sweetheart. Ah, that's it!' Stella put her middle finger above the younger woman's clitoris and made tiny sweeping movements down, as if dusting a thimble. Cindy moaned in obvious ecstasy, thighs tightening as her climax neared.

'Plead for your slippering, or I'll stop stroking your clit.'

'Have to come! Have to . . .'

Stella stilled her finger in place. Cindy pushed hard against the immobile digits. 'Stella, please!'

'Plead for the slipper.'

'All right! I beg! I beg!' She added something inaudible, then grunted like an animal in labour and bore down upon the pleasure-giver. 'Oh yes, yes, yes, yes, yes!'

'Yes, you'll take my slipper on your backside till you've learned obedience,' Stella whispered. 'And I'll make your bad bottom very sorry indeed.' She returned her fingers to the girl's throbbing clit. 'But first you're going to squirm and come against my fingers again whilst Paul observes you. It's a little game we play called Neighbourhood Watch.'

The Quiz Mistress

Lights. Cameras. Action! Bobby Welson felt his heartbeat speeding as the studio filled with the familiar tune. For the first time he was on TV, taking part in a live broadcast. Himself and two other nineteen-year-olds formed a panel on the regional quiz show, *Learn.*

'Coleridge wrote "*And not a drop to drink*",' Katrina Keel, the presenter, producer and researcher began. 'What was the name of –'

'The quote's actually "*Nor any drop to drink*",' Bobby blurted out.

There was a pause. The kind of pause his teacher used to leave before ordering him out to the front to taste the cane on his bent-over bottom. The kind of pause that said *oh dear, you're in lots of trouble now.*

'Thank you for putting me right, Mr Welson,' Katrina said. She rephrased the question and continued – but her eyes said that they had unfinished business. Bobby licked suddenly dry lips.

At last the programme ended. He looked entreatingly at her tall firm body in the black suit and ivory silk blouse.

'Mr Welson – will you wait behind, please?'

She made the question sound like an imperative. He nodded, squirming in his seat as his colleagues left for the television studio's hospitality suite.

'I could use a drink myself!' he joked feebly.

'You don't deserve one,' Katrina said.

She walked closer to his chair.

'Stand up.'

He did. Couldn't quite bring himself to make eye contact.

'Why did you show me up in front of thousands of viewers?'

'I didn't mean . . .'

'Little boys often don't *mean*. But they still do wrong.' She slapped her palm against her outer thigh three times in quick succession. 'They still have to be punished on their exposed young rumps.'

Had she gone mad? This couldn't be happening! Face reddening, Bobby stared wildly round the studio, then gazed at her shoulders, unable to meet her cold grey eyes.

'Can't I make amends? There's this little Mexican Bistro near here –'

'You want me to eat with you?' Her eyes trailed his slight body dismissively. 'You're not fit to kiss my shoes!'

Lost for words, he gazed at her glossy high-heels, the black-stockinged feet within them. Her strong ankles, firm no-nonsense legs.

Katrina looked him up and down, walked round the back of him, head to one side, coolly appraising.

'That's a thought, boy. Kiss my feet. Show your respect. Say sorry in the nicest way you can.'

'I won't! You can't make me!'

His voice sounded unusually high, kept rising.

'Can't I? I could tell the management you made an indecent suggestion. You might end up spending tonight in the cells.'

Damn. She had him now. Bobby fought to keep a hold on the situation.

'I didn't mean to show you up! I didn't think!'

'Then we must *teach* you to think. How do you think we'll manage that?'

She flexed the long wooden ruler she used to keep her place on the question sheet. Bobby gulped.

'Bend over the back of that chair.'

He glanced at the doors.

'But what if the cameraman comes back into the studio?'

'He'll see you get a good thrashing on your bent-over backside.'

'But I'm too old for that!'

His bottom twitched nervously at the prospect.

'You're never too old, boy.'

Bobby opened his eyes pleadingly wider. 'And if I don't?'

'I'll tell the management you've been pestering me.'

No way out. He'd have to do what she said – he could lose his reputation, his job, maybe even his flat if she pressed charges. He had on warm trousers, so how much could a rulering hurt? Inhaling hard, he lowered himself over the wooden chair, its hard back sticking into his belly as he put his palms flat on the seat.

'Good boy. Now unbutton your trousers.'

He looked round.

'You're joking!'

'I've never been more serious in my life.'

'But . . .'

At the thought of her seeing his yellow underpants he felt both ashamed and excited.

'Do bad boys usually get punished with their trousers on?'

'No.'

Fingers fumbling as if chilled, he located his belt, his button, his zip, edged down the beige linen.

'Push them down to your ankles and leave them there.'

He did, feeling the warm studio air around his naked thighs, feeling the increasing vulnerability of his balls.

'I'm going to ruler you for five minutes over your pants. Reason is, I prefer to ultimately inspect a red bum rather than a white bum. These cheeks will be nicely warmed by the time I tell you to disrobe.'

Bobby hung his head, glad that he was facing away from her. He didn't know what to say, what to do. He was just arched over here, waiting. Waiting for the ruler to strike down on his helpless upturned backside.

'Have you been thinking about what comes next?'

She sounded different to before – more vicious, almost taunting.

'Yes.'

'Address me as ma'am!'

'Yes, ma'am.'

'And what conclusion have you reached?'

He gulped hard, tensed. 'That I deserve a spanking.'

'Say "I deserve a spanking, ma'am!" '

He felt the first hard crack across the centre of his raised bottom cheeks.

'Ow!'

He jerked up, swivelled round. She was raising the arm with the ruler again. The weal stung like crazy.

'Cuts surprisingly deep, doesn't it? Lasts surprisingly long.' She smiled at his obvious discomfiture. 'Get that bum bent again. I've hardly started with you yet.'

Closing his eyes, he pushed his bottom out. Tensed some more this time. Wished he'd worn thicker underpants.

'Yellow makes me angry,' she said conversationally. 'Makes me see red!'

'I didn't know . . .'

'You know now, you silly boy. Never mind, they'll be coming off in a few minutes once I've warmed your backside a good deal more.'

She toasted his right buttock with the flailing stick. He cried out again, even though he'd told himself he wasn't going to.

'Don't make a noise without permission!' she snapped, laying into that same smarting buttock again. Then she dealt two swipes to the left, then two more to the right, further down this time. After evening them up, she continued to rebuke his pantied cheeks with merciless zeal.

God, this hurt more than he'd thought! Grunting under his breath, Bobby kept his belly across the chair back, though his arse cheeks swung from side to side as he tried to second-guess where the next blow was coming from. Taking aim at his upper thighs, upper cheeks, lower underswell, Katrina whacked and whacked.

'You cowardly slug. Now for some serious correction! Pull your pants down, slowly.'

He'd been dreading this moment. He put his fingers to his waistband, hesitated. Hell to be denuded like this! Still, she was brighter than him and older than him – best just to do what she said, humour the woman. Surely her arm must be tiring by now? A few hard taps on the bare and he'd be home and dry.

Well, home and wet. His cock seemed to be leaking a lot at the tip. As he put his fingers to his pants it pulsed up at him. He was glad Katrina couldn't see it. Such ignominy – a boyish thrashing exciting his traitorous prick! Confused, he edged the elastic away, slowly unveiling his hot little buttocks. Did they look as red raw and sore as they felt?

'Leave your pants at the top of your thighs. That's it. Outlines your arse quite well, gives me something to aim above. No point in wasting my hardest whacks on your upper legs.'

This time the ruler's blow wasn't deflected by the material. The sound ricocheted around the room, hard wood on soft nude buttocks.

'Uh! Aah!'

With difficulty, Bobby kept his palms on the chair seat. He felt scared, stupid, desperately defenceless with his trousers round his ankles and his pants at his thighs.

'Now take them both off fully and come and lie over my lap.'

His cock ached some more. How wonderful to be this close to the incredible Katrina! Then his manhood deflated slightly. How awful to be across her knees like some overgrown kid.

'Hurry up! You'll get double if you're late.'

As he kicked off his trousers and pulled his pants the rest of the way down, he looked round. She was sitting in a chair in the centre of the stage, staring at him. As he watched, she pulled a thick leather glove from her voluminous jacket pocket and slid it over her strong right hand. Patting her lap, she contemplated him coldly. 'Twenty hard spanks on the bare.'

He moaned inside. Kept his mouth shut, his eyes fixed. Walked tremulously over to her.

'Do I really have to . . .?'

'Lie down!'

He did as he was told. She smelt of rich woodland scent

and athletic womanliness. Her thighs were embraced by midnight black nylon. He went over them slowly, holding his breath and closing his eyes at the shame of it all. Put his palms on the floor.

'Stretch your legs back a bit. That's better! Hurts more if they're tense and unsupported – and I aim to hurt you a lot.' He could tell. His bum seemed to wriggle of its own accord as she surveyed it. Started to palm it, round and round and round.

Was she still holding the ruler, or intending to use the glove? It was hard to say. He daren't look round; he stared at the wooden floor as he lay across her knees and waited for his thrashing.

'It's quite sensitive already, isn't it?' she whispered.

'Yes!'

'Do you know how much of a baking it's still to get?'

He opened his mouth to ask for clemency, for a reprieve, and she slapped down, down, down.

'Aaah!'

He cried out and bucked and reared. The glove obviously had a reinforced palm. It felt like a table-tennis bat.

'Stay still, boy!'

She spanked harder, harder, harder. Heat upon pain upon heat, a roasting assault on his helpless bare backside.

'Please stop,' he whimpered, feeling his cock hardening and softening as it rubbed against her pubis.

'For speaking without permission you've already earned yourself a triple dose.'

He heard a door in the distance open, heard a voice. 'Christ! I think someone's coming,' he moaned, twisting his head to try and look back at her.

'Then they'll see you being disciplined over my lap, see your naked bad bum.'

He tried to push back and escape, but uncertainty had exhausted him and she held him down.

'Do you know where we're going now?' she asked.

He shook his head.

'We're going to the next set where I can chastise you properly.'

'The next set?'

'Upstairs they've been recording *Trapped*, a medieval drama. They've got a fully equipped dungeon through there.' She squeezed his disarmed crimson globes till he winced and whimpered. 'You should hear the actors screaming in the stocks!' She looked pitilessly at Bobby. 'Only difference is, you're not going to act.'

She'd flipped this time. He shook his head.

'I'm not going!'

'Oh, you'll go. Put your trousers on now. Follow me, boy.'

'Where are my . . .?' Picking up his trousers, he looked around for his yellow underpants, but they were gone.

'I've got them.' Katrina gave him a quick peep inside her blouse, where she had them tucked between her breasts – large, luscious bra-less breasts with hard brown nipples. 'If you don't do as you're told I'll tell the doorman that you stripped and indecently exposed yourself to me.' She smiled. 'I'll bet the crotch is stained with your semen. Am I right?'

Blushing, Bobby looked away and struggled into his trousers. Walking stiffly, he followed her past the security guard.

'Got a fan with me tonight,' Katrina said. 'I'm giving him an extensive guide of the studio. Isn't that right, Mr Welson?'

Bobby nodded mutely.

'Not like you to give up your free time, Miss Keel!' said the guard, looking surprised.

The upstairs set looked reassuringly normal at first. Bobby walked through a banquet hall into a cosy but anti-quated living room.

'Silly boy! You haven't been good enough to go there. Come with me.'

Nervously he followed her back to a door with a lock on it. Watched mutely as she took the key from a large bunch on a hook.

'Disobedient prisoners get sent to the basement punishment chamber!' She smiled, and using the ruler between his shoulderblades, she prodded him down to a long, narrow room. It was centrally heated and thickly carpeted with a grey slate effect. The walls were papered a mellow stone and held manacles and long heavy chains.

'What will you . . .?' He stared at the whips, the knouts, the tawse. She could do anything!

'Take your trousers off again. Now stand in the centre of the room so that I have access to both the front and back of you. Stretch your arms up. That's right.'

Numbly he did as she asked. Watched as she used a pulley which lowered two arm chains from the ceiling. Standing on a chair, she moved above him to clip the adjoining handcuffs round his wrists.

'Legs far apart, if you please!' When she'd exerted a slight pull on his arms, she edged his legs apart, the movement stretching his upper body further. Then she used the ankle cuffs to hold him in place. Now he was standing upright, with arms and legs extended, chained in the position of an X. He could do little more than flinch his exposed sore rear.

'Tell me you've been a bad boy.'

Bobby gritted his teeth. Damn her – he wouldn't say it!

'Tell me,' she said again more coldly. Walking forward till she was only inches from him, she put her palm under his balls and began to caress their heavy swell.

'Oooooooooh!' Despite the chains, Bobby's knees buckled forward slightly, and he moaned with pleasure.

'You like that, don't you?'

He loved it, craved it.

'Yes!'

'Say "Yes, ma'am." Then tell me you've been a bad, bad boy.'

'I've been a bad, bad boy.'

He flushed as he said the words. His friends at work would never believe this! But the way she touched him made him feel . . .

'Beg to taste my cane.'

He grunted with fear this time. She took her hand away.

'Beg, now.'

'Oh, ma'am please, not that!'

Katrina walked over to the wall and selected a long rattan. She set it on the ground before him. 'Look at it. Imagine how it'll feel on your exposed arse. Get ready to beg.'

She returned her ministrations to his balls. Bobby felt confused. He'd thought he was only to enjoy her touch if he did what she wanted!

'Oh yes, ma'am, yes, ma'am!' he moaned in his bonds as she teased and tickled the exquisitely sensitive flesh of his undercarriage. He could feel his spunk building up in him second by second. Any moment now . . .

Katrina stopped. 'Beg.'

'Oh, Christ, yes – I beg!'

'Tell me how much you deserve the cane. Tell me how hard you need it.'

She put her palm just millimetres from his balls, the promise of infinite pleasure there if he did what she asked.

'I've been so naughty . . . need the cane on my arse till I beg for mercy . . . need a red hot arse.'

'Mmm, you do.' She picked up the implement of correction. Bobby winced. That rod looked wicked.

'I've already felt the glove, the ruler, ma'am,' he reminded her.

'I'm going to cane you twice as hard for insolence, boy,' Katrina said.

She walked round behind him.

'Mmm. It's reddening nicely, now.'

He heard the swish of the rattan, felt the searing, branding line of pain across his upper thighs.

'Aaah!' He wriggled, started to beg.

She immediately laid a second on his upper cheeks, and a third in the middle. 'I think I'll administer the fourth one on top of the third,' she said thoughtfully.

'No. Please.'

'What will you do to please?'

'Kiss your shoes. Lick your feet. Crawl. Kneel.'

When she was caning him hard like this he felt that he loved her, yet hated her. Felt he'd do anything to make the punishment stop. Katrina ran the cane teasingly over his tender buttocks. 'If I unchain you will you do exactly as you're told?'

'Yes, ma'am. I swear I will, ma'am!'

She stroked his flaming cheeks consideringly.

'I'm not quite sure – on the one hand, your bottom does feel as if it's burning, as if it's had enough.' She thumbed the globes. 'But on the other, you were so very, very wicked in showing me up in front of the nation tonight.'

Bobby's cock, which had been pulsing with hope, began to deflate again.

'I'll apologise so good! I'll do anything you want. Have mercy, I can't bear it, ma'am!'

'I might decide that I want you to bear it,' she whispered, as he whimpered and writhed in his chains. He'd give anything to have his hands free to protect his exposed rear end.

'It hurts so much, doesn't it?' she taunted, coming to stand at his side so that she could trace his well-warmed globes with one hand whilst she teased his swelling balls with the other.

'Don't punish me any more, Mistress.'

'Ah, so you recognise that I'm your mistress now!'

She looked into his face as she teased his scrotum and tormented his arse. He moved the little he could in his bonds, wishing that he could close his legs for even a moment.

'Poor little Bobby. If I want to I can cocktease your prick and berate your backside all night.'

'I know, Mistress – but I could please you so well.' He ran his tongue over his lips, hoping that she would see its insinuating promise.

'What would you do?'

'I'd put my head between your legs, lick you so hard.'

'I doubt if you know where the clitoris is, you pathetic imbecile!'

'I'd find it! You could show me! Please, miss – I'll do exactly as you say.'

Katrina looked him up and down. Aware of her gaze, he stared submissively at the floor. His arse was on fire.

'All right. But if you fail me at all you'll take my cane across your useless backside again.'

He nodded. 'Yes, Mistress. Thank you, Mistress!'

He flexed his arms as soon as she unchained and uncuffed them.

She glared as he moved his hands back. 'Don't touch your punished arse!'

Every cell in his brain, his body, was crying out for him to be allowed to do so. But he daren't disobey her. She could punish him here all night if she so desired.

'I won't, Mistress. I'll be a good boy, Mistress.'

'You'd better be,' she muttered, putting her feet on the floor and lowering herself back upon a low open-plan couch, pulling her skirt up. Leaving on her stockings, she started to edge her crotch thong down.

'Won't my mistress uncuff my ankles?' Bobby whimpered, looking down.

'I've unchained them – but I'm leaving them cuffed together to teach you humility. You can hobble over here to me like a whipped dog.'

Bobby took an awkward half-hop in her direction.

'Means you can't kick out or run away if I decide to torment your wicked bottom some more.'

'I'll please you so much . . .'

The journey to reach her labia was agonisingly slow and hugely shameful. Once he almost fell, and had to flail his arms to keep his balance, stay in place. His ankles were being chafed by the metal cuffs. His shoulders and arms still remembered the pull of being chained upwards. Every step sent new pulses of pain through his well-flogged rear.

At last he reached her quim. Knelt on the ground between her spread-apart legs.

'Lick hard and well, boy. Make me come good, or else you'll suffer.'

She slapped her palm against her thigh again. She'd done that before his ordeal started. When would it end?

'Beg to lick my Mistress,' he moaned, putting his tongue just above her clit and beginning to tease it gently. Katrina shut her eyes.

Scarcely breathing, Bobby tongued again and again and again, finding a rhythm. Soon her tendermost parts started to move against his face, and he knew she was nearing the edge.

'Lick!' she urged, 'Lick harder, fool!' She wound strong fingers through his hair and forced his head closer. He increased his pace. Her thighs tensed up, quim lifting into his lips. Sex lips pulsing.

'Uh!' she muttered, 'Uh! Ah!'

Unsure what to do, he continued tonguing as he peeked through his lashes at her. Her face was stretched with ecstasy, though the little noise she made was coolly controlled, unemotional.

'Suck my toes, boy, and say thank you,' she said after a few seconds, pushing his head away.

'Thank you for letting me lick you, Mistress,' Bobby murmured, then took her big toe in his mouth and kissed its tip.

He wanted to kiss more than her toes! He'd love to . . . His brainwaves sent sensation to his balls, which immediately sent his prick into action, leaking and looking for release. It reared up, rubbing against the couch end, just as Katrina opened her eyes.

'Stand up, boy, and put your hands above your head.'

He did as she ordered, again fighting the urge to cup his arse, to protect it.

'What have we here?'

She put the ruler beneath his shaft and slapped upwards ever so lightly. Pleasure and pain twanged through his penis. Bobby groaned. 'Please, Mistress, have mercy. Don't thrash me any more!' Without being told, he sank on his knees before her, put his arms round her calves, supplicating. 'I wish only to serve my mistress. Please don't take your hard whacking ruler to my shaft!'

'What else is your pathetic prick good for?' She played the cruel wood over his six stiff inches again.

'You could ride it, Mistress. I'd keep it hard for as long as you wanted. For hours and hours!'

'Would you? I suspect you'd come right away, like some twelve-year-old boy who's just wanked for the first time.'

'No, Mistress – I'd keep it rigid and thick, keep it up.'

'We'll see.' She pushed him flat on the floor. 'Spread your legs. Further! Don't move a muscle without being told. Keep your cock to attention.'

She squatted above him, put her soaking slit to his pulsing prick. Bobby's ball bag twitched.

'Easy!' She kept him waiting whilst she teased her sex lips over the eye of his cock. He wanted to come so bad, but he did not dare.

'I may just wank myself off,' she said, 'rather than slide down this pitiable pole.'

'Please, Mistress – it's a good pole, a hard pole, a big pole.'

'I've seen a lot bigger than this,' she replied. She shook her head. 'I suppose it'll have to do. Remember – stay in place. One quiver out of turn and you get the hardest thrashing.'

'Yes, Mistress. Thank you, Mistress!'

He bit his lip to hold back the moan as she impaled herself all the way down over his cock.

Smiling grimly into his face, she raised herself up, then pushed down again on his pleasure-crazed prick until her strong thighs weighed down his weaker thighs. With difficulty he kept his arse on the floor.

'Keep still, very still,' she taunted, circling her hips teasingly over the first half of his shaft. He so wanted to thrust upwards. Erotic charges were squirming through his scrotum, and he whined his lust.

'Did I tell you to make a noise?' She slapped his face, both sides. He shook his head. He wanted to cry. Wanted to climax. Wanted to take his arms from his sides and unbutton her blouse, suckle her tits for hours. 'You've made me angry. I may come off of you.'

'Please, I'll stay so still! You can punish me later. I beg!'

'I could tie you down over the punishment bench.' She pushed down harder on his cock. Pushed harder still. He noticed that her breathing was increasing.

'I'd hand you the birch myself, Mistress. I'd ask you to use it on my bum.'

'And what about the tawse?' she gasped, grinding hard.

'I'd crawl over on my hands and knees to fetch it from the wall. I'd bring it to you in my mouth, like a dog that deserves to be beaten. I'd lie on my belly and take it hard.'

'Yes, you would, and I'd use it for hour after hour on the sensitive crease at the top of your thighs.'

She was moving above him like a piston now. His cock couldn't take much more. Try as he might, it was going to spurt right up her.

'Then I'd wet your arse with the hose,' she said. 'You'd really beg if I beat you after that.'

'I'll beg now,' he moaned. 'I'll say and do what you want. Oh Christ, Mistress, anything!'

'Then do nothing!' she cried out, and her mouth tensed in and she came.

His cock let go and he strained upwards. She must have seen the look on his face.

'What did I tell you?' she said.

He was beyond words, still coming.

As the last pulses of pleasure leaked from him, she pulled away. His dripping cock was already beginning to shrink.

'He's small now,' she said, 'but I'm going to tease him till he's large again. Then I'll command him to obey me.' She looked levelly down at Bobby's wretched face. 'I'll chain you up and stroke your prick for maybe half an hour. You can enjoy it, maybe even leak a little, but you're not allowed to come.'

His prick and balls swelled slightly at the thought of her teasing hands.

'And if I do?'

Katrina looked around at the rods and belts that graced the walls. 'Take your pick.' She smiled. 'If you're wilful I'll use more than one of them.' And Bobby realised that though the quiz was over his most testing time had just begun.

A Bonding Business

Most sexual dissatisfaction results from a lack of sensitivity on the part of the male or a complete refusal to experiment on the part of the female. Elliot Whitechapel, however, though sexually dissatisfied, could lay the blame at neither door. A person of impeccable standards, he read *Cosmo Man* supplements, bathed twice daily, and knew not only where the clitoris was, but the kind of gentle attention it required to achieve optimal results.

Similarly, his partners were not averse to stimulating him in a variety of ways, and lubricated fingers regularly probed his anus and massaged his prostrate to produce a delightfully explosive come. Small hand-held vibrators were teased round his balls, wine, honey and fresh cream were sucked from his shaft, and a generally good time was had by all.

But not a great time, not great. And as a man with money, power and a directorship at the head of a hotel chain, Elliot believed that he was entitled to the best.

And the personal best he aspired to was S&M. *S&M!* Even the sound sent a thrill through him, made his most memorable straight encounters seem tame. Ah, to hold his beloved down, then slowly strip her naked. To take his time spreadeagling her arms and legs before tying them to the corners of his four-poster bed. Oh, to deliciously tease those helpless bared buttocks with a finger, a tongue, the roasting, reddening pressure of a downward slapping palm.

Strange that his freedom could be enhanced by someone else's captivity, that intense pleasure could be gained through inflicting mild pain, but it was the case with him and he would not try to fight it any longer. Somewhere there had to be a submissive female out there with similarly unmet needs.

At first Elliot had tried to subtly introduce his preferences to new girlfriends, giving them chainmail jewellery, slave bracelets, the kind of presents he hoped would invoke comment, steer the conversation on to appropriate punishment-led paths. But the women had given him grateful smiles without subservience and soon he had moved on to the next girlfriend and the next.

'Fancy going to the cinema tonight, Wanda?' he had recently asked a girl he'd been dating for three weeks. He had read the preview and knew the film contained some adult caning.

'Sure, it'll make a change from the wine bar,' she had replied.

Heart thudding, he'd queued for popcorn, coke, a film guide. *Soon*, the adrenalin in his body had been promising him – *very, very soon*. A couple of hours from now he would hopefully know unimaginable excitement, ecstatic sex, the pulling-a-woman-over-his-knee realisation of his dreams!

Breathing competing for precedence with his heartbeat, he had sat through endless trailers, adverts, credits, but at last the film had got underway and they reached *the scene*.

Arm around Wanda's shoulders, hand running feverishly up and down her side, Elliot stared fixedly at the screen as the sexually aroused masochist was bound and punished for some misdemeanour, as the camera cut to the dominant's hand and effective rattan coming down. Surreptitiously he shot a look at Wanda, only to find her munching unaffectedly away, oblivious to the sudden hush of the auditorium. His erection, which had been straining wildly against the confines of his suit, immediately lessened, returning to something flaccid and unsure. Still ...

'Enjoy the film?' he had asked as he walked her home, striving for nonchalance but finding none, aware that this was the nearest he would ever come to admitting his sexual dominance. 'Sure,' – that dreadful Americanised *sure* again – 'though the caning session was sick.'

'Sick?' Even as he echoed the words his stomach lurched its message at him, and he choked back the acrid taste that invaded his senses. 'But they both enjoyed it! Surely if it's by mutual consent it's not sick?'

'It's a perversion,' said Wanda, who put foreign objects into her vagina and who would have a multiple orgasm at the mere prospect of giving herself an enema.

Elliot sighed. Perversion, he decided hollowly, was whatever you yourself weren't into or didn't understand. Dispiritedly he dropped Wanda at her house, explained as kindly as possible that he wasn't ready to get more fully involved yet, and beat a hasty retreat knowing that he never wanted to see her – or think of her – again.

The book lay on a high shelf devoted to soft and medium porn, artfully hidden above the bookshop's door. *What Color Is Your Handkerchief?* was its title, and it was a lesbian S&M reader, a guide to the American scene. By wearing a handkerchief of a certain colour or folding it a certain way, Elliot learned, you could indicate your punishment preferences and so find the right partner for you.

It was beautifully simple. It was also – assuming a heterosexual American equivalent existed – beautifully safe, for he could go to the USA and indulge in his proclivities without the kind of blackmail or ridicule he might encounter at home in the London clubs.

And so over the next few weeks he delegated more and more tasks to his considerable staff, then took himself off on a two-month sabbatical to the States.

'You get off on this, honey?' The woman who joined him at his table was overmade-up, over-perfumed and underdressed.

'Maybe,' he said, embarrassed, returning his eyes to the S&M encounter on the stage.

'She's not really into it,' the woman said, indicating the slender young girl who'd already been stripped by her master and bound by her wrists to the oak beams overhead.

If she wasn't, Elliot thought, hugely aroused, then she

was a damn good actress, for though she writhed and moaned loudly as the whipping intensified, her face was erotically charged, lips slick and eyes lustfully heavy as she whispered her desire. And later when her tormentor cut her down and lightly touched her Mount of Venus, she came with a cry, and her body suffused with the mottled sex flush no one could fake.

'I have a dungeon back at my place,' his table mate said conversationally, 'and I only live three blocks away.'

Unable to conceal his irritation, Elliot shook his head. Shrugging, the woman got up to go and what he saw in her eyes wasn't submission or desire, but despair.

'Have a drink on me,' he said quietly, handing her a hugely generous bill. Again his erection had died. Hope, he was beginning to fear, was dying too.

S&M catalogues, S&M outfitters, S&M theatres: suddenly the world was full of the sadomasochism he so craved, but it was all too commercialised and crass for Elliot's taste. Some of the floor shows had been too extreme for him, others too obviously enacted or surreal.

The same was true of the many club members he had met, with their particular likes and dislikes. Somehow their fantasies and his never quite matched, never quite produced the level of excitation he knew he was capable of, believed he deserved. One woman wanted to be tied so tightly that she couldn't move, whereas he longed to see her heated bottom writhing. Another begged him to use the martinet on her inner thighs, yet he craved a woman who'd pretend to loathe each painful stroke.

And so, two whole weeks before his holiday was scheduled to finish, Elliot Whitechapel found himself on a plane back to England, a titillating cache of S&M books and magazines in his bag. Providing he got safely through customs, he thought wryly, he'd be a relatively happy man. But if he didn't, if he was stopped . . .

At the prospect of the mortification awaiting him, Elliot ordered another drink and quickly followed it by a third. Gradually he became aware that he was being watched, and turned to find the girl in the next seat staring at him with large serious eyes.

And suddenly Elliot was tired of being sensitive and egalitarian, of being unappreciated no matter what he did. 'Like what you see?' he said gruffly. The girl blushed hotly, bit her lip, laced her ringless fingers in her lap.

Elliot felt his conscience lurch with guilt. 'God, I shouldn't have said that! Blame it on the booze,' he apologised, touching her arm lightly.

The girl shrugged. 'No, it's OK. I was staring at the number of drinks you've consumed. I got drunk the first time I flew as well, and it doesn't help.'

She had a slightly breathless melodic voice which was very, very soothing. Tuning in to it eagerly, Elliot relaxed in his seat. 'I've flown many times,' he volunteered. 'It's just that I've had a rather stressful trip.'

'Business or pleasure?'

'Oh, definitely pleasure!' Elliot smiled his assured director's smile as he recalled how exciting his first-ever stage show had been, and a pulse began to beat strongly in his groin. Beside him the girl reddened and looked away again, body restless with confusion. She really was extraordinarily shy – or extraordinarily sub?

Determined not to raise his hopes too far, Elliot summoned forth the voice he used to intimidate his more difficult employees. 'Tell me your name.'

'Olivia.'

'Olivia. And what brought you to the States, Olivia?'

'Business,' she said, smiling impishly, darting a sideways glance in his direction. 'I'm doing American Studies as part of an Arts degree course. My parents paid for the trip as my twenty-first birthday gift.'

'I'd love to have given you your dumps!' He said the words lightly, thinking *if I'm merely embarrassing this girl, if I've got it all wrong . . .*

Olivia ran her tongue across her lips and looked quickly away. 'You're not too late,' she said throatily. 'My birthday's today.'

* * *

He had looked forward to their first date together all week, had played numerous dom/sub scenarios through his head and now, as they walked up the stairs to the restaurant, he decided to test his conjecture. 'Oh, I haven't given you your dumps yet,' he said casually, ready to back off at the first sign of anger and distress.

Lightly, he gripped her arm and brought the palm of his hand back, slapping at her dress-sheathed buttocks three times, four, five. 'It seems strangely like punishing someone for coming of age,' he said with a forced laugh, and when she swayed with desire against him he knew he had come home.

Stiltedly they walked into the restaurant and nibbled at the Tandoori prawns, gazes searching then falling only to search – to consolidate what they had seen – again and again. 'Dessert, sir?' the waiter asked, taking away their barely touched plates. Elliot stood up and threw down the appropriate notes.

'We don't have time for dessert,' he said authoratively. 'We've a little unfinished business to take care of right now.'

'Twenty-one!' Elliot said triumphantly. He leaned over and kissed Olivia's scarlet buttocks before resting his hand lightly against her spank-warmed skin. 'Does it hurt much?'

'What do you think? Those last five . . .' she licked her lips, 'they stung like crazy!'

'Want me to take your mind off it?'

'Yes, please!'

Tenderly he untied her, rolled her over on to her back and touched her clit, yet more heat springing beneath his fingers as she rubbed against his fingertips and quickly came. God, he wanted to be inside her! Elliot guided her hand to his thickened crotch. Perhaps she wouldn't want to make love this quickly? After all, it was only their first date!

'Which way do you want me?' Olivia whispered, staring at his cock. 'Like this or hands and knees, doggy style?'

'Doggy style,' Elliot ordered, and came as soon as she pushed her reddened rear against his loins.

'Teasing bitch!' he said, spanking her again, recovering quickly. Moments later he entered her and began to thrust, coming so hugely that every pleasurable sensation he'd ever known seemed to culminate a hundredfold in his prick.

'Got to go soon. I've a tutorial,' Olivia murmured when they woke up the next morning.

'You didn't ask for permission to leave,' Elliot said. He kept his gaze firm, even as she smiled at him sleepily. At last her grin faltered.

'Sorry! Maybe I can make amends like this?'

Sexually sure of herself, she slid between his hard thighs, covering his shaft and scrotum with little licks and kisses. 'You may continue to tongue me,' Elliot said quietly, 'though I'll have to take my belt to your backside to make sure that you don't make the same mistake again.'

'Not the big wide belt you took off last night?' Olivia's eyes were huge with mild fear and anticipation.

'The very same.'

'And it'll make me better?'

'It'll make you bond to me,' Elliot said.

He caressed her hair from root to ends as she sucked his shaft, hoping that in the months to follow he could take her to her limit, knowing that the bond between them would strengthen each time he punished her then pleasured her till she came.

Labour Pains

'And I've to wear *those*?' Katie Reed looked at the vest-style white top and micro-sized black skirt on the table before her.

The entertainments manager nodded, and added a feather duster and pair of ankle-strapped stiletto shoes to the flimsy fare. 'There you go! One Modern Maid's outfit. Take it away.'

She'd be taken away by the police for indecent exposure if she went out in this lot! Katie sat back further in her chair. 'I'll have on panties and a bra?'

'Not if you want to work for us, you won't.' The forty-something looked at his Rolex then back at her and gave a man-about-town kind of grimace. 'You're getting off lightly, love – most Strip-O-Grams actually have to strip.'

Two days later Katie climbed into a taxi and squinted at her work card. 'Hall's House, Maitland Road, please.'

'That's Russell Hall the interviewer, isn't it?' Russell Hall who made pornographers cry and page three girls tremble. Just her luck to be landed with a moralising local celeb. But what could a girl do? Her student grant stretched as far as a piece of used chewing gum. She needed this well-paid work.

Deep breath. Stomach in. Smile up. Holding her feather duster over her shoulder like a bayonet, she rang the interviewer's doorbell and heard the same chimes that introduced his radio show pealing within. Some of Russell's so-called friends had set him up, knowing he'd placed a genuine advert for a cleaning lady. She was to waltz in as he interviewed live on the radio, and knock his jug of iced water into his lap.

Then she'd get paid and go home and get out of this minuscule maid's outfit! Katie widened her smile as a man in his thirties opened the door. 'I'm Michael, a colleague of Russell's,' he said, winking. 'He's recording in his home studio now.'

'And I just go in and ...?'

'Flutter around dusting his desk for a minute or two, making sure he sees your assets. Then swat the contents of that freezing cold jug over his egotistical balls!'

The *Do Not Disturb: Interview in Progress* sign on the studio door looked blackly daunting. *Rules are made to be broken*, Katie reminded herself. She looked back at Michael and he gave her the thumbs-up, then tucked two twenty-pound notes between her tits.

Four minutes for forty quid. Do it. Do it! She fluttered into the room, noting Russell Hall's open mouth and sudden closing words. '... parliamentary reform?' he asked weakly.

The man he was interviewing stared at her thighs then muttered, 'Yes.'

Katie took a deep breath, then pushed her unfettered breasts into their line of vision, bending over the desk in order to polish an imaginary speck. Russell pointed mutely and pucely to the door, indicating that she should get out, and make it pronto. It was time to show him her arse!

Turn quickly. Stand straight. She stretched towards an ugly painting on the wall, knowing the action would prove that she had no pants on, and flicked the feather duster firmly against the canvas's side. She froze as it fell from the wall and crashed into the spare microphone below it, bending the mike at an unnatural angle. The picture hit the floor and bounced twice, then lay upright, a white score visible across its surreal front.

'We now bring you a statement on current atmospheric changes from the Minister for the Environment,' Russell said carefully, slotting in a tape from the section marked *Thursday's tape*. As the recorded message transmitted to the listening locals, he turned to his gaping interviewee. 'I apologise for the confusion. Let's return to my hospitality suite.'

He ushered the man through the door, saying 'Join you in a mo, sir,' then looked back at Katie: 'Get your backside on that settee and contemplate the thrashing you're about to get.'

He had to mean a *verbal* thrashing, an *emotional* thrashing. He couldn't ... Katie paced the large room, examining the twin decks. She put the unused recorder's volume on low then slotted in a cassette tape. The action failed to take her mind off things.

Maybe the best scheme was to escape? She opened the studio door to find Michael sitting on a chair. 'Russell says I've got to stand guard,' he murmured apologetically. 'Seems he wants to tear strips off you for vandalising some priceless work of art.'

Priceless! Oh, Christ. Returning to the studio, she sat down on the elongated settee. As she felt its warm cover against her bare bum, she wished again she'd been allowed to wear panties, wished that Russell wasn't re-entering the room. She sat, trembling, as the recorded tape ended and he went on the air live again, castigating local councillors and vocally flagellating businessmen. Then came his exit: 'Join us tomorrow for more inquisitions past and present from Hall's House!'

He pressed a button, took off his headphones and pulled his chair out until it was in the centre of the room. 'Now get over here and lay that posterior beneath my palm.'

'You must be joking!'

'Young lady, I'm not the joking kind.'

'I know, but ... 'A bum-saving answer seemed very far away. 'I'm not one of your interview MPs!'

'No, you aren't. They're not destructive.'

'I didn't *mean* to ruin your microphone and painting!'

'But you did.'

She'd have to pay somehow. A thought came to her, and she pushed a hand inside her top, coming out with the two twenties. 'Look, your friend gave me this for playing the maid prank. You can have it back.'

'Do you know how much a Yakohamo original costs?'

'A what?'

'That Japanese mural you ruined.'

57

'Em, no.'

'A damn sight more than forty quid, I'll tell you.'

'I realise that, but weren't you insured?'

She swallowed when Russell Hall flexed his palm as if readying it for her rump. What on earth had made her try to blame *him* for her carelessness? 'I just took receipt of it yesterday after an auction,' he shouted. Worse and worse. She'd spoilt his latest acquisition, done irreplaceable harm.

He stood up and looked down at her, his eyes cold. 'I could go to the police if you'd rather.'

'Please don't!' She'd been fined for shoplifting four years ago, had been caught at twelve with unpaid-for mascara down her glove. This was the third bad thing she'd done in her life and it hadn't been deliberate. But knowing her luck she'd probably do time!

'Better to have a sore bum for an hour or two and get it over with,' said Russell Hall, sitting down on the settee next to her and patting his lap with obvious inference.

'When you said a thrashing that's what you meant?'

'What else?'

'I thought maybe a strict talking-to.'

'That's for children.'

'Oh. Right.'

She stared at his suited knees, one of which was almost touching hers. She couldn't just lower herself across them. She just couldn't! 'If I have to pull you over it'll hurt more,' Russell said.

'You'll have to catch me first!' Limbs languorous with doubt, she made a half-hearted attempt to stand up. Felt his strong arms wrap around her lightly clad waist.

'I like a girl who puts up a bit of a fight.'

'You ain't seen nothing yet!' Katie muttered, trying to angle her stiletto toe so that it grazed his ankle. She might have acquiesced to this spanking, but that didn't mean she had to make things easy for him too.

'We'll have to whip the temper out of that backside.'

'In your dreams!' she muttered, aware that she was being moulded to fit his lap even as she verbally resisted him and that he now had one strong leg effectively trapping hers.

She tried to swat with her right hand, but he pinned it to her back. Did the same to her left after scooping it out from under her body. Katie felt him transfer both her wrists to one of his large hands, hold them high up her back. Now her arms and legs were completely immobilised. She wriggled as he used his free hand to squeeze her defenceless rump through her skirt.

'You know this'll have to come up.'

Katie forced deep sarcasm into her voice. 'Why, haven't you seen a woman's bum before? Can't you use your imagination?' Physically, he might have the judging seat but she'd still do her best to put him through a mental trial.

'Oh, I've seen lots of bad bottoms.' He laid on the lightest of slaps across the dividing crack, a teasing warning. 'Spanked a fair number, too.'

'Call girls, were they?'

'No, one or two were Strip-O-Grams.'

Damn, she'd laid herself wide open for that one! Just as he was now laying open her knickerless arse.

Katie felt the cool breeze from the window floating over her bum as he finished pulling the mini skirt all the way up, revealing both buttocks. It now bunched at her waist, further accentuating the naked cheeks below. God, this was embarrassing. Even as she willed herself to relax, she tensed both cheeks involuntarily. 'Now, now. We don't want a puckered bum. We want a nice smooth canvas that'll redden very prettily,' the local celebrity said.

'Split personality, are you? Who's this *we*?'

'Michael and I. Bet he's listening outside. I'll bring him in to watch if you fail to behave yourself. He's the one who booked you. Am I right?'

A shrug. 'We have a client confidentiality clause.'

'Pity, that.' He fingered her taut bare orbs. 'Secrecy leads to lots more palm prints. Why not confess all for the sake of your backside?'

'All right. It was him!'

'And now *you're* the one in my bad books.' She felt him lift back his arm, squealed as he toasted the centre of one helpless buttock. Caught her breath as he warmed its creamy twin companion, repeated each slap further up. Both previously cool globes felt like they were colouring up already. 'Ouch! That really hurts!'

'You're not here to have your passport photo taken,' Russell Hall said. She hadn't realised a man's palm could make a woman's bottom sting this much. A sting that soon turned to an ongoing throb as he spanked her on the full swell, spanked over spanks and under spanks and to the side. 'Ah! Oh!' Little gasps of surprise erupted in her throat, her body jerking then flattening in an assault towards Eden. Each contact with his fingers and palm increased the baking glow.

'I'll tell the police!'

'I'll tell them more.'

'I'll tell my mum!'

'That you went to a stranger's house without your bra and knickers?'

'I'll . . . ouch!' She wriggled against his trousers as the chastisement went on. Why couldn't her brain forge some forgive-me phrases, words that would stop him searing the top, the centre, the sensitive underhang of her lap-held arse?

'Are you sorry you ruined my painting?' he murmured at last, breaking off the slaps to pique each quivering inch of her overheated bottom.

'I am! I'll never be so careless again!' Surely now he would release her? Katie held her breath and lay wearily across his knees, her rear end smarting.

'I suppose Michael's partly to blame.'

'He is! He engaged me for this prank. He paid me forty pounds!' Any moment now he'd lift her from his lap and phone her a taxi.

'And he didn't warn you about my collection of Chinese sculpture or contemporary art?'

'He didn't.' She was desperate to reassure him. 'I was just to knock your iced water into your lap.'

'Were you, indeed?' Russell Hall fondled her crimsoned cheeks with restored intensity. 'Soaking an interviewer's suit – that's not a nice thing to do.'

'I didn't want to,' Katie whispered, backpedalling. Damn her runaway mouth!

'Have you heard of the saying *sauce for the goose*?'

She nodded, slithering about on his knee. She had a feeling her ordeal was far from over. 'I think it's appropriate in the circumstances, don't you?' Katie shrugged. 'You don't want to get that skirt and vest wet?' She shook her head and closed her eyes, knowing what was coming next. 'Then strip.'

'I want to go home!' she muttered as he let go of her hands.

'To the policeman and policewoman I'd have to call? They'll enjoy parading that red rump around the station before they book you for vandalism!'

'All right! I'm stripping.' She stood up on unusually weak bare legs, and pulled off her vest top to reveal jutting-nippled breasts. It was just nervousness that was making them harden, she told herself as she edged her mini skirt down over her tingling rear end.

'Shoes off too. Let's see you as Nature intended.' God, did he have to eyeball every inch of skin as she unveiled it? He was really enjoying this.

'Happy now?' she muttered, focusing somewhere in the region of his record collection, then at the blank grey screen of his TV, then at the crooked mike.

When she at last met his gaze he was smiling. 'Let's get you over that little table in the corner where I've put the iced water. I moved it there when I saw how accident-prone you'd been!' Katie walked over to the marbled drinks table and stretched out on its surface. She winced and shifted her posture, feeling the marble cold against her trouser-chafed stomach and pubic purse.

'Satisfied?' she muttered.

'I hope you'll satisfy me yet,' he replied. He had no chance, even though her groin did feel uncomfortably distended. He'd never benefit though – she could wank when she got home.

'One cooling jug of water coming up,' said Russell Hall. She sensed him lining himself up above her. Cried out as the cool stream splashed over her hot sore bum.

After the initial contrast, the effect was very nice. Some of the sting subsided. 'Now I'll spank you for planning to soak my balls with this,' Russell murmured, taking his weight on his legs then half squatting over her back. Katie lifted her head for a neck-straining moment to see that he was sitting facing her rear, both hands free to chasten it. She let her head flop down again as he laid on the first slap.

'Aaah!' This spank hurt more than the ones he'd dished out before, yet the water should have cooled her poor bottom. 'A wet arse hurts more than a dry arse,' Russell Hall said.

'Done a physics course, have you?'

'No, but the University of Life has taught me how to pain a bad posterior.' Damn, he had an answer for everything – and a slap to accentuate it. She inhaled fast and tried to drum her bare feet against the Axminster as he smacked both writhing globes again.

'I've said I'm sorry! What more do you want?'

'To fuck you till you come real sweetly.'

'Don't you mean *really* sweetly?'

'I'll tease you till you're grateful to come at all!'

'Dream on.'

'Oh, I'm very much a realist.' She sensed him reaching for something just out of her line of vision on the floor.

'What are . . .?' Felt the exquisite light touch of something on her exposed labial leaves and clit.

'I'm touching your sex with your feather duster.'

'Why?' She drew in her breath as he played the plumes across her pussy again.

'Because I can.' A pause. 'And because it's a challenge, I suppose. I mean, you said that you wouldn't want me inside you. I'm hoping that you'll change your mind with the right kind of persuasion.'

'No way!'

Yet there was a way – and he was using it. She clamped her teeth together to hold the moans of pleasure in. 'Mr Hall – no more like that! Oh, please!' Sensation was speeding to her mount again and again in a series of exquisite action replays, causing her to wriggle like a sandworm and try to push her surging bud into the table's unsatisfying edge.

'All right! Shove it up me. Make me come!'

Russell took more of his weight on his hands, freeing her back a little. 'Spread your legs, then. Wider, so that your pussy's completely open to me. Now stay like that.' A pause. 'I'm going to fuck you from behind. You're to keep holding on to the far end of the table. If you let go I'll withdraw and thrash you again.'

'Yes, Mr Hall.' She hated him, but ached for his cock. That feather duster had taken her sex towards the summit. She closed her eyes and mouth in silent gratitude as she felt him move to kneel behind her, felt his prick starting to nudge its way in.

'Stay still,' he warned. 'You're too clumsy when you move.' She wanted to push against his shaft, taking it in deeper, deeper, deeper. She rubbed her nipples against the marble, wishing he'd take their soft warm surroundings in his hands. His belly was slapping against her scarlet bum. His fingers were gripping her waist. His sex was plunging in and out of her sex. 'God, I can dole out a spanking!' Russell Hall muttered. 'You've got the most scorching hot little bum!'

He thrust in, almost out, further in. 'Was it in your contract that you were going to get fucked?'

'No!' How dare he make such an assumption.

'Then your pussy's an additional perk?'

'I didn't intend –'

'Fancy a Strip-O-Gram being so turned on by a bit of plumage.'

It was increasingly hard to think: 'I'm not a Strip-O-Gram.'

Closer, closer. 'Oh? What would you call yourself?'

'A . . . A Modern Maid.'

'Made to please, huh?'

'Forced to please insufferable pigs like you!'

Pigs that could admittedly angle their cocks with delicious dexterity. Strange the way you could crave the muscle movement yet hate the man. 'I reckon your pussy's full of pleasure,' Russell murmured. 'Reckon it's as hot and wet as they come.'

Whimpering, writhing: 'I'm fantasising about someone handsome, that's why!'

'Sweetheart, it's a bit late to play hard to get, pretend you don't want it. You're butt naked over my coffee table, having begged me for a fuck!'

She climaxed then, her dingo-like howls echoing through the studio. Russell Hall thrust the last of the sweetness out. She lay there, contracting against his cock as he pumped on, aware of his sweat and her sex juice running down the backs of her thighs and tender petals. 'Should have shafted you while you still had that tart's skirt on,' Russell said.

'It's a maid's outfit,' she muttered, as his thrusting increased. She wondered if she could build up to a second peak: there was still a healthy blood supply to the area. She felt a small surge of disappointment as he enhanced his speed.

Damn, he was about to ... 'Does your firm do a Nympho Nurse? A Willing Waitress? A grown-up Schoolgirl?' the interviewer muttered, then groaned and gripped her waist as if he were about to fall off the planet, and squeezed forward, then stayed pulsing in her passageway.

'Beauty!' he muttered. Slowly she felt him pull out, turned as he threw the sheath in the basket. 'Can I get you a drink? A snack?' He seemed almost human now.

'No – just a pair of your wife's pants, please. And you can call me a cab.'

'Her pants?' He'd flinched at the mention of his wife, but now his brow cleared. 'Mm, see what you mean. She's taken her silken ones away with her on vacation, but I'm sure you'll be glad of her cotton leftovers if it means the taxi driver doesn't get to see your ruby-red backside!' He paused for a second to pat that self-same *derrière*, tucked his now-flaccid flesh into his zipper, then left the room.

Maybe his wife had a long skirt she could borrow as well? Katie crossed the studio and reached for the handle of the door. 'Fell for the whole thing!' Russell was saying.

'Told you it was worth a try,' Michael's voice added.

'I've procured girls for mates who're into spanking by pulling a ruse like that before.'

'Great arse and legs,' Russell added crudely. 'She wasn't half kicking them by the time I'd finished with her, the stupid little bitch!'

Yes, she had a great arse. Yes, she was little – but no, she wasn't stupid. Ten minutes later Katie sat gingerly in the taxi as it drove her back home. She was bright enough to recognise the *on* button of a recording desk, clever enough to have completed a media action course. When Russell Hall put in the cassette bearing tomorrow's date his listeners would only hear the first two minutes of the stock-market review he'd promised them. He'd then take off his headphones and retire with his interviewee to the hospitality suite while the tape continued to run.

Thereafter, the nation would hear Mr Morality himself blackmailing the teenage Katie into suffering a spanking and a shafting. She had a feeling that Russell's radio manager and his wife's divorce lawyers would be shafting him from now on.

Staff Training

'Give *you* the job?'

Charles Grieve looked doubtfully at Angela Reynolds. Granted, she'd only been his girlfriend for two weeks, but their relationship might well last a long time. Which meant that she'd be seen as having unfair advantage in applying for the post as his personal assistant, a fact she very well knew.

'You'd have to admit you knew a member of the panel –' he started.

'My memory's bad!' Angela grinned.

She looked so bright and lively that Charles found himself smiling back.

'You'd have to be a model worker,' he warned.

Angela gazed into his eyes. 'Believe me, Charles, I'd be very, very good.'

Three weeks later the interviews for the Revon boarding-school headmaster's PA took place. She was still his girlfriend, but she shook his hand and said she was pleased to meet him. Charles nodded, refusing to articulate the same lie.

'Tell us all a little about yourself,' he murmured awkwardly. She did so. The other two men and women interviewers looked suitably impressed.

'She's to be your PA – what do you think, Charles?' asked the chairman.

'She'll do me,' said Charles calmly, knowing that she would. He felt his groin tighten at the slight *double entendre*. He hadn't seen much of Angela's body yet and he'd like to see more.

She came. She settled in. Perhaps she got complacent. During her second week on the job, he realised he was going to have to bare her misguided little bum.

'My PA didn't inform me of the arrangements,' he said into the receiver, then apologised profusely. He put down the phone and switched on the school tannoy system, and rubbed his hands. 'Miss Reynolds – report to the headmaster's study right away.'

Five minutes later she rushed through the door, her chestnut hair tendrilling free of its chignon. 'Two of the younger boys were scrapping near the kitchens. I intervened –'

'It's not your job to intervene!' He knew from long experience that you had to run a boarding school with firm discipline. 'There are school monitors for that. Anyway, that's not why I called you here.'

'Oh?' Angela sat down in her chair and picked up her dictation pad.

'Write this down,' said Charles. 'I, Angela Reynolds, am about to receive a good thrashing for doing shoddy work.'

'You can't . . .' Angela's mouth and eyes opened wide as she looked up at him. A sudden still life, she held the pen near the pad.

'Oh, believe me, I can,' said Charles, flexing his palm.

'I could go to the authorities . . .'

'Go on.' He held the phone out to her. 'Just remember that word'll get out that you lied about not knowing anyone on the panel. You'll be dismissed without reference. In this climate you may never work again.'

Angela licked her pink-lipsticked lips.

'Charles! Couldn't we just . . .?'

Obviously coming to some decision she walked over to him and sat sideways in his lap, her long legs stretching out, heels swinging. She kissed his neck just above the collar, moved her teeth to his ear.

'We could just end your feeble attempts at seduction and teach you a lesson,' Charles said.

Putting one hand on her shoulders and another above her belly at the waist, he tipped her over till she was wriggling across his knees, her skirted bum beneath his exploring digits. She drummed her high heels on the ground and muttered 'Bastard!' and 'You rotten pig!'

'I'll take these insults out on your arse later,' Charles said calmly, fondling her extremities. 'Back to your initial crime, miss! How many spanks do you deserve for failing to inform me of my Gentlemen's Club lecture yesterday?'

'Oh God! I meant to. Then that truancy officer needed a report, and . . .'

She was trying to twist back entreatingly. He held her down. 'This looks very bad for the school, you know. And very painful for your very punishable little backside.'

'I'll make it up to you!' Angela added.

He slapped her teasing right hand away from his inner thigh. The caresses would come later. 'You've just earned yourself another five minutes' worth of spanks.'

Her skirt was close fitting, but when he'd finished rolling it up it stayed round her waist, outlining the start of her pert young bottom. Her briefs were just that – a micro scrap of lemon silk which showed the topmost swell of her arse and cut high to show the flesh above her grey-stock-inged thighs. Mercilessly, he pulled down her pants and suspender belt and nylons. He didn't want anything to get in the way.

'Lock the door!' Angela gasped.

'No, I'd quite like some of the other staff to see you up-ended like this. It would make them think twice before they misbehaved.'

Her newly bared bum was small and taut, with well-rounded fair cheeks that didn't look as if they'd been span-ked before. She wriggled with shame, obviously aware that he was staring down at them. The crease between her but-tocks opened, closed. He ran a teasing finger down its sensitive interior. She'd wriggle some more in a second when she felt his palm!

'You haven't told me how many spanks you deserve for your first infringement,' he said gloatingly. 'So I'm just go-ing to wallop you until my arm's too sore to go on.'

Angela said something rude about his fatherless state

again. He slapped down hard on her right buttock, swiftly followed up with a sharp smack to her left.

'Oh, you –!'

The third and fourth spanks seemed to unvoice her, and she settled for another gasp and the tiniest of whimpers instead.

'Such a bad girl,' Charles murmured, tracing the blurred pink imprints of his palm on her restless untested bottom. 'So thoughtless. So incompetent. I may have to schedule regular staff training to take place.'

'No!'

Angela tried to bring her palms back to protect her bum, but he took both wrists in one hand and held them in front of her. 'My dear, I've hardly started. There's no point in begging for forgiveness yet.'

He put his spanking hand into action, slapping first one globe then the other, before bringing his palms further down to warm the backs of her thighs. Her buttocks jerked at each five-fingered slap, then she flattened herself further over his lap, then half raised up again. Her calves flexed and relaxed as she got into a rhythm which vainly tried to protect her fast-heating rear.

'It's so sore . . .'

'Sore enough to remind you to diarise all my appointments?'

'Yes, Mr Grieve. Please, yes!'

'I hope so, Miss Reynolds.'

He stopped his administrations to fondle her reddened writhing bum. It felt as hot as he'd expected, looked alluringly vulnerable. She gave a little shudder – of excitement? mild fear? – each time he stroked her, obviously anticipating the next forceful slap.

'You're now going to fetch the cane from the glass case and bring it to me,' he said conversationally. 'Then you'll put your belly over the desk and stick your arse out as far as it'll go, and ask me to teach obedience to my newest member of staff.'

'I won't do it!' Angela muttered.

'Won't comply with the boss's orders? Oh dear.'

Angela slithered about some more. Charles ran his right hand from the top of one buttock to her thigh, then did the same with its partner before letting his thumb taunt the dividing crack between her well-warmed cheeks.

'Put your pants on now, then,' he said, 'and come back in an hour to collect your dismissal details.'

'Not that!' Angela gasped, trying to move her head around enough to make eye contact with him.

'Well, do as you're told and fetch that stinging cane!'

Slowly she unbent herself from his lap and started to smooth down her skirt as she straightened.

'Keep that up above your hot little backside,' ordered Charles. 'I don't want to waste good thrashing time unbaring your bottom again. You've enough violations against you as it is.'

'Yes, sir.'

She was learning – albeit slowly. He watched as she awkwardly crossed the room, her naked buttocks two glowing red ovals beneath the rucked-up blue band of her skirt.

Fingers slipping against the inset that passed as a handle, she pulled the glass panel along and reached for the cane which lay on a red velvet cushion, a warning to hundreds of naughty boys and girls.

'It's long,' she whimpered, holding the bamboo in two upturned hands, and turning to face him.

'Means a man can get a good swing at his target,' Charles explained.

Angela was still staring down at the behaviour-modifying instrument.

'Bring it over here,' Charles ordered. '*Now.*'

Taking small, feet-close-together steps she did so. Handed it to him. Winced as he swished it once, twice, thrice through the air. 'Much as I love to have your naked arse beneath my palms, I couldn't get enough leverage with this thing to thrash your ineptitude out of you,' he said as she stared mutely at his lap and waited. 'So we'll save further sessions over my knee for later – get yourself over my desk.'

Her bum looked smaller when she'd obeyed – doubtless

because he was now viewing it from a little distance. There was still enough flesh to get his cane into though. And small bums, in his experience, hurt more than larger ones did. The tops of her thighs were still finger-struck pink, but looked pale when contrasted with the hotly slapped curve of her bare bottom. As he stared she flexed her palms against the far edge of the desk.

'Six strokes to conclude your punishment for not keeping my work schedule in order,' he said evenly. 'Then ...?' He let the question hang in the air, noting how she squirmed against the wooden surface and stiffened her thighs. She'd be thinking about how much the cane was going to hurt her tendermost places, about what came next. 'This'll sting,' he added. 'But then you deserve to be warmed up, don't you?'

'Yes,' Angela whispered contritely.

'Say "Yes, sir." '

She did. She'd come a long way from the girl who'd rained insults on him about his parentage. Not that he'd forgiven her, or forgotten.

'Say "I promise to do my job more efficiently" after each stroke,' he instructed.

Angela swallowed noisily, and flexed her deliciously taut calves as best she could.

Taking his arm back, he brought the implement squarely across both buttocks so that it landed in the centre, cutting across the crack in her arse to neatly render her globes into pink quartets.

'Aaah!' She jumped up, hands going to her bum, and turned round to face him, hair totally free of its clasp now, face redder than her arse.

'You're leaving?' queried Charles. 'It's been fun.'

'No, I ...' Angela stopped, then walked shyly up to him and put her palms against his chest, thumbs against his shirt, locating the nipples. She lifted her lips to his and kissed him. He remained passive, looking down.

'Now, where was I? Oh, yes – five strokes to go.'

'Isn't there a way ...?'

'Later. Much later.'

He saw desire and fear and excitement in her slightly glassy eyes.

'I have to repeat the first stroke,' he said gently. 'You do understand?'

'Please don't, sir!' Angela looked down at the carpet, then back at the desk. She licked her lips twice, bit her lower one. 'It stung so much . . .'

'It'll subside to a dull ache. The point is, you'll remember it every time you're arranging a meeting for me, every time you have to take dictation or telephone some scholarly body on my behalf.'

'I'll remember. Oh God, I'll remember,' whispered Angela, putting protective palms over her roasted bum.

His hand on her lower back, Charles guided her over to the desk, helped her get in place.

'I'm repeating the first stroke,' he reminded her, 'for insubordination. Thank me nicely in advance.'

'Thank you for caning me, sir,' muttered Angela through gritted teeth, trying to make her belly merge with the wood. He admired the clear red line against its background of lighter red. A good hard spanking made a nice preparation for a caning, toasted the flesh, rendering it more supple, making the erring party more ready to acquiesce.

Charles flexed the cane so that it made a warning swishing sound. Angela jerked her bum, then relaxed again. 'Just practising,' Charles said. 'I do that after a girl's been particularly bad. It strengthens my whipping arm a great deal.'

'I beg . . .' Angela whimpered, turning her head to look imploringly back at him.

'Face the front. I expect an obedient useful salaried PA from now on.'

As if realising the error of her ways, she fell silent. Charles took aim, taking care to land the cane as close as possible to where its predecessor had been. The thin red line immediately darkened to a deeper one. Angela let go of the desk and bucked and yelled.

'Oh dear. Oh dear, Oh dear.'

Immediately realising her mistake, she bent herself over the surface again and gripped at the far side of the desk as if it were a lifeline.

'I didn't get up! I didn't! I didn't!'

'I should hope not, miss.' He ran the cane over her sore bared bottom. 'We'll be here all day if I have to keep giving you the first cut over again.'

Outside he could hear the second-years on their way to the tuck-shop.

Angela groaned, 'I wish you would lock the door!'

'Address me as *sir*.' He flicked the cane against her thigh tops to emphasise his displeasure. He knew no one would enter the room without his permission. He had everyone's respect. But he didn't want *her* to know that! It added to her humiliation to think that the matron, the janitor, even his pupils could come in at any moment and see her reddened wriggling buttocks feeling the merciless lash of his cane.

'I'll be lenient, and move on to stroke two.'

'Thank you, sir. Oh, thank you!' She buried her head more deeply between her arms. Her bottom twitched. Her thighs quivered slightly. He meted the stroke out just below the last one, creating a wider red band. Hadn't he read that some headmasters of yore had chalked two parallel lines across the trouser seats of each recalcitrant bottom? They had then directed all their wrath towards these same luckless strips of flesh. Charles smiled to himself. It was a variant to experiment with in the future, if his pretty PA misbehaved herself again.

Angela had cried out at the second stroke, but kept her body in place.

'Oh dear, you've made me angry. You've made me very, very angry,' Charles said sadly. He stepped closer to her waiting bum and palmed it for long, long moments whilst she squirmed.

'I didn't move, sir,' she whispered.

'No, but you were supposed to promise to do your job more efficiently after each stroke.'

'Oh, Christ!' Angela twisted her flushed face round to

look at him. 'I just forgot! I wasn't meaning to be disobedient!'

'Like you forgot to remind me of my Gentlemen's Club
obligations?'

'Oh, please!'

'Please double my punishment, sir? Please parade me
with my bared bottom in front of the entire school, sir?'

'Please don't give me extra punishment. I'll do anything
you want!'

'What I want from my staff is –'

There was a knock at the door. An authoritative knock.
Angela jumped up and stared wildly round the room,
which offered no hiding place.

'Oh, hell! Don't let them see me! Don't . . .'

Charles brought her gently back to the desk and helped
her over it.

'Keep in position, my pretty dear – that's right, showing
off your disobedient bared young bum. Maybe my visitor
will recognise that it's an essentially impudent little arse,
will want to give it a good hiding too.'

'Don't let them . . .' Angela started again. She looked
too overwhelmed to move this time. And there was nowhere for her to go.

'I may bring in lots of people to watch your staff training. They won't have seen teaching practice like this for a
long, long time.'

He heard her moan with shame as he opened the door
and slipped quickly out. The deputy headmistress stood
there.

'Ah, Charles – I wanted a word about the teachers' an-
nual review.'

Charles nodded. 'I'm just on my way to the library,
Celia. I'll bring the papers to you in twenty minutes if you
like.' In keeping with his story, he went to the school's
large book-filled hall and borrowed a managerial book.

When he got back to his room and opened his door,
Angela had pulled down her skirt and either put on or
hidden her pants. She stood, red-faced, by the window.

'I couldn't bear to keep bending over the desk.'

'You'll have to bare it later then, take it twice as hard.'

Her eyes half-closed and her mouth fell open in a look that spoke of both anguish and arousal.

'How much later? I don't think I can take much more – I can't sit down!'

'You won't be sitting down for quite some time.' He took his own seat behind his desk. 'In fact, we're going to have you running around in the gym hall. I noticed you were clumsy earlier, needed some athletics practice. Be at the gym at midnight tonight.'

'And if I'm not?' Angela tried to look imperious, and failed. The top button of her blouse had come undone. Her lips looked full and wanton. He wanted to enjoy her now, but knew that tonight's lesson would make their ultimate union even more sweet.

'If you don't keep this appointment you are free to leave my employ. Perhaps you could go and work for someone whose standards are as inferior as your own?'

'I've already apologised for my mistakes!'

'Apologies don't restore my credibility.'

'Maybe I could –'

'You can follow these instructions before turning up for staff training tonight.'

He told her what he required. She blushed, staring at the ground. He dismissed her. Watched as she turned and walked towards the door, heel taps uneven, head down. Taking his seat, he monitored her progress. If she looked back, she'd ultimately be his! She stopped as she reached for the handle, cast a quick glance back at him. He nodded, watching her disappearing bare calves. What had she done with her stockings, then? Perhaps she knew there was no point in wearing them. She doubtless planned to go to her cottage in the grounds for a cooling bath.

For the rest of the afternoon Charles organised the school sports day, his mind thrilling to the sport to come. Miss Reynolds had only been given a brief tour of the gym hall when she started working for him. She was about to become much better acquainted with its many charms.

Thoughtfully he picked up the cane that she'd left on his

desk, and ran it through his fingers. He'd have to remember to take it with him tonight.

He wondered if she'd show up. Not that he'd really sack her if she didn't – she was a first-class PA who'd only made one error of judgement. Given that they'd been growing more intimate, this specially prolonged foreplay would simply make their first merging one that she'd never forget.

Midnight seemed a long way away – but he had preparations to attend to before then. He checked the timetable: there wouldn't be a class in the gymnasium after 4 p.m. Some of the older boys went there to work out in the evenings, though. Luckily their curfew was at ten.

Hugging his plans to himself like a thermal vest, Charles completed his business then went to his bungalow behind the school, where he ate, bathed and put on a clean white shirt and linen trousers. Half an hour before the intended punishment session, he donned his long black headmaster's cloak.

Now to lick the gym into demanding form! Not to mention its luckless occupant. Swishing his cane, Charles strode through the darkness to the large hall and unlocked it. He hooked all the wooden shutters over the windows before putting on the cruelly bright overhead lights. He'd leave the key in the inside of the door, so she could lock it – or unlock it – if it got too much for her. Not that his previous girlfriend had complained . . .

Ensuring there was a distance of eight feet between each obstacle, he set out bars that you jumped over, a low-arched grid that you slid under, ten cones that you wove your way around. Then he took out a stop-watch and a whistle and put the basketball under the relevant high net.

At five to twelve the door opened ever so slightly, and an eye and nose appeared. She was here! The door opened further, and she slipped in, looked back and locked the door behind her. She'd done exactly as he said.

'Nice,' he said, walking over to her and pacing round and round. 'Very nice. But you haven't come here to be complimented on your dress sense, have you, Miss Reynolds?

'No, sir,' Angela whispered, swallowing.

'Why have you come?

'Because . . . because I was bad!'

'*How* bad?'

'Very bad.'

She'd forgotten to say *sir* this time. Before, in his room, she'd been starting to humiliate herself verbally. Now he could see that a little of her spirit had returned with her pride.

'*Very* bad,' he confirmed. 'Very bad indeed. Very disobedient. And what happens to naughty girls who are disobedient?'

'They . . . have to learn.'

'Have to learn?' He marched steadily round and round, tapping the cane against his leg. 'Come on, you can do better than that. Say "They get caned on their wilful little bums." '

Angela looked at her gym shoes then at the ground as if they would provide a way out of her dilemma.

'They . . .'

'Say it or you'll go over my knee again as well as taking six of the best!'

'They . . .' she half-sobbed, 'get caned on their wilful little bums, sir.'

'Then I don't think that bum should be hidden by a skirt, do you?'

'N – no, sir.' Eyes downcast once more, Angela reached for her skirt hem, looked up at him supplicatingly.

'Lift it right up over your back as you bend over. That's it! Good girl.'

Standing behind her, he caressed her taut bottom through the full navy knickers. 'I'll lay two parallel strokes over your pants, my dear, then I'm going to set you a little test.'

He kept her waiting for a goodly while whilst he lined up his swing to warm the centre of her buttocks. She tensed her bum muscles every few seconds in evident anticipation. Her white ankle socks and plain white short-sleeved blouse made her look gloriously vulnerable. One gym shoe was trailing a lace.

'You really shouldn't have covered your bum before when someone knocked at my door,' he said regretfully, tracing the merciless wood down her pantied globes.

'I felt so silly.'

'You *are* silly. Very foolish indeed.'

'Next time . . .'

'You're planning to be bad enough to warrant a next time?'

'No,' Angela muttered, head bent towards the ground. 'I didn't mean –'

'I don't know what you mean – but I mean business.' He brought the cane down across the lower fleshy swell of both arse cheeks and she cried out and let go of her stance. Rubbed her bum hard, making an extended gasping sound; a whine through breath.

'Bend over. Grasp your ankles.'

'Just the two?'

'That's what I said.'

Two over your panties!

'Then you'll . . .?'

'Then the test.'

Shoulders, calves and bum tensing, Angela took up the unprotected position, her small round buttocks lucklessly disarmed.

'Pull your knickers higher so that I see some naked thigh,' Charles said thoughtfully. 'Mmm, that's better. Now I can focus on both cheeks of that wilful little *derrière*, see exactly where my cane has to go.'

Angela groaned.

'Save your anguish for later, dear.'

He gave a light smack at each waiting orb, and she shivered. Again he let her anticipation build.

Then he delivered the stroke beneath the underswell of her buttocks. Her knees bent forward several inches and she gasped, but straightened quickly and stayed rooted to the spot. 'Good. You're learning.' He took a seat on the long low bench that was parallel to the topmost wall, 'Let's have a look at that punished bum.'

This time she didn't demur, but went over his knee. As

she did so she let go of her skirt, which fell back down to cover her modesty. That would never do!

'Don't be shy,' he murmured tauntingly. 'Show your superiors your pretty pants.'

Head pressed against the bench, she twitched ashamedly as he pulled her skirt up, traced his palm over both compact spherical cheeks.

'Does your backside hurt?'

She nodded. He spanked her hard.

'Hurt more when you forget to say "Yes, sir"?'

'Yes, sir. It really hurts, sir!'

'You'll appreciate a little gamesmanship to take your mind off your punished posterior, then.'

Angela sagged more heavily against his knees. He slid his hands beneath her sex to help her up. She was wet and hot and open.

'Charles ... please,' she whimpered, putting her lips to his neck as he encouraged her upright.

'Soon, Miss Reynolds, you'll be given a chance to show your appreciation of this extra staff training. But for now we've work to do!'

He turned her towards the obstacle course he'd arranged. 'You go up and over this one, run on, crawl under that one. Run on again – fast as you can, of course! – then weave in and out of these cones without touching one, far less knocking it down.'

'Yes, sir,' Angela murmured. The hectic flush of her face subsided slightly as she surveyed the room. 'Do I come back to you when I'm finished, sir?'

Charles showed her the stop-watch, switched it on with obvious relish. 'I'll tell you when you're finished, my pretty miss!'

He sat down on another long bench to watch her antics. Her short sports skirt flapped up and down as she started running, giving tantalising glimpses of small buttocks in navy blue pants. Her pert breasts seemed to strain through her white blouse as she pumped her arms in a bid to move forward faster. Her mouth was a set line of concentration as he observed the stop-watch clocking up the time.

Angela completed her first circuit and looked back at him. He waved her on. 'Keep going!'

She obeyed, her pace a little slower. On her third circuit she bumped her right calf against one of the cones.

Charles blew his whistle. 'Penalty! You were warned.'

Angela stopped in her tracks. 'I was getting tired. I –'

'I must insist that all my staff take a medical. I can't have employees being this unfit.'

She held her side. 'I'm just a bit out of condition!'

'Then we'll start by shaping up your backside.'

She stood, licking her lips, staring somewhere in the vicinity of his chest, fingers straying to her long brown locks.

'Come here.' She shuffled over to stand before him. He pulled the bench two feet away from the wall. 'Kneel facing the bench, then drape your belly over it. Use one hand to steady yourself, then reach the other back to pull down your pants.'

'I tried to do right! I tried!' Even as she protested, she started to edge down the navy cotton.

'I know you did. And I'll take that into consideration. It's almost over now.'

'And we'll . . .?'

She looked back at him, eyes glazed, lips opening.

'Probably two or three times.'

He stared as she edged her pants off. His cane had left its imprints on her bum, both midway and above the thighs. They were obviously still stinging. The strokes he'd doled out that morning had already faded away.

'One on the bare for second-rate athletic performance,' he said sadly, watching the waiting bum tense and untense. It seemed to have taken on a life of its own in its quest to be a good bum, a sweet bum, a bum that didn't get spanked or caned.

'Raise that arse a little higher, if you please,' he ordered, and heard her groan.

He used the cane near the top of her rump and watched the acquitted flesh of her lower cheeks tremble slightly. He hadn't caned that particular strip before, and the line came up well.

'Uh!' she expelled, driving her tummy forward, palms coming back in almost the same movement to protect her tormented flesh.

'Not another transgression! I told you not to touch!'

She rubbed each curve, then took her hands away, holding them a half inch or so from her well-thrashed bottom.

'Put your hands on your head.'

She obeyed him.

'Keep them there.' He gave an exaggerated sigh, and his crotch twitched. 'I thought I was finished with you, but now you'll have to go over the horse.'

He took down her skirt, then put his hands under her armpits and half lifted her up. He walked her gently over to the long wooden horse that his pupils loved to leapfrog.

'Up you go.'

Angela gave a little jump, then a bigger one, her hands on the horse's seat, desperately seeking propulsion. Her bare bottom pulled in with each muscular effort, its hot redness a contrast to her white blouse.

'I hope you're trying.' He swished the cane through the air. Angela gave another start, and got herself halfway up the equipment. Her gym-shoed feet drummed against the side as her toes sought further purchase. 'Such an awkward girl. So very slow.'

He put his palms under her arse and hoisted her right on to the contraption. Then he took her hands and tugged her arms slightly till they lay before her on the green baize, and got one slender leg to drape over each side of the gym apparatus so that her bare bottom was fully exposed to his touch.

'Keep your arse there and thank me for each spank.'

Whimpering, Angela thanked and thanked, her moans of pain turning, as he caressed her sex, to cries of pleasure.

'Now for some measurements of your internal fitness,' Charles murmured, carrying her over to the scatter cushions in the corner before laying her down on her tummy and sliding inside. She was as deliciously ready for him as he'd imagined, and he felt equally well-primed as he moved into her, staring down at her blush-red bared bum.

Finally they slept, safe in the knowledge that the cleaners wouldn't arrive till 7 a.m. They woke at six.

'Shall we have breakfast at my place?' Angela murmured, kissing him.

'Could do,' Charles said, 'though you may prefer a long cold shower.'

'How so?'

'Because yesterday you called me some vile names, and today your bare bottom must pay for these insults.'

'I thought you'd have forgotten ...' He saw curiosity and excitement and fear in her eyes.

He shook his head.

'Over your study desk again?' At the memory, her small hands flew to her still well-pinkened buttocks.

'No – that isn't humiliating enough for a girl as bad as you.'

'Then what ...?'

Charles smiled. 'Given that you used the language of the farmyard, I've decided to give you a thrashing in the school farm's barn.' He smiled. 'There's a nice thick bale of hay we can bend you over. I must remember to wear my leather belt.'

Room Service

These sheets were hardly rumpled! Donna looked at the double bed: she'd get away with not changing it. If a few of the other hotel rooms were equally tidy she could save over an hour. This part-time job as a chambermaid didn't pay very well and was totally perkless. Who could blame her for cutting corners now and then?

Smiling to herself, she hurried out into the corridor – and into the hotel manager, Arnold Boscome. 'You're looking very pleased with yourself, Miss Telford.' At six foot one he towered above her five foot three. Donna gulped, and stared down at the clean bedding she was still clutching. 'Em, yes.'

'I like a contented staff – makes for a convivial atmosphere! Only I wonder if you'll be as happy after I've inspected this room? Donna gripped the sheets more tightly and forced her eyes to confront his. This was something she hadn't anticipated. 'Really, sir – it's fine!'

She tensed her thighs together and nibbled at her lower lip as they entered the room and he edged back the top of the duvet. Thank goodness it looked unwrinkled and white. As she stared he pulled the quilt further down, then further – to reveal a gentleman's black sock.

'Oh dear. Oh dear, oh dear.'

Donna licked her lips, mind searching wildly for a way to excuse such laziness. 'We've had complaints about unchanged beds of late,' Boscome continued. 'Obviously well-founded complaints.'

'I . . . I'm a mature student, sir. I've got essays to do. I also have to work on my dissertation, and . . . uh . . . sometimes I'm short of time.'

The manager looked her up and down, minutely inspecting her flushed face, her black chambermaid's dress with the crisp white apron. 'You have time to study. Time for boyfriends – I've seen young men collect you here before. Yet you don't have time to do the work I pay you for? That's a sackable offence.'

Worse and worse! Donna made her eyes entreatingly big. 'Don't give me the sack, sir. I'll do anything you want to make it up to you, sir.'

'Anything?'

'Yes, sir. Please!' There was a pause. A very long pause. A heart-thumping pause.

'In that case get your lazy backside over my knee.'

Donna felt herself blushing further. Excitement and fear caused a flipping-over thrill throughout her lower belly.

'You must recognise that you need to be taught discipline,' the manager said.

'It was only a few sheets!' she muttered, stalling for the sake of her arse, for thinking time.

'And a few lost guests. And a tarnished reputation in the industry. Take your thrashing.'

'Oh, piss off.' False bravado made her utter the words. She wasn't a baby!

'I'll pretend I didn't hear that.' Boscome stood up and reached for her wrists. 'You can go over easy and retain your pay packet, or . . .?' Or be broke and probably homeless. She couldn't survive on her pitiful student loan.

But she couldn't just submit. She couldn't! She had her pride, her dignity to think of. 'I'll go to the management!' she said.

'They'll doubtless agree you need your backside warmed, and you'll still be sacked for shoddy work, silly.' He pulled her closer by her hands, then sat down on the edge of the bed, staring up at her. 'Ask for your spanking now, and ask really nicely. I'll make it hurt all the more if you delay.'

'How many?' Donna quavered, standing her ground. Her boss turned her sideways on to his knees, murmuring, '*I'll* ask the questions!' She took a step back, but he used his full force to pull her down, down, down, till her head and shoulders lay across one corner of the bed. Transferring his right hand to her skirted arse, he used the elbowed weight of his left arm to hold her in place.

'I'll wallop you harder if you struggle.' Her legs, stretched out to the full behind her, felt weak and tremulous. His thighs felt taut and strong.

'That's better! Now, as I spank you I want you to think about how bad you've been, and maybe after your bum's sore you'll start to tell me all about your wickedness.' All she could think about now was the helplessness of her still-skirted behind. 'Time that we edged your dress up, my sweet,' Boscome added, hoisting her rear end higher into the air to increase her vulnerability, 'I like to feast my eyes on the bottom I'm about to spank.'

Donna dug her nails into the duvet as she felt him roll the material up above her waist, revealing her black tights and thin purple panties. 'Bad girls don't get to keep their tights on,' the manager murmured, peeling the covering of nylon away.

'Please don't take down my pants!' Donna gasped, screwing her eyes shut tight at the shame of it.

'That depends on whether or not you're good.'

She'd be good! She'd be brilliant! She whimpered through her breath with humiliation and desire as the forty-something man began to caress the cheeks of her backside through the painfully inadequate silk covering. 'I'm going to make this bottom sting,' he said coolly, 'and then we'll have a little talk about your behaviour before I decide whether or not to warm it up some more.'

He caressed her waiting cheeks again and again. Donna writhed, wishing he'd just get it over with, but when the first whack ricocheted down she opened her eyes wide and yelled.

'Oh, don't start snivelling now. You'll really have something to cry about in ten minutes!' Her boss added a second angry spank to the neighbouring cheek.

What must her bum look like, upended like this? It was a well-rounded creamy one with a tight furrow, probably ideal for spanking. And how did her thighs look, stretched out behind her, stripped bare? Thank goodness he'd let her keep on her pants, for though their thinness spared her nothing, they at least left some of her dignity intact.

She tensed both buttocks as Boscome slapped them again. He seemed to be finding a hard, fast rhythm. She whimpered as he whacked alternate helpless globes with repeated zeal. 'I'll change the beds properly!' she cried, not sure if he heard her above the noise of the spanking. She prayed that another chambermaid or new guest wouldn't come in and see her pinioned over her employer's merciless lap.

'What else won't you do again?' Boscome asked, stopping his painful assault on her rear to stroke her cheeks through her knickers. Donna tensed some more: had he found out about her other shortcuts at work? 'I . . . I aim to please, sir,' she muttered, 'but I don't know what you mean.'

'I think you do.' He palmed her arse round and round and round. 'Tell you what, I'll make it easy for you. If you admit your crimes you'll only get one other spanking. If you lie to me, you'll get two.'

'What makes you think . . .?'

'As I said earlier, other guests have made complaints about you.'

He had her, then. She might as well admit to each offence and get it over with. 'Well . . .' she wriggled at the thought of the punishment which would follow, 'I've just been emptying the ashtrays instead of washing them most days.'

'And?'

She winced at the thought of the hiding each new admission would bring her. 'And hoovering around the furniture instead of under it, sir.'

'Doing half your job, in other words,' Boscome murmured, starting to fondle her raised hot bum with renewed firmness.

'Yes, but I'll never make the same mistake again!'

'No, you won't, because every time you don't do your

duties you'll remember how your bottom felt after I'd finished with it. How will it feel?'

'Sore, sir – very sore!' Almost sore enough to make her beg. Donna searched for a way to lessen the severity of her additional spanking, 'I'll remember. Please, sir, I'll remember!' she said.

'The chambermaid's been naughty, so we have to pull her knickers down,' said Boscome evenly. Donna held her breath, waiting for him to peel down the heated silk. 'Reach your hands back, girl, and bare your bum for me.'

She swallowed hard. 'Couldn't I –?'

'Bare your bum.' He was unyielding. If she didn't want to lose this job she didn't have much option. Trying not to think about the ignominy of her position, Donna obeyed.

'Mmm, coming along nicely,' the manager said, pulling her hands away when her briefs were just below thigh level. He settled her more firmly so that her palms were on the floor this time. Now she felt the air on her exposed bottom. Her half-mast panties seemed to underline and accentuate the vulnerable soft flesh that was to be thrashed.

Were her buttocks as red as they felt? Her poor rump was already smarting all over, each pert cheek obviously well fingermarked from underswell to lower back. Her plump thighs felt equally scalded. How much more would she squeal when she felt his powerful right hand on the bare?

'Sir, I'll never do it again,' she pleaded as he palmed her stripped sore flesh.

'Is that your plea for clemency?' He palpated her globes more firmly. 'I'm sure you can show more humility than that!'

She felt the changing movement beneath her as he pulled his arm back. Then she tensed her buttocks and thighs as she waited for the renewed punishing slaps.

The first landed on the centre of her right buttock, and was immediately followed by one which stung her across the dividing crack, heat radiating out towards both bum cheeks. She grunted and opened her mouth to protest, but he'd already moved his ministrations on to her left orb and started to wallop that with the same hard-handed zeal.

'Uh! Ah!' Donna raised her head and palms from the floor, but found that her boss's determined arm was stopping her getting any further. She drummed her toes on the carpet and let out another yell. 'I'm doubling the intensity now because you're making so much fuss.' He thrashed harder, harder, harder as she drove her denuded pubis forward, small firm breasts pointing forlornly towards the floor.

'I'll make the beds!' Donna gasped. Two more merciless spanks rained down. 'I'll wash the bloody ashtrays as often as you like!'

'Swearing is disrespectful and earns you another five minutes thrashing.'

She bit back the thought. Her bottom was getting really, really sore. Her entire being was beginning to concentrate on these baking twin rotundities. Her body took on its own rhythm: tense, wince, cry out, momentarily relax. Her sex rubbed against his knee each time she pushed forward, sending increasingly urgent pulsing sensations through her swollen groin.

'I'll do anything!' she gasped.

'I may avail myself of that promise later.' He kept spanking her as he spoke the words. There was no relief.

'I could please you with my mouth . . .'

'You'd have pleased me much more if you'd just done the work I paid you for.' Her comment seemed to anger him – leastways the next four spanks came down extra hard.

Now the tops of her thighs felt as fiery and scarlet as her poor upturned buttocks. Her normally cool *derrière* was turned into two burning globes atop fingermarked legs. 'I could spank you for another hour,' said her boss in a casual tone. 'I do weight lifting at the gym so my arm muscles are very well developed.' He subjected her bare bottom to another three full-force spanks.

Something gave way inside Donna's mind.

'I've been a bad girl,' she gasped, 'a girl who deserves to be punished. I need . . . I needed this spanking to teach me a lesson, but from now on I promise I'll be so dutiful, so good!'

'I think you will, for a while,' said Boscome thoughtfully, ceasing the walloping to trace his palms over her violated flesh.

Donna whimpered as pain radiated through her bottom and pleasure spread upwards through her mons. 'Spread your legs a little further,' Boscome instructed. Swallowing hard, she did so. Felt his fingers sliding under her tummy, then moving down to find the ecstasy route.

'Thank me nicely,' he said, beginning to tease the wet hard bud of her sexuality.

'Thank you, sir!'

'For deigning to touch my clitoris, sir,' he coached. Donna closed her eyes. This was so humiliating. 'I can't hear you,' said the manager, taking his climax-promising fingers away.

She couldn't stand it – the sense of loss. She had to come. Had to come quickly! 'Thank you, sir, for deigning to touch my clitoris,' she said between gritted teeth. Boscome returned his digits to her fervent flesh, but kept them immobile above her clitoral hood. 'Would the bad girl like to say anything else?'

Aroused beyond bearing, Donna tried to rub herself against his hand. 'Whatever you want! Tell me what to say! Only let me come, I beg, sir.'

'In your own words, please,' her boss murmured dispassionately, sliding one promissory finger down her desperate labial lips before taking it away.

'I don't deserve your fingers on my clit. I must beg for it, beg for it really nicely!' Voice almost disembodied in its desperation, her entire focus centred on her pleading clit.

'I suppose I might as well fondle it now I'm here,' said Boscome, starting his delicious slow ministrations again.

Round and round and . . .

'If I see some dust across the room, I'll stop,' he warned.

'Yes, sir,' Donna moaned, moving hungrily against him.

'If my fingers get bored with touching you . . .'

'Yes, sir. Yes!'

She rubbed greedily against his hand, the fingers that had brought such pain now bringing unimaginable pleasure.

'Easy,' said Boscome. 'If you get too excited I may stop.'

'I beg, sir. Oh, please, I beg!'

'I think you do. I think you're starting to beg quite nicely.' Rubbing, rubbing, the *nearly there* signals were going off all around her sex. 'Now just stay still for the next five minutes whilst I fondle you for my own delectation. I'll have to punish you some more if you start to wriggle about.'

He pleasured her especially sweetly and Donna groaned. And writhed despite herself. The sensations were just too exquisite. 'Oh, dear,' said Boscome, still teasing her tender parts. 'You've disobeyed me again with all this wiggling.' She tensed her thighs as her orgasm approached. 'What happens to naughty girls who disobey?'

'They . . . get thrashed.'

'That's right. And what do we thrash their wicked bottoms with?'

She had to say what he wanted or he wouldn't let her come! 'With . . . with a belt, sir.'

Alarm spread through her brain, arousal spread through her sex lips. Arousal won.

'And how many lashes should we dole out to this particular bottom?'

'S – six!' she muttered, moving.

'Only six? And you forgot to say sir. That's extra punishment!'

'Ten, sir!' Donna groaned, and came.

'Further wilfulness!' Boscome said a moment later, helping her on to her belly on the bed. He lay down beside her and she put her arms round his waist, burying her flushed face in his shoulder. 'After you've paid lip service to being sorry, we'll have to have a chat.'

'Yes, sir!' Donna sighed, nuzzling into his neck with her lips as her small hands moved down to unzip him. She triumphed in his sighs of satisfaction as she lowered her mouth . . .

Two days later she felt less triumphant. 'What did I tell you?' He strode into the hotel laundry where she was depositing the towels. 'You've left a wet footmat in Room 613.'

'I didn't mean –'

'You never mean. Bend over that table in the corner.'

Donna felt the heat rush to her face and sex simultaneously. 'Go to hell!'

'Hell is for bad girls. Haven't you been bad?'

She shrugged. 'I guess, but . . .'

'Butt with two t's is all I'm interested in at the moment. Yours needs correcting very hard.'

'Yeah? By you and whose army?' Her mind raced ahead for further insults, further put-downs. She couldn't just give in to him immediately, do as he asked. It was humiliating, demoralising being subjected to this. She was a grown woman!

'Oh, I'm mastering the show single-handed,' Boscome said. He walked her over to the unpolished wooden desk.

'I won't let you, you bastard!'

He smiled. 'Less of the histrionics. You want to keep your job and you want to come and you want me inside you. You know in the end you'll bend across it anyway.'

'Yeah. Right!' Best get it over with. He pushed her into place and she gripped the furthest edge with suddenly tremulous fingers. 'What if someone comes in?'

Boscome looked her up and down. 'That's a silly question, isn't it? Obviously they'll see me taking my belt to your arse.'

Donna whimpered at the image. 'Three over your dress, three over your knickers, and two on the bare,' Boscome said. He stroked her full but lean bottom through the twin layers of material. 'That way your arse is nicely warmed up for the hardest strokes.'

Donna lay there, waiting, waiting, waiting. Thinking about her defenceless backside, about the laundry maids that could waltz through the door. Some of them thought she was uppity because her main role was that of student. How they would gloat to see her reduced to this!

She tensed up as she sensed Boscome's arm draw back, jumped as the first lash of the belt struck home, midway down her bottom. It stung, but the protection given by her cotton dress and pants assured that the pain wasn't too sharply defined. As she got used to the muted burning, Boscome laid on a second cut.

The third went slightly higher than the first and second, creating a wide band of heated hurting. 'Pull your dress up now,' Boscome said. Donna winced. Took her time edging up the shift, dreading further exposure. Already her wriggling had ensured that part of her panties had worked their way into the crack of her arse.

Which meant that her lower cheeks were already bared. Boscome aimed the first two lashes there and Donna almost shot over the table. 'Aaah! Aaah!'

'You should have thought of how this would feel before you left a used bathmat in place.'

'I know! I . . . had a lot to do. I'm sorry!'

'This thrashing will *make* you sorry,' Boscome said. He laid on the third stroke high up her bum, which, if anything, hurt more than the others. Donna wailed and jumped up, started stumbling towards the door.

'We haven't finished teaching you your work duties yet.' Gently but firmly Boscome took her upper arms and propelled her back to the waiting desk. Her feet dragged against the floor. 'I can't bear it!'

'You're going to have to, unless you'd rather leave my employ today.'

'No, not that!' Donna laid her tummy over the table again, half-sobbing. She moved her scourged young bottom from side to side as she waited for the onslaught to renew.

'Time to pull your pants down,' her boss said.

'Christ, no!'

'Time to pull them down.'

'Do you want *me* to . . .' She gulped, her red face blushing further.

'Of course. I've better things to do with my time than undress you. Get these knickers off.' Snivelling, she reached back and edged down her cotton panties, feeling them slither to her ankles as she got back into place. 'What

92

a pity you only have two to go,' the manager murmured. 'It's such a wilful-looking arse. I could punish it for hours!'

'Please don't, sir. I'll be so obedient, sir. I promise to please you!' She spread her thighs insinuatingly.

'Just concentrate on being disciplined,' Boscome said.

'Yes, sir, I'll concentrate, sir.' She cried out loudly as the wide expanse of leather made searing contact with her bared disarmed bottom, and put her hands back to cup the scalding globes.

'Were you given permission to touch?'

'No, but . . .' She looked back at him helplessly.

'Stand up. Hold your right hand above your left hand. That's it.' Donna winced with shame as he flicked the belt over her waiting palm.

He didn't do it hard – but it was shameful, being treated like a schoolgirl. 'Back over that table for your final stroke,' Boscome said.

'I can't endure . . .' He stared at her until she looked away. 'Please, sir, go easy.' Face as flushed as her buttocks, she got back in place over the desk.

'That bottom still doesn't know who's in charge.' The manager played with her exposed waiting rear.

'It does, sir. I swear it!'

'And haven't I already warned you about swearing?'

'I didn't mean –'

'I don't think you know *what* you mean, but I know what your arse needs. Fewer words and more humility might help.'

Donna's fingers opened and closed against the end of the table. She was acutely aware of her disrobed and well-warmed buttocks. Was he enjoying just looking at her small pert *derrière* and curvaceous thighs? Was that why he was taking his time in laying on the final stroke? 'Tell me you deserve to taste my belt again,' Boscome ordered.

'I deserve . . .' She remembered he liked her to say things in her own words.

Donna cleared her throat. 'I've been disobedient. It's only fitting that you take it out on my rear end, that you teach it compliance.'

'And?' Boscome prompted.

'And . . .' she bit back a near sob of frustration and humiliation, 'and I ask nicely for the belt.'

'Push your arse out further, then. Good girl.'

Bottom obscenely upended, she inhaled hard. Let out her breath in a wail as the strap struck low down above both thighs, making her bottom jiggle. 'Thank you, sir,' she moaned, determined not to anger him further.

'What else would you like to thank me for?' Boscome murmured. She heard his zip go down.

His hardness moved against her cervix, her clitoris moved against the desk, his belly pushed against her heated scarlet buttocks. 'Thank you for granting me permission to come, sir,' Donna whispered. And promptly came.

Buckling Under

Belts and bourbon – he loved them, though not necessarily in that order. Jack Slones hiccuped gently, and tasted whisky sour. As for the belts? All the women on the bus were wearing coats or buttoned-up jackets. Not a waist-cincher or slinky studded strap in sight.

Forget sex and subservience, he told himself. Forget women. Concentrate on finding some brass to spend on brandy and beer! He'd overheard his alcohol counsellor telling her friend about this pub on the town's outskirts: '. . . half-price drinks to attract custom from the city. Near that farmhouse that sells fresh produce just off the Bay-grass Road.'

Baygrass Road here he came! Jack stared hollowly into his wallet as the bus drove past yellow rape-seed fields and greeny-brown fallow. It was three whole days till he got his next unemployment Giro and he was running a hell of a thirst. He had enough cash for a couple of cognacs and the charm for a one-liner or several to the hopefully man-starved landlady. After which . . . ?

Find and keep a job his Life-After-Liquor counsellor had said. The bitch was determined to make him as respectably dull as she was. Wanted him to quit the burglaries, the casual sex and the booze.

'*The Quail's Quencher*, mate? Here's your nearest stop,' the driver called. Jack staggered from the bus, ambled along the half-lit lane till he neared a red-brick mansion. A sign by the gate offered *Free-range eggs for sale*. The pub was just across the park: he could see its bright-lit promise. All he needed was a few more quid. The decision to act was hard, the actual actions easy. He took the bush-dark pathway at the side of the house.

A long drive. A short drop to the cellar window. He got his glass cutter from his rucksack and carved out a neat little circle, undid the lock. Eased the frame forward, pushed up from the sill, angled his limbs through the gap. Home and dry.

A dry cellar. A *hot* cellar. Unusual, that. His eyes hadn't yet adjusted to the blackness, but he could feel the cushioning impact of a carpet under his soft-soled shoes. Maybe they used this place as a study. Why, only the other month he'd broken drunkenly into this flat and seen . . .

Now he heard footsteps. Jack's heartbeat leapt and he turned to flee, barged into something and lurched heart-stoppingly over. Floundered. Fell. '*Get him!*' A woman's voice. Two shadows rushed at his scrabbling form, held his arms behind his back. He felt the cold hard clunkiness of handcuffs.

'Shall we call the police, madam?'

'No, wait.'

That was good. That was definitely good. Even his drink-dazed brain recognised that. Maybe she was going to take pity on him. After all, he hadn't actually found her lingerie drawer or her petty-cash jar yet. Her commands came again through the darkness. 'Take him to the showers to hose off the scent of whisky. Then spreadeagle him naked to the four-poster and leave him to sleep it off.'

An iron-furred mouth. Prickling lids. An indeterminate time later he filtered back to the waking world to find his limbs feeling lightly stretched, weighted. 'Ah, our careless criminal is with us again!'

Jack opened his eyes and moved them in the direction of the mocking female voice. Swallowed hard as he focused on the black leather hood she wore with its slits to see, speak and breathe through. He must be dreaming again. Yet he wasn't usually aware of his hangover's parching symptoms in his dreams.

'Do you want to urinate?' He shrugged warily. 'Such a shy boy. I think you do!' He moaned low and long as the woman pressed the heel of her hand against his drink-distended belly, gasped with relief as she moved the source of the pressure away. He let his gaze travel down, down, down, from her bare throat and *décolletage* to the fine mesh black top that clung to her globular mammaries. They swelled beneath their fishnet splendour like creamy water-filled balloons.

And those gossamer dark stockings, that drop-waisted charcoal skirt! His testes drummed to a tense new throb. At twenty-eight he still had the torso of a younger man: slim yet hard, toned without trying. The do-gooders kept warning of beer bellies and builder's cleavages, but the excess flesh had stayed away.

Except from his cock, which seemed to grow longer, to crave more deeply, through every year that passed, despite its owner's Bacchanal excesses. Was that what having a secret unsatisfied longing did, made your sex-drive strengthen and strain to be let out? He'd broken dates and hearts and even windows in his drink-powered tantrums, but no lover had ever tied him down to helplessness with her belts.

Wonder and dread and an undercurrent of almost unbearable anticipation trilling through the sexual paths to his belly, he tugged on the ones they'd used to bind his wrists and ankles to the mahogany four-poster bed. Belts – Christ, he usually loved the things! Loved looking at them, fingering them, imagining what they'd feel like if someone brought one down on his disarmed bared bottom. But this wasn't some fetishistic fantasy he was in control of. This was for real!

'If you'd just let me go. I've never harmed anyone.'

'Doesn't it harm them when you violate their property?' The voice behind the mask. The voice of a jury.

'I . . . suppose.' Jack nodded, then looked away.

'And why should I release a destructive force?'

Just his luck if she was Shannon-Moll the Cannibal. This called for some play-acting. 'Madam, trust me – I'll never do it again!'

'Not if you're properly punished, you won't.' She put

her hands on her hips. For the umpteenth time Jack's attention moved to the strap around her waist, a wide ebony band with a thick round silver buckle. His cock hardened, his bowels softened. 'What are you going to do to me?' he croaked.

'Take my belt to your arse.' She was studying his crotch. Jack followed her gaze towards his vertical pulsing pole. His full bladder was equally insistent. Yet he daren't ask to use the toilet lest she again massaged that tender place.

'You feel helpless, don't you, Jack?'

Best to tell the truth, not make her mad. 'Yes, ma'am.'

'You feel like one of your burglary victims.'

He closed his eyes, wished he'd never trained their gaze on her opulent mansion. 'Yes, madam, yes.'

'Good.' She thumbed his helpless testicles till the need to come brought tears to his eyes. 'I'm going to teach you that crime doesn't pay. Then we'll have a chat with that wicked weapon.' She skimmed a slight but sense-serving palm up his shaft and Jack instinctively arched the little he could towards her, the belts on his wrists and ankles tightening against his limbs.

'Jones! Kronenburg!' He tensed as she called two of her henchmen in, let out his breath as she snapped, 'Untie and hold him. Take him to the bathroom. Give him some mineral water and sweet biscuits, then return him to me.'

Fifteen minutes later, washed and watered and fed, they brought him back. 'Now you're ready to really feel each lash,' she murmured as they marched him in to his basement jail. She was standing beside the bed with the belt from her waist in her hand. It looked even longer and thicker than it had when she'd been wearing it. 'I want you to dwell on your criminal actions each time the leather comes down.'

'I will, Mistress.' He hadn't planned to say that subservient word: it was just there, as if it had always been there, waiting for this moment. Fancy him, Jack Slones, being this obsequious! In most relationships, despite his inner desires, he was soon fucking the new girlfriend's sister or mother, screwing with her bank balance or her mind.

'One stroke for breaking the glass.' She ordered the men to tie him over on his belly. His heart thudded, his thick need rubbing against the duvet. His bottom suddenly felt defenceless and small. 'What if I can't take it?' he muttered, as she traced the cool buckle over both buttocks in a taunting prelude, again and again and again.

'Like your robbed victims, you really don't have any choice.' She brought the belt down hard, a sudden wide streak of shock and heat. He bucked forward, straightened as best he could, and moaned into the pillow. 'And a second stroke for the shock you caused us by breaking in.' She laid this one upon his bottom's fullest swell. 'Hurts, doesn't it?' she murmured sweetly, using her gloved fingers to rim his arsehole till he wanted to be filled there more than he'd ever wanted anything. 'Like you hurt those girls in your past.'

'How did you know?'

'We've been through your rucksack, seen your address book and your driving licence with the drink-driving suspensions. Read that self-indulgent little diary you insist on keeping. If only these lovesick young girls could see you like this!'

'I just – they let themselves be used!'

'The way you let the drink use you?' He was trying to think up a witty rejoinder when she brought the belt down over the backs of his legs, a burning lash that underlined where buttock met thigh.

'I'll never ill-treat a woman again!' He closed his eyes and waited, tense, as he felt her gloved palm slide between his legs to hold his pounding cock in a casual cradle. 'Rub against the glove, Jack, till you come like a schoolboy having a wank for the very first time.'

'Couldn't you just –'

'I could punish you more if you don't obey me. Rub now, or I'll remove my hand.'

With his wrists bound, this was all the relief he would get and, Christ, he needed it. Especially because the thrashing had brought the blood to his sore bum and his shaft. Chafing himself against her palm like an Alsatian frigging a lamp-post, he panted and shuddered and spurted. 'Take him to the showers, then dress him and set him to work in the timber yard. I want enough firewood to last me through the winter, or else!'

'Yes, Mistress.' The men unbound his extremities, half lifted him to the side of the bed. His cock was sensitive now, dripping semen. He wanted to get down on his belly and crawl across the floor towards her. Instead, he stared at his naked feet as they led him towards the door.

'Wait!' she called clearly. He waited for a kindly touch, a look. 'You may as well know what your sentence is.'

He turned, nodded.

'You'll do manual work every day for the next six months. Once a week you'll receive the pleasure of an orgasm as reward for your labours. You'll also receive a punishment for past misdeeds.'

'Punished by only getting to come once a week?' he joked. She walked behind him and pushed a dry gloved finger up his arse until it reached his prostate.

'The punishment is that I'll be wearing a belt – each week a different belt. You'll unbuckle it and hand it to me, get into the position I order. Then you'll tell me how many strokes you think you need.'

That didn't sound so bad! He'd say four, have a hot-bummed thrill then a climax. If he got bored with her games he'd find a sneaky way back into the outside world.

A week later, he found himself being led to an attic room. In the intervening days he'd worked hard and eaten well and drunk nothing. Well, only water and orange juice – when what he wanted was malt whisky, clear sharp gin and Madam's quim. Those masked features, that unmasked half-bared body, the way she'd used the strap . . .

She was standing to the side of wooden bunk beds, with their convenient bondage poles. The masked men let go of his arms and he walked unaided to the lower bunk, clambered on to it, then crouched, awaiting her bidding.

'You've worked well, Jack.'

'Thank you.' His throat ached at the unexpected compliment.

'Yet your diary shows such laziness for the past year.'

He'd done nothing more effortful than ambling to the pub.

'I'm sorry, Mistress, I've been insufferably indolent.'

'And what should we do about that?'

He tried not to think of the watching masked men. 'You should . . . punish me.'

'What with?'

He swallowed, wanting yet fearing this: 'With your belt.'

Unsure what to do with his arms, his legs, he used them to crawl closer. This time her belt was made of three braided red ropes held with an African carved wooden clasp. He took the strap off and kissed it, handed it to her. Lay down on the bed.

'No – let's have you bent over that dressing-table stool this time. Mmm, that's it. Gives me a clearer target.' He howled as the implement came down on him, held on to the little stool's glossy legs. 'One for the jobs you turned down. Two for the time you've been a burden on the State. Another for living off immoral earnings . . .' He'd been more of a bad boy than he'd realised, and now his bared arse was going to pay.

He flinched, covered his bottom then got back in place as she toasted his rear with the strap, praying that she'd find a reason to make his hungry cock feel good again. He hadn't been allowed to touch himself all week. They'd shackled one of his legs to the bed at night, had locked on a chastity belt that kept his fingers away from his phallus. Ah, the irony – a form of belt preventing him from caressing his cock to a ceiling-shot come! Normally he just imagined a waist-wrapped strap and grew hard and climaxed even harder. Or looked at some lady's chainmail buckle and felt his balls contract.

'Come here, Jack.' Through a haze of confusion and bum-based pain he heard her voice, and scrabbled from the stool to obey it. 'I liked warming your arse for you, Jack. Come and check how wet I am with your tongue.' He'd never . . . Girls had always sucked *him*. Sometimes he'd pushed their heads down hard. He felt a hot rush of shame. Should have treated them better. No one deserved . . .

Not true. He alone deserved to be treated like this. He'd been a booze-led bastard. Now that the drink was no longer in his brain or in his veins, he felt as if he had the potential to be clean and good. But first he had to act dirty, debase himself, sort of settle the score by doing whatever his mistress wanted. By licking her crotch.

She'd stretched out on the velour-draped settee. He crawled to its foot and edged himself up till his tongue was above her shiny clitoris. The carpet was plush beneath his knees. He licked experimentally at the peeking point of flesh, adding to its glisten. Heard her excited snort of air.

Aha, so even his mistress wasn't indomitable! She had her weaknesses, her needs. He used his fingers to unpeel her sex lips from each other, traced his tongue up the inside glistening leaf. Teased down again, back upwards. 'Mmh!'

She made a half-grunting, half-heavy breathing sound and shifted her naked legs and hips until his mouth was above her sexual hood again. He licked twice, enjoying the low clicks in her throat, started to flirt away from her most sensitive centre. He'd make it *her* turn to beg.

'Williams! Hemingway!' He'd almost forgotten her various bodyguarding men, now heard their footsteps crossing the room towards their mistress. 'Mr Slones isn't really trying. Put him in the sixty-nine position. You may have to hand me my belt.'

He raised his head as strong hands grabbed his arms. 'But you've already given me my thrashing for this week!'

'At last you're remembering life's rules. Perhaps you'll start to live by them?' His captors finished turning him and he found his nose pressed against her salty slit, her palms sliding over his naked arse, a belted arse that he wanted left to recover for the week! He put his mouth to her mons with new-found enthusiasm. Found a rhythm in his head and transferred it to his tongue. Felt her thighs closing in on his face as he licked, pubic purse bearing down, breath speeding. 'Oh, oh, oh, oh, oooooooooh!'

He'd hoped she'd suck his own sex, but it wasn't her way. She was the boss. It was her house. He had to learn to be humble. 'Do you want to fasten my cock back into the chastity belt?' he murmured obsequiously.

'After you've enjoyed release,' she said, and he was so grateful that he almost wept.

This time she held a rubber vibrating pussy in her hand. He wanted it, yet hated it. This was so demeaning! Ordering her henchmen to keep his arms extended from his shoulders, she placed the pulsing sheath over the leaking manhood between his legs. 'Look at my tits, Jack. Imagine being allowed to suckle at them some day.' He was imagining! Jesus, to bury his head between those cushiony thrills.

'I'll be . . .' The sensations took him down, down, down, words and phrases rushing to his brain as sensation swelled in his lower belly. 'Mistress, I'll do whatever I can to please you, I swear!'

'Shoot now, then, Jack. Don't keep that pretty pussy waiting, or Mrs Belt will have to come off and find a soft target again.' He looked at the new strap she'd fastened round her waist – the one she would use on him next week – and came and came.

Weeks merged into months. Every seven days he took his punishment like a man then orgasmed like a schoolboy. Climaxed by being tied across the spin drier, by rubbing himself between her toes, by sliding inside a hole cut in an orange. In between he watched his mind grow clear and his body grow strong. The purposelessness he'd felt in the outside world didn't apply here. He had field work, household chores, a sexual routine.

'You've been a good slave,' she said, as she walked into his basement sex cell one day. He wanted to kiss her feet. He wanted to lie in her arms. He wanted . . . 'Unbuckle the belt from my waist.' He trembled as he kissed it. It was made solely of looped-together chrome hoops, hard and lengthy. Would she really be this cruel?

'This one would seriously bruise you, wouldn't it, Jack?'

'Yes, Mistress.'

'Then why are you lying on your tummy ready to take it?'

'Because the rules are . . . because I promised to obey.'

'And will you now obey society's rules? I mean the ones that make sense for all, the fair ones. Don't steal, don't abuse your partner. Don't drink if it turns you into an idiotic beast.'

'I'll obey, Mistress.' He buried his head in his hands and waited for the lash to fall. It never came.

Instead, a soft hand – an *ungloved* hand – stroked his bottom. 'Lie over my knee, Jack. I'm going to give you an old-fashioned spanking for your previous wrongdoings.' Awkwardly he pulled himself on to her silk-skirted lap.

That same soft hand was surprisingly firm. He squirmed as her many slaps made his cheeks feel warm, his cock feel hotter. It was trapped between his thighs and hers. 'Now lie on your back.' He turned over, wincing as the chintz cover scraped against his pinkened bum. Opened his eyes wide as he felt her fingers sliding over every centimetre of his scrotum. Jesus, that felt good!

'As you know, I get off on punishing you, Jack. I may as well slide down on this thing while it's here.' He stared up into her masked face as she clothed his prick in a see-through condom, angled herself above the head of his shaft, then enveloped it. She was melting syrup, liquid wonder. 'Oh, thank you, thank you, thank you!' he said.

His mistress impaled herself right down to the root. As she fucked him, she unbuttoned her ebony top and let her breasts hang free, heavy cream pendulums. He lifted his head in rapture and a nipple grazed his open mouth.

'Lick my belt, Jack.' She was still wearing it. He bent up and she moved over his face, her pubic purse still thrusting down on him. He tasted the cold chrome, felt his flesh start to build. 'Carry the image of it in your head from now on, Jack. Before you transgress, just picture how it feels against those helpless bared cheeks.'

She leaned back till his cock was standing almost totally upright, and started to move down on him harder, faster. The chrome rings round her waist glittered coldly. His spanked bum cheeks rubbed against the bed. 'Come exactly when I order you to,' she said through closed teeth, her own private Eden obviously approaching. 'Not a second before.'

'Yes, Mistress.' Signs of impending satiation were spiralling through his balls. He tried to concentrate on other things, belatedly aware that none of her many bodyguards were in the room with him. For once he was untied, essentially free. He wanted to stay captive to her quim, remain deep inside her oiled gripping treasure. This jewel spelt home.

'Easy,' she whispered, as he strained into her especially hard. Every sense in each cell told him he was coming, coming, coming. 'Hold it, Jack,' she murmured. 'Let's see that new-won self-control.' She was arousal personified, but he wanted to please her. He tried to detach himself from his excitement by counting up how much money he'd lost in confiscated cheques. She'd made him phone Social Security at the end of his first week, got the Giros redirected here, made him sign . . .

'Are your balls awfully sensitive, Jack?' She stroked them as she rode. He groaned. God, she had a fiendish touch! 'What about this bit?' She moved one damning finger back to his anal hole and tickled it. 'Should we explore it later? Maybe get some of the others in?'

The scene seemed to further excite her well-fucked sex and she cried out, pushing hard, hard, hard against his cock, her breathing beneath the mask something humid, frantic. The fierce wet contractions set his own ecstasy button off, and he shot forcefully into the sheath. She flopped over him for a few moments, and when she pulled free of his body, he took off the condom and knotted it, then dropped it carefully into the bin.

'Six months ago you'd have just thrown that out of the window, Jack!' Had he been here six whole months? Time felt irrelevant. 'That means your sentence is over. You're free to go.'

He looked at her dumbly as she got up and cleaned her sex with scented tissues. 'I . . . God, please, I want to stay.'

'Why?'

'Because you know how to punish me until I come and come. Because I feel safe here. Because I love you.'

'No, you love what we've given you – a sense of inner discipline. You now have these strengths within.'

He thought of his two-roomed rented flat. His previous pub-based life. He wanted something more. 'I could stay on and work here.'

'You can work outside. We've found you an apprenticeship with a man who makes society gowns.' Floaty chiffon and folds of silk. He loved fabric, and fashion.

'I'll put in long hours for him, Mistress, if that's what you want.'

'It should be what *you* want – you and the next lovable girl that you meet.'

'But I want you.'

'I'll show her how to use a belt on your bum. Until then you can come back here every two weeks to confess your sins and receive the proper reprimand.'

He nodded, pondered. 'Madam – do I get to see your face?' He wanted to note the exact shade of her hair, know if she had cruel eyes, if she wore lipstick.

'You may.' She left him waiting for a moment, then unpeeled the concealing mask.

'Miss Gold!' He stared at his alcohol counsellor. 'But how . . . ?'

'Fifty of us clubbed together to buy this place. It's kept for our more recalcitrant cases. Men who don't respond to our conventional attempts at reform.'

'And all the bodyguards have been . . . ?'

'Alcoholics, shoplifters, layabouts. We've got them working in the kitchens and the fields.'

'Even Jones and Kronenburg and Williams and the chef?'

'Oh yes. Jones's urge to be taunted with nipple clamps was making him forge cheques to spend in exorbitantly expensive sex clubs. Now we regularly make him wear the metal pegs for twenty minutes at a time. He begs for release, of course, but his cock is very happy. He's due to start work in a London patisserie in a few days.'

Truth is stranger than fiction. A few hours later Jack walked free of the farmhouse, a thrilling mix of what had happened and what he'd like to have happened misting his vision. Wonderful, the way she'd had a belt for every week, for every thrashing! Awful the way she'd withheld her soft sexual centre till the end. Still, there was one more fiction in his head – her fiction, her cruel but ultimately life-saving fiction. The only lie.

A lie worth repeating. After walking for ten minutes Jack saw a youth in his twenties standing by the roadside. He had his hitching thumb out, was glaring at the passing cars. An empty gin bottle lay at his feet. His eyes were running on empty. He ran a penknife under his nails, a macho warning. 'Got a few quid on you, mate?'

'Not until I start my new job tomorrow,' Jack admitted. 'But there's a pub near the village back there selling half-price beer.' He smiled, knowing the boy would remember the smile for the next six months, come to understand its meaning. 'Just ask at that red-brick farmhouse which sells the eggs. They're guaranteed to show you the way.'

Teaching Practice

The coach, Kerry decided, was Britain's answer to the singles bar. A few hours of touring and already three blushingly new liaisons had been formed. Widening her eyes, she smiled at one of the guides. 'So, Adam, what's next on the agenda?' In truth she already knew the reply.

Lisa was! Lisa, the other guide, who fancied Adam. Lisa, who obviously thought *Exploring England* should be retitled *Lisa Prescott Speaks*.

'Lisa's taking everyone on to York Minster,' Adam said, smiling, 'after dropping me off at the hotel.'

Was she now? When the rival's away . . . 'I think I'll join you,' murmured Kerry, forcing a note of fatigue into her voice. 'This heat . . .'

'Of course!' Suddenly he was all professional courtesy, opening a window, suggesting she might like to move nearer to the front of the bus.

'I'll be fine when I've rested,' Kerry murmured, unbuttoning the top of her blouse. She could imagine his eyes darkening with lust when she swayed against him and he was forced to carry her to her bed.

Side by side at Reception, Kerry leaned ever so lightly against the inscrutable lecturer and guide, breathing in his cedar aftershave. Normally she wasn't this forward, but it had been months since she'd desired anyone this much. Months since she'd done anything about it! Not since she and Peter had split.

Her thoughts were interrupted by the receptionist. 'The touring party? Oh, we weren't expecting you until later.'

'The others have gone into town,' Adam said calmly. 'We came on ahead.'

'Ah, I see!' Kerry blushed at the girl's obvious implication and dipped her head till her silky brown hair coated her hot face. Keys jangled past her into an outstretched palm. When she looked up, Adam was staring. 'Let's get you into bed.'

The stairs seemed to last for ever. Kerry trembled slightly and a sudden gnawing hunger seared her gut. 'Maybe I should eat something,' she murmured.

'Later,' Adam said firmly. 'I'll have room service send something up.

Room. Service. Service with a smile. Go for it! As Kerry unlocked the door she turned to him. 'Want to tuck me in?' For interminable seconds he stayed silent. Then: 'Oh, surely you can do without me?' With a quick wave of his hand, he was gone.

Breakfast next morning was a tense affair or rather a non-affair. Miserably Kerry concentrated on her cold toast and warm tea. 'Feeling better this morning?' chirruped Lisa. The younger girl nodded. 'Good, we're going to a very special museum. It would be a shame if you missed out.'

Nothing was missing from the museum – it was huge. An entire floor was devoted to replicas of Victorian shops: an apothecary, a cobbler's lined with boots. Whilst some of the students lingered in the velvet-seated library, others moved on to the washhouse, the telephone exchange, the bank.

Enchanted, Kerry set off alone. Here was an old-fashioned printing press, there a . . . She opened the door to reveal a small schoolroom. With difficulty she lowered herself into a seat and slid her legs beneath an equally low-slung desk.

'Kerry!' The door swung open again. The low male voice startled her.

'Adam! God, this brings back memories.'

Adam walked over to the blackboard and picked up the chalk. 'It does, huh? Let's see how much you remember.' He was smiling at her. Kerry smiled back.

'Well, I was good at English.'

'Today we'll do maths. If three men take two weeks to dig a hole . . .' He went on to write up an impossibly complex problem on the board.

'No chance!' Kerry murmured.

'My dear girl, I'd like you to try.' Adam had stopped smiling and was frowning slightly. Suddenly uncomfortable, Kerry stared at the inkwell, long dry.

'If I had some paper . . .'

Adam slid his hand into his jacket pocket and brought out a notebook. Slowly he walked over and handed it to her. Kerry didn't start to breathe freely till he moved away.

For the next two minutes she was all too aware of him pacing up and down as she tried to still her frantically racing brain, but she couldn't concentrate. Aware of his eyes upon her, she took a guess.

'Finished?' He hadn't smiled for ever so long now.

'As ready as I'll ever be.' Her voice sounded tremulous and small.

'Bring it out to the front, then, girl.'

Beginning to perspire slightly, Kerry pushed the little desk away and walked stiff-kneed from the chair. Conscious of the sudden rush of heat which swelled her sex, she walked over to the suited man and held out her task.

'Stay there.' For a moment he studied it, then his voice went deadly quiet. 'Oh dear, you've got it wrong.' He reached for the cane. 'I'm afraid that you'll have to be punished.'

The door swung open. 'So there you are!' Lisa Prescott stood there, a slight flush darkening the sides of her face.

'I was looking everywhere for you two. I –'

'Kerry was telling me about the various Education Acts,' Adam said smoothly. 'She's quite the historian.'

Lisa looked at him sharply. 'We'll all be history as far as the hotel's concerned if we don't get back in time for dinner tonight.'

Food, drink, conversation. The meal for Kerry was a blur. Again and again her gaze sought Adam's and neither looked away. Would he come to her room? The hours crawled by in an agony of fear and anticipation. The entire party moved on to the bar then to the TV lounge. Kerry found herself hugely conscious of each small movement of her limbs. Where, when and for how long would he cane her? As the clock struck midnight, she stretched long and hard. 'Oh, well. Time I went to bed.' She could see several of the men staring at the sudden uplift of her breasts.

With self-conscious heaviness, Kerry moved to the door. As she sidled past Adam he slid a piece of paper into her hand. 'A little unfinished business,' he murmured. Kerry fled.

When she reached her room, she unfolded the paper. It contained her written work. *See me. Nine a.m.* was written beneath it in red ink.

The following day Kerry went down to the first sitting of breakfast. Everyone had the morning to themselves – she could only pray none of them opted for a return trip to the museum. Terror and lust competing for precedence in mind and body, she began the twenty-minute walk to the room.

Arriving, the young student paid her admission charge, hoping the woman wouldn't recognise her. 'Bright and early,' the cashier said. 'You're our second customer to-day.'

Was Adam the first, then? Adrenalin surging, Kerry began the long walk down the reconstructed street. In case the woman was watching, she made brief forays into the other shops and buildings. The schoolroom door, as last time, was closed. On an impulse, she knocked.

'Come in.'

With shaking hand she turned the big brass handle.

'Ah, Kerry!' He was sitting behind the teacher's desk, threading the cane back and forth.

'You wanted to see me, sir?' As if from a long way away she heard her voice.

'Yes, that last assignment – it really won't do.'

Kerry stared at the desk, at the cane, twitched her bottom.

'It was slovenly,' Adam continued, 'poorly worked out, wrong.'

'Sorry,' Kerry muttered, shifting her stance, her gaze lingering desperately on the small shuttered window. 'I've never been good at sums.'

'Then we must teach you,' Adam said softly. 'Can you count to six?'

Kerry stared at him. 'Of course! I . . .'

The man walked over to the door and jammed it shut with a small chair. Then he walked back to Kerry and flexed the cane.

'Bend over.' He indicated one of the small desks at the front of the schoolroom.

Kerry swallowed. 'You can't be serious.'

She felt his hands on the small of her back, guiding her over, holding her there whilst the other reached beneath her skirt and stroked her labia through the fast-dampening cloth. When he moved his hand away, she whimpered.

'Take your punishment,' he murmured. 'Then maybe you can have some fun.'

Too weak by now to rise, she felt him slowly inch her skirt all the way up, felt his palms on the cotton-clad roundness of her cheeks. Firmly he began to edge her pants down, stopping when they came to the part of her thighs just below the sulcal crease.

'Please,' Kerry whimpered, hips obscenely spread.

'Say *please, sir*,' Adam murmured. Kerry shook her head. She sensed his arm draw back, felt the first searing stroke across her centre swell as cane met flesh. Despite herself she cried out. Adam traced the cane gently down her bum. 'Let's try again,' he said pleasantly, 'with more politeness and respect for your betters. You're already due another five.'

He laid the second one on higher up. Christ, it hurt! Kerry pushed her belly against the wooden lid as she felt the flesh stinging, then tightening. 'Not so hard,' she whimpered.

'What have you to add?' Kerry closed her mouth tightly and clenched her buttock muscles. She was damned if she'd give in.

'You're getting the third stroke over the second for staying mute.' He swung the rod. Pain seared across already smarting hemispheres.

'Please, sir!' she gasped, half getting up then forcing herself back into position across the desk. Part of her desperately wanted to put her hands protectively over her punished bottom. The other half wanted to see how much she could take.

'That's better. You're being a good girl now.' She closed her eyes as if to shut out his words. Prayed that no one would come in and find her upended with her pants down like this. Adam set the long smooth cane in front of her. 'Kiss it and ask nicely for the other strokes.'

'Kiss my arse,' she muttered, mustering a little pride. She heard the bamboo scrape against the desk as he picked it up, heard the whoosh as it cut through the air. 'I'll kiss it! I'll kiss it!' she groaned, flinching wildly then jumping up to rub her punished backside.

The bamboo tasted surprisingly neutral against her parted lips. 'Right, angel, let's get you over the desk again.' Going back over took all of her willpower and determination. She had to take this caning – it might win him away from Lisa. She mustn't act like a baby now!

Still, it was difficult to keep her hands away from her scarlet bum, to keep them holding on to the desk legs, especially when she sensed his arm moving back again. 'Please, sir, be kind.'

'Kind to someone who's seduced me away from the influential Lisa on a coach trip? Kind to someone who can't even do basic maths?'

Kerry knew he'd show no mercy now. She clenched her teeth together and dug her nails into the desk, then howled as the fifth cut warmed her upper thighs with painful precision. 'Aaah! They're tender!'

'As tender as these bits?' He fondled her sore hot cheeks.

'N . . . no.'

'Where do you want the last one then?'

'Nowhere!'

'I can see I haven't taught you self-discipline yet.'

'Across the middle,' Kerry said, defeated. The flesh was at its roundest there: maybe such a padded area wouldn't ache so much.

'Right, I'll dish it out lower down,' Adam said, fingering the area he was about to punish. And promptly did.

There was a silence after the last stroke ended. Kerry lay there, backside throbbing heat. Then she felt strong fingers caressing the contours between her thighs. God, she wanted him! She arched back hungrily and felt the rough material of his suit brush her bottom cheeks.

'Easy,' Adam murmured, teasingly parting her labia, sliding a first then second finger deep inside. She heard the sound of his zip going down and arched back further. She had to come!

'Please do it,' she whispered, 'Please . . .'

Slowly Adam entered her, then almost came out again finding his rhythm with long measured thrusts. With his hands still pinning her to the table, she could do little but push back slightly with her bared bottom, making encouraging and increasingly desperate little cries.

'Damn you, you bastard. Damn you!' she cried as he played with her, then shivered as he placed the cane before her eyes again.

'Look at it,' he instructed. 'Just imagine how it'll feel coming down.'

Building, Kerry felt her breasts swell further still, begging for his fingers. Hot need pushed down from lower belly to mons. The pulsing rose to something beyond pleasure as Adam's groin ground hers against the desk, and his fingers slid down and around her clitoris and stroked.

Going, going . . . Kerry cried out as the ecstasy took her over the edge. A few seconds later Adam moaned and strained forward, his sex pushing further into hers.

Please don't let me see Lisa, please don't let me see Lisa, please don't let me . . . As they entered the hotel, the words cut like a refrain through Kerry's head. 'Ah, Lisa!' As Adam spoke her rival's name, Kerry forced herself to smile. Though she'd washed up as best she could in the museum powder room, she still felt disorientated. The colour in both sets of cheeks intensified as Adam ran an exploratory palm over her arse.

'Coming for morning coffee, Adam?' Lisa murmured. Kerry studied the ground. Was this it, then, a one-morning stand, a never-to-be-repeated experience? Adam's fondling of her hindquarters increased. 'I'd love to but we're about to tour the gymnasium. I promised Kerry, you see.'

For a moment after they entered the fitness hall she didn't understand. Then Adam turned her to face the wooden horse, his grip on her waist showing he meant business. 'In schooling your mind, we mustn't neglect your physical education. Be here at twelve tonight, or else.'

The surge of lust to her loins unsteadied her and she reached out to finger the wooden frame. Liquid pooled between her labial lips, fast wanting the friction of release. Unbidden, her eyes were drawn to Adam's belt with its thick black contours. 'Oh dear,' she whispered. 'I never was much good at gym.'

Payback

'Welcome to *Stepping Out!*' Jeff said, as the first female customer walked into his new fitness club.

'This is so handy for me – I teach at the secondary school across the road,' she murmured, looking around.

'We'll hopefully be seeing a lot more of you then,' he added, eyes taking in her high firm breasts in the tight red T-shirt, her cute round bottom in black leggings, her wide friendly smile.

At the end of the aerobics class she told him her name was Amanda Breen and that she planned to become a regular.

'Got the form? I'll sign up for six months élite membership. It's time I did something to fight stress!'

'Then you've come to the right place! Élite membership gives you unlimited use of our toning tables, our sunbeds and sauna for a year.'

'Sounds fantastic,' said the auburn-haired twenty-something, pulling on a clinging pink cashmere sweater. 'You won't be able to keep me away.'

It was true. She arrived for every lunchtime stretch 'n' tone class for the next fortnight, tanned herself on the Tuesday and Thursday nights. Each Monday and Wednesday saw her wired up to the toning tables. Soon her limbs took on a sleek supple appearance and fetching golden sheen.

'She's certainly getting her money's worth,' said Jeff's business partner, William.

'No – she's getting *our* money's worth,' muttered Jeff, staring down at the letter he'd just received from his bank.

Amanda's cheque had bounced. He half expected her to bounce out of his life, but she breezed in as usual that lunchtime.

'Hi there – can't wait to get dancing to these rap records for the next hour!'

'Can't wait to get paid,' Jeff said grimly.

'I don't understand . . .'

'Maybe this'll explain?'

He showed her the letter.

'I'll write you another one immediately. My salary must have gone in late.'

She worked at a posh school. Her clothes looked good. Surely she couldn't be a debtor?

'All right, but there should be some penalty for all the worry you've caused us so far.'

Amanda blushed slightly. 'I see!' She cleared her throat. 'Em, what do you suggest?'

'Well, when I was little and didn't use my pocket money wisely I got a good spanking. I don't believe in hitting kids of course, but if grown-up girls misbehave . . .'

'You wouldn't!' Amanda gasped, reddening further.

Jeff's cock lengthened at the thought of turning her arse a similar shade. 'Report to my room after your aerobics session,' he said, 'I'll tell the teacher you'll be needing all your strength for later so she shouldn't work you too hard today.'

'And if I don't?'

'I'll go across to the school and tell your superiors that you write bad cheques, that you set a bad example to your pupils.'

Amanda licked her lips and stared at the carpet. 'I'll report to you in an hour, sir,' she said.

She did. She was still wearing her close-fitting leggings. A faint line of perspiration stained her polo-shirt under her breasts.

'That was a hard workout!'

'Not as hard as the spanking I'm about to give you.' Jeff flexed his fingers, relishing the cruel contact. 'Now bend over my knee.' Sitting on the tall wooden chair, he patted his lap.

117

'Couldn't we just –'

'Just do it!'

'Pig!' she muttered.

'You get twenty extra spanks for that.'

Amanda quivered as she lowered her belly over his thighs. 'Twenty *extra* – how many were you planning?'

'That depends on how repentant you are after I've spanked you over your pants.'

Amanda inhaled sharply. 'Don't you mean my leggings?'

'No, dear. You don't get to keep that much protection on!'

He stroked her small pert bum through the black lycra till she wriggled against his cock and her thighs trembled. 'Put your hands back and edge your leggings down. That's it. Nice and slow.'

'I can't believe this is happening!' Amanda gasped.

'Oh, it's real all right. I'm watching you show a virtual stranger your pretty pink panties.' He stroked her arse again and again through her knickers, enjoying her shame. 'I can see the crack of your arse. I can feel the dampening folds of your hot little pussy.'

He played with her protected pink petals some more. Then, balls swelling with anticipation, he pulled her half-mast leggings all the way down and threw them across the room.

'Have you been spanked before, Amanda?'

She shook her head.

'You'll be surprised how hot your bum gets – really stinging.'

'Just do it!' she muttered.

'Oh, I like to take my time.'

'How long . . .'

'. . . Before you get back to work? That depends on if you do and say the right things. I want you to be very very nice.'

Raising his right hand, he brought it down with medium force over her relaxed left cheek. The warmed buttock immediately twitched, then she pushed her body clumsily forward. Jeff treated the alternate buttock to the same level of severity. Amanda gasped.

118

'Save your whimpering for later. I've hardly started.'
For five minutes he walloped first one knickered orb then
the other, holding her more firmly with his left hand as she
moved her head from side to side and started to drum her
feet.

'Keep quiet. I'll know when you've had enough by the
colour of your bottom. Any more noise and I'll have to
teach you obedience by pulling down your pants.'

'Not that!' gasped Amanda. 'Please!'

Jeff leathered her harder.

'Aaah!' she yelled, as his palm lashed the tender crease
where arse cheek meets thigh.

'Didn't I tell you not to make a sound? You'll get the
rest of your spanking on the bare now. Reach your hands
back and roll your knickers down.'

'I won't!' Amanda wailed.

'You'll get double.'

'But it already stings –'

'Exactly! Why earn more?'

Obviously fearing a further thrashing she hesitated for a
second then reached her uncertain fingers back and worked
the pink satin down.

Leaving the scrap of material at her ankles, Jeff contemplated her stripped bare bum. It was red round the centre
where the force of his palm had punished it, with fingertip
pink marks all round the outer buttocks and over the tops
of her thighs.

'Mmm, you've warmed up nicely. Now the real spanking
begins.'

'What do you mean?' Amanda breathed, head hanging
closer to the floor with humiliation or exhaustion.

'So far I've just been preparing your buttocks for much-
needed chastisement. A bad girl's thrashing should be on
her bare bottom and should take a long long time.' He
stroked the enjoyable heat of her pert twin rounds. 'I want
you to tell me how wicked you've been. The humility in
your response will determine how often my hard hand con-
nects with your soft little backside.'

'I've been bad,' Amanda said in an emotionless voice.

Jeff spanked her four times.

'You're not really trying.'

'I . . . I'm a wicked girl. I deserve to be over your knee with my pants round my ankles being made to beg!'

'Better,' said Jeff, prick pulsing as he fondled her heated globes. 'But still not good enough.'

He brought his hand down full force three times in the same place, the outline of his hand traced in red against her writhing posterior. He did the same with the other cheek. Amanda bucked and yelled.

'I'll crawl on my belly . . . kiss your feet.'

'Kiss anything else?' Jeff murmured encouragingly.

'Take you in my mouth . . . Suck your balls.'

It was an offer he couldn't refuse. Jeff closed his eyes with erotic anticipation as she slid from his knee on to her own knees. Breathed in as she unzipped him, breathed out low and long as her lipsticked-lips enclosed his titan tool.

'God, yes!'

Her mouth was warm velvet, her tongue a teasing source of hot wet pleasure. Jeff raised his hips closer to her face and groaned.

Looking in the mirror across the room he could see her reddened arse, his handprints still enlivening it. Lucky she could teach school standing up – her bum looked too tender to sit down. He remembered the way it had felt under his hands, the way she'd wriggled and pleaded. Just like her lips were pleading for his frenzied fountain now . . .

As her tongue played the eye of his cock, Jeff felt the *almost* signal go off in his balls and his sex sac tightened. Amanda put her right palm under his scrotum and stroked gently. Her bum trembled with the movement, hot cheeks jiggling as if hit by an imaginary birching rod or cane.

'Ah . . . ah!' Jeff imagined her arse being taught a lesson by the martinet he kept in his bedroom cupboard. Amanda sucked especially hard and he came.

'Wow! You needed that!' Amanda grinned, wiping her lips.

'Not as much as you needed a walloping.'

The smile disappeared again.

'Get into your pants and leggings.'

He kept his voice cool though his milked cock felt hot and his pulse was beating overtime.

'Don't you want . . . ?'

To pleasure her? Of course he did. But some women made more effort in the end if you kept them waiting.

'Want that cheque from you?' he said, deliberately misunderstanding. 'Of course I do.'

'Right! I'll just . . .' Amanda winced as she edged her punished arse back into her knickers and outer clothing. 'God, my bum feels as if it's on fire!'

Jeff looked her up and down, trying to keep his features dispassionate, though he longed to be buried deep inside her. 'Then you'll better not enrage me further and earn a good hard dose of my belt.'

She wrote her cheque, then stood waiting for his response. He looked down at the paperwork on his desk for silent moments until she muttered that she'd see him later, and slipped out. Then he poured himself a much-needed drink.

For the next week, Jeff relived the scene whilst he wanked at home and in the gym staff room. He saw Amanda each time she came into the club, and though she made small talk she couldn't quite meet his eye. She must fancy him, else she simply wouldn't have written another cheque, wouldn't have come back to further stretch 'n' tone classes. At any stage in the transaction she could have walked away.

'Did you sort that membership defaulter out?' William asked.

'I'm dealing with it.'

Dealing with her in his dreams nightly! It wasn't often he got to take a beautiful brunette to task like that. He wished he had photos of the event to enliven his solo sex sessions until he got the opportunity to spank someone again. Was she also remembering the way he'd come inside her mouth, as if his balls would release their sexual sap for ever? Did she imagine how powerfully he could take her to the edge of her climax and beyond?

Then another letter arrived from the bank. Her second cheque had also bounced! Jeff felt excited and angry. This time he had no intention of waiting for her to show up at the gym. It was imperative to his pride that he made sure she really learned her lesson. Which meant spending an entire evening alone with her and her devilish *derrière* after the last aerobics class. Settling his features into as stony a mask as possible, he was waiting for her outside the school when class finished for the day.

'Miss Breen – a word, if you please!'

She blushed when she saw him, and quickly left the two teachers she'd been walking with.

'Jeff, what on earth –?'

'Call me *sir*. Your cheque's failed again. I'm going to take the full cost out on your cheating bottom.'

'But –'

'Butt with two t's is all I want to see! You're coming to the club with me now for a prolonged sore session that'll last for several hours.'

'I can't!' She looked around wildly as if the playground held a handy buttock shield. 'I, er, haven't had my tea!'

'Oh, I'll feed you,' said Jeff. 'The last thing I want is you passing out from hunger.'

He marched her over to the fitness club and settled her at a table with two sandwich packs, a coffee and a slice of cherry cake. Amanda ate one sandwich and sipped half the coffee, but her gaze flitted round the room like a startled butterfly and her mind seemed to be elsewhere. On her arse, probably, Jeff thought, feeling his length stiffen. He hoped she was remembering his warning about the belt. The silly little minx had it coming to her. She'd now had at least a hundred pounds' worth of work-outs and sunbed and toning sessions for free!

'The last class finishes at six, but I want you in my office at five for a warm-up spanking.'

He sat waiting impatiently behind his desk. Waiting, waiting. At ten past five he walked out of his office to find her sitting at a table in reception, staring unfocusedly at a magazine.

'It'll hurt more now because I had to come and get you,' he said in a low voice as another three aerobics students walked past them. Amanda hung her head.

'Come with me.'

Still gazing at the floor, she followed him into the men's staff-room, closing the door behind her. The teachers were all female ones, so they wouldn't be disturbed.

'I didn't expect to see you back here after our last session,' he said sadly, taking a seat but leaving her standing.

'I didn't intend –'

'You must secretly enjoy being spanked.'

'I don't! It's just ... the pupils I teach are all rich – the school expects certain standards. I've been buying designer clothes and shoes to impress them, but I'm still on a junior teacher's wage.'

'So I'm supposed to supplement your income?' He shook his head. 'Do you know how hard it is building up a business?'

Amanda licked her lips: 'I ... no.'

'Know what it's like to have the pressures of self-employment?'

'No, sir.'

'Then I'm going to teach you. Going to show you how painful life can be.' He stared up at her classy matching skirt and jacket. 'Turn your back to me, then take your jacket off and pull your skirt down. I want to see your bum being unveiled.' He leaned forward, eager to note how pale it was prior to the first full spank.

Flushing and staring somewhere at the centre of the room, Amanda shrugged out of her jacket then undid the button and zip of her skirt and eased the linen off. Stood fidgeting in her tights and cream silk slip.

'Now your underskirt.' The silkiness came down to reveal thin dove-grey tights, that outlined her slightly plump thighs and gently curved tummy. 'And your nylons.' She continued her unwilling striptease, limbs increasingly shy and stiff. Jeff contemplated her stripped smooth curves.

'Turn round and face me.'

She did.

'We've been at this stage before, haven't we, Amanda?'
She nodded, blushing.

'You know you don't get to keep your panties on.'

This time she knew better than to argue. She was learning. Blushing further, she unhooked the lace-trimmed lemon bikini briefs and pulled them over her unmarked cheeks, down past her thighs and calves till they lay discarded on the ground.

'You can keep your blouse and bra on for now.' He hadn't seen her breasts yet, but he was hoping to. She'd been hot as hell after their last session. He hoped this one would make her just as ready for sex.

'Now bend over the desk.' He watched her closely as she obeyed him. 'Good girl, but push your belly down harder so that your bum sticks up.'

She followed his commands. Her bottom was as deliciously rounded and taut as he'd remembered.

'I've spanked this wilful little rear before. I obviously didn't do it hard enough if it's back here being disobedient again.'

'I could pay you in instalments –'

'I can take it out on your hide in instalments!'

'I could stay away from the fitness club.'

'But you still have to pay for the classes and pampering sessions you've already had!'

Obviously knowing she was licked – or was about to be – Amanda buried her head in her hands and sagged more heavily against the table. Her bare bottom twitched uncertainly as Jeff walked up to it. For long long moments he didn't raise his palm or make a sound. Fearfully Amanda looked back at him, biting her lip, her eyes wide with the anticipation of what was to happen. Jeff smiled grimly. 'I hope you're thinking about the penalty for being bad.'

Silence. He'd soon change that. He drew back his arm and brought his right hand hard across her creamy young bottom. Amanda wriggled and squealed. Jeff repeated the gesture on the same globe, then meted out two slaps to the other cheek.

'Will this make you more obedient?' He moved his flailing fingers further down to toast the tops of her thighs.

'I could suck you,' Amanda moaned.

'Later, if you're good. Much later.'

His piston was primed within his underpants, throbbed with wanting as he stared at her heating arse.

He spanked her till his arm felt tired, till his entire concentration had turned towards the long strings of clear wetness trailing from her sex centre.

'What's this?' he teased, stroking a finger lightly inside her labia.

'Please,' Amanda begged.

'Please what?'

'You know!'

She thrust back against his fingers.

'No, I'm not a mind-reader, dear.'

She'd need some further foreplay before she begged for his cock – and he wanted to hear her ask for it nicely. He slid his right arm under her belly, circled his middle fingers round, round, round, just above her clitoris till she moaned.

'Please, sir . . .' She rubbed her desire bud frenziedly against his flirtatious fingers. Jeff stopped his movements but kept his middle digit pressed tantalisingly in place.

'I need to come now!' She pushed her clit harder against his immobile finger.

'Then beg for my prick inside you.'

Mutely she shook her head.

'Oh dear, I'm going to take this obliging finger away.'

'I'll bring myself off, then!'

'That'll be difficult when I tie your hands above your head.'

He took away the contact from her clitoris. Amanda wailed, 'All right! All right! Please slide your length inside me.'

'Pretty please,' Jeff instructed.

'Pretty please!'

She was desperate to come – so was he. He unzipped himself. For weeks he'd thought of an evening spent like this. He knew he'd spend himself quickly. But this was just their first session, the start of a long night ahead!

She was warm liquid sensation. She gripped him eagerly. He slid all the way in, pulled back a little, found his favourite rhythmic thrust.

'God, yes!' Amanda sighed with relief as he filled her up, arse pushing back against him. He looked down at her scarlet globes and felt his pleasure build.

'So shy, hiding your tits.' He moved his hands forward, reached under her blouse, fondling her breasts through the obviously lacy bra: a present for later.

Amanda groaned and rubbed her nipples against his fingers, rubbed her sex against his stiff long stick.

'Ask to be allowed to come.'

'Please!' Her voice held the breathless hoarse tension of near-orgasm.

'I'm sure you can ask more nicely than that!'

No answer. He circled his cock round and round, put one finger against her craving clit, threatening to take it away again.

'You know what to say,' he murmured cruelly.

'Jeff . . . sir! Please.'

'Please what?'

Thrusting harder, faster, deeper, his hand dripping with her sexual excitement, his palm heated by her crotch.

'Need to . . .' she gasped, pushing back to meet each lust-crazed lunge. Tendrils of auburn fringe clung to her head. Her tits were rubbing against the desk. Her thighs were frantic.

'Sir, need to . . .'

'What do you say?' Teasing, taunting with his pussy pleaser.

'Pretty please!' She said it of her own volition and the signal went off in his groin and he strained into her, spurting as if he'd never stop. 'Aaaaah!'

He stayed hard, kept thrusting as he felt Amanda's thighs tense in, signalling her almost-orgasm.

'Ah . . . ah . . . ah!' Her more protracted but spaced-out cries echoed his as her wild rapture climbed towards the heights.

'Yes ... yes ... yes!' she gasped, then came, crying out like a little animal, fingers flexing against the desk leaving perspiration marks. He stayed inside, bucking hard as she writhed and groaned, a long ecstatic erogenous appreciation. Her throbbing canal squeezed out the last pulsing pleasure of his own climax and he groaned out loud.

'You needed that!' he teased into her hair, reaching forward to hold her breasts, the nipples pushing through the bra like warmed bullets.

Amanda pushed her hair back from her forehead. 'You're telling me!'

For several moments he lay motionless across her back, idly licking her long smooth neck, his belly against her punished bottom. Then he remembered he had work to do. She hadn't finished paying for her bounced cheques yet!

'Put on your clothes and go and sit outside in reception. Say goodnight to everyone as they leave.'

'But they'll know I've been fucked, and –'

'You can make up excuses to explain why you're so agitated and flushed.'

'You wouldn't!'

Amanda got up shakily from the desk and tried to go into his arms, but he held her at arm's length firmly.

'I'm afraid I have to. You have to remember not to create bad debts.'

'But I thought –'

'That because I deemed to enter you you'd paid your dues? It doesn't work like that.'

Inside, he knew it *could* work like that – but then she'd be more of a girlfriend than a lover. When it came to punishment for pleasure he'd found too much familiarity bred contempt.

Stonily, he handed her both parts of the suit and her underwear, stared as she fumblingly put them on over her chastised bottom and finger-flicked thighs. Finally she looked round in vain for a mirror then ran her fingers through her hair. 'How do I look?'

She looked delectable.

'Red on all four cheeks – but most people will just see two of them!' he replied.

Her lip trembled, eyes wide with excitement and apprehension. 'And you'll really make me sit out there on my sore bum in reception for thirty minutes talking to strangers?'

'Just be thankful I'm not warming your posterior all that time.'

One hand on her shoulder, he edged her out of the door. She winced as she took a seat near the juice bar.

'Sit down properly on both buttocks.'

She looked around fearfully before doing so, but everyone was in an aerobics class.

'I've some paperwork to do in my office,' he said, aware that he was giving her the opportunity to leave again if the heat was too much for her. 'I'll come out for you around six.'

He looked back at the door. Her body looked very proper in its blue linen suit, but her cheeks were hectic. As for the bum in the lemon panties beneath . . . !

Jeff relaxed in the big armchair for the next half hour, sipping a gin and tonic. Gradually his balls returned to normal. He was glad – they might well be in use for a second time later tonight! For now, though, his prick was at peace, which was good as he needed to be able to concentrate on her wilful little *derrière* for a while. He wouldn't be able to do that so well if he was painfully stiff.

As he heard the last stragglers milling around reception, Jeff sauntered out.

'I was just telling Gillian that I've booked a late sunbed session!' a pink-cheeked Amanda said.

Jeff smiled to himself: sunbed, huh? It was half true given that he was about to tan her arse.

'That's right. I'll just switch everything on.' He went into the little sunbed room and adjusted his twitching undercarriage. When he came out the others had left the club.

'Now, my bankrupt little friend . . .'

He marched Amanda into the gym, put three of the plastic steps they used at aerobics on top of each other to form a punishment bench. It looked both high and hard and stable. Amanda gulped.

'Take off all your clothes and bend over that. Put your palms flat on the floor and stick your disobedient rump out.'

'What are . . . what are you going to do?' She stood before the makeshift bench in her skirt suit and looked round at him.

'What do you think I'm going to do?'

'Hurt my . . . hurt my bum.'

'Belt your backside,' he said crudely.· 'Say it after me, girl.'

She shook her head.

'Are you disobeying an order?' He stroked her spanked waiting bum through the linen skirt. 'What happens to bad girls who disobey?'

'They . . . get punished more.'

'Where do they get punished, Amanda?'

She whimpered, refusing to say the shameful words.

'On their wicked little posteriors. You've said sentences like that before to get out of a thrashing. I'm sure you can learn how to say them again.'

He walked in front of her.

'What's this?' He unbuckled his belt.

'It's . . .' She licked her lips.

'It's going to teach you a lesson.'

'How . . . how many?'

'That depends on your saying the right thing.'

'I . . . I'm sorry,' Amanda said.

'That's a start. But my belt's still very angry. And when it's angry it comes down hard on a recalcitrant bum.'

He stared at her till she looked away.

'Take off your clothes.'

Each button seemed to fight going through the buttonhole. Her fingers fumbled with hooks and zips till at last she stood naked, gazing at the floor. She had nice tits – large, with cheeky pink pouting nipples leading on to a small toned waist.

'Bend over the bench.'

Swallowing hard, she did as he asked. Her pinkened globes were an upended waiting target.

'Nice, very nice.'

Her bum cheeks twitched at the thought of what awaited them. Let them wait . . .

For long moments he surveyed the sight. With each lengthening of the pause Amanda's buttocks grew more agitated. They tensed in at the centre, jiggled slightly as she moved her thighs and feet.

At last Jeff pulled the belt back halfway and flicked it over both buttocks simultaneously. Amanda flinched and let out a piglet-style grunt. Jeff repeated the belting four times, each stripe falling beside the next till her backside was all over fiery, uniformly marked.

'Want to try saying sorry again?'

'Suck your cock.'

'Boring,' said Jeff. 'We've played this scene before.'

He used the belt another two times further down across the top of her thighs. Amanda rocked on the makeshift bench as if she was about to get up to protect her posterior.

'Stay where you are or you'll get extra.'

'But I can't bear –'

'I've bared it for you, sweetheart.'

She groaned loudly, but stayed in place.

'As the whole point of your coming here is getting fit,' said Jeff, 'I think it's time I put you through your paces.'

Amanda looked back at him tearfully.

'Yes, let's have you limbering up the ropes.' He watched as she stood up. 'Don't bother covering your bottom with your hands, darling. No point in trying to stand on ceremony here.'

'Just for a moment?'

Her fingers were spread over her sore flesh as if to keep the belt at bay.

Jeff shook his head warningly. 'You've got to *earn* the right to protect your bottom.'

'But how?'

'I want to see your naked little body shimming up these ropes like it was born to it!'

'And if I'm no good?'

She peeled her palms away from her posterior reluctantly.

'You'll have to learn.'

Her face was hot, and, as a glistening strand dripped from her close-cropped crotch, he realised her pussy was even hotter. They'd really get athletic by the end of the night! For now, though, she had to realise that she couldn't write bad cheques – it amounted to stealing.

'I may invite your bank manager here to see you get your just desserts,' he said.

'No – don't!'

Amanda put one hand on top of the other and started up the rope. Jeff stood back to take in the view. Her reddened arse jiggled as she strove for purchase. Her nipples were straining forward with effort and excitement as she began her ascent.

'Higher,' he said as she entwined her ankles round the foot of the climbing cord.

'I . . . I can't!'

'I'm your trainer – you'll do as I say!' He slapped lightly at her left cheek and reflexively she kicked him away, her naked foot connecting with his shoulder.

'Oh dear,' said Jeff. 'Fancy kicking your superior. I'm going to make you very sorry indeed!'

'I *am* sorry . . . didn't mean . . .' She jumped from the rope, looked wildly at the door.

'Thinking of going someplace?' Jeff asked.

Amanda put her hands supplicatingly on his chest. 'I could kiss it better, sir.'

'Forget kissing.' He slid his palms down to her well-warmed bottom. 'And the only place you're going is over my knee!'

This time he sat down on the stepping bench and dragged her over his lap.

'Not again!' Amanda wailed.

'Well, if you won't behave I have no option.'

He fondled her flaming pained buttocks. 'How many lashes of the belt do you deserve this time?'

Amanda sighed. 'Two?'

'You've only had six so far. Isn't ten a nice round number? That would mean you'd take another four.'

He caressed her curves till she wriggled and pushed against his prick.

'Another four, sir,' she sighed, obviously keen to get it over with and enjoy the sex session her thrashing was leading to.

'Four well-spaced-out lashes with the belt.' He smiled. 'I think we may have you do twelve press-ups in between each lash. Wouldn't that be fun?'

Amanda writhed some more. 'I've never been any good at press-ups!'

'Maybe this leathering will change all that?'

He brought the broad strap down on her undisciplined little bum until she moaned and ground her pussy against his pulsing penis. And, bounced cheques or not, Jeff knew he'd soon be making a sizeable deposit from his sperm account.

Colouring Things

This was one of the most luxurious rooms he'd ever seen – and its owner was an equally rich, dark-eyed beauty. Overawed and excited in turn, Colin Chalmers stared at her, then at the cream-papered walls.

'You want the skirting boards and cornice painted scarlet, Mrs Merringrew?'

The woman nodded, her eyes fixed on the current décor. 'Yes, for contrast, you understand.'

Colin understood that his prick twitched with desire every time he looked at her. That open mink coat! That dove-grey silk dress and sheer-stockinged long legs! She was out of his league, though – educated, well-groomed, married. The most she'd ever let him do for her was paint part of this room.

Her *bed*room. His groin tautened again.

'You'll put down papers,' she said, turning away towards the door.

'Em – yes, ma'am.'

He watched as her black patent heels clipped her from the room. She must be going out to lunch somewhere salubrious across town. His own stomach rumbled. He'd have to stop soon and eat the sandwiches he'd packed for his meal.

Still thinking about food, he stepped back, wondering which section of the wall he should start on. Stepped back into the open pot of scarlet paint.

Even as he turned round, the red rush of gloss went everywhere. Over the lush white carpet, the foot of the bed, the dressing table's edge.

'Here are the papers,' Mrs Merringrew murmured, coming back into the room. She stopped and stared.

'*Oh God, I'm sorry*,' Colin gasped, hands going to his mouth like a naughty schoolboy.

'You're going to be *very* sorry.'

'I could clean it up . . .'

'With your tongue? I think that could be arranged.' He stared at the ruined wool, not quite taking in her words. He'd never seen a woman look so angry. 'I'm going to have to take you in hand,' she said.

Unsure of what she meant, Colin stayed rooted to the spot.

'Get on your belly over that bed,' Mrs Merringrew ordered.

'What are . . .?' His voice cracked with nervousness.

'Don't ask stupid questions – just do as you're told!'

'And if I don't?'

'I'll tell your boss. You'll have the shortest-ever apprenticeship. He'll probably want to tan your hide himself.'

Was tanning his hide what she planned? He hadn't been spanked since primary school, but could still remember what it felt like. Ten minutes of overwhelming buttock misery, then your nerve ends forgot. And to have her touch him in any way . . . God knows, he'd fantasised so often about being stroked by a woman. 'I'm putting my belly over the bed, Mrs Merringrew,' he said obsequiously.

'Address me as Mistress,' she said.

Wasn't that what servants had once called their employers? In a limited way he supposed he *was* her servant. She'd paid his firm to do a job for her. He'd failed. Now she was taking it out on his bum.

'I'm not usually this accident-prone,' he said hesitantly to fill in the silence.

'By the time I've finished leathering your backside you'll never dare to have an accident again.'

Sitting on the bed beside his denimed arse, she stroked its quivering contours over and over.

'These'll have to come off, boy.' Waiting for her to remove them, he closed his eyes. 'Stop wasting my time.' Her voice was cool, controlled, compelling. 'Undo the button and zip quickly. Get these jeans at your ankles now!'

Burying his face in the duvet, he undid them and pulled them down, down, down, feeling the hairs on his thighs and calves standing up with uncertainty. They weren't the only part of his anatomy that was standing up!

'I hope you're not getting hard?'

Colin pushed his erection further into the bed and murmured 'No, Mistress.'

'Because I'll punish you extra if you get excited – and if you lie about it, too.'

How could he not get turned on when he was partially disrobed in front of her? Colin closed his legs tightly trying to hide his arousal some more.

'I'm a champion swimmer. My arm muscles are like iron.' As if to prove it, she slapped suddenly down at his nearest buttock, then at its partner. Colin grunted slightly. She had a hard, ricocheting slap. As the shock of the first sting radiated out across his taut cheeks, she laid on a third, fourth, fifth painful lesson across his arse crease.

'How many?' he whimpered, writhing.

'As many as I decide you deserve.'

After twenty or thirty full-force spanks, he felt his bum starting to glow and tingle fiercely. 'Let's have a look at what we've achieved so far,' murmured his mistress, squeezing his cheeks. He winced, held his breath as he waited for her to undress him. 'Take your underpants off now, boy. Do I have to wait all day?'

'No, I . . .' He cast a shy glance round at her. 'This is so embarrassing.'

'You *should* be embarrassed, coming here like some misbehaving little urchin and ruining my beautiful home.' She palmed his underpanted rear. 'If I have to take these off by myself you'll feel the brunt of my garden cane, and I promise you, that's *really* sore.'

'Yes, Mistress.' Dying inside, he edged down his Y-fronts, pulled them over his legs and kicked carefully free of them. She felt his bare bottom.

'Mmm. Colouring nicely – but you've a long way to go.'

Colin whimpered. He was out of his depth. Aroused yet ashamed. Hurting. His mind searched for ways to appease her, to avoid the thrashing that was coming next.

Walking over to the dressing-table, the sultry beauty picked up a hand mirror and held it so that its glass faced the larger wall mirror behind him. By doing so, she forced him to look at his own fiery bum. Red handprint blurred over red handprint. You could see all five fingers, the flesh at its most scarlet in the centre where it had been lashed by her palm.

'Now get down on your knees in front of the paint stain.' Darting a quick glance at her, Colin clambered from the bed and knelt awkwardly beside his mishap. 'See how red it is? And you've just seen the paltry pinkness of your arse.'

Colin licked his lips.

'I intend to turn your bare bottom to that colour – a hand obviously won't get your backside to a deep enough scarlet.' She smiled as he looked up at her pleadingly. 'You'll have to go over the dressing-table and taste my husband's slipper across your cheeks.'

Her husband! At the mention of his name, Colin cringed closer to the ground. 'Mistress – is he due home soon?'

'Could be any minute now.'

'What if he finds us like this?'

'Finds out what *you've* done wrong, you mean. He'll probably take his belt to your disobedient young seat.'

'I could pay for the damage.'

'Oh yes, boy, you'll pay all right.' She took hold of his hair as he knelt at her ankles. 'Get over that dressing-table and stick your bottom right out!'

Stepping numbly over the paint stain, Colin did as she commanded. One by one he put the lipsticks, powders and perfumes that graced the tabletop upon the floor. He was terrified he'd earn further strokes by breaking something. Turning his back, he tried to keep his bobbing cock away from her, knowing she'd slipper him harder for this carnal crime.

When the dressing-table was bare, he went sideways over it, so that one of his ears was towards its mirror. He shut his eyes tightly – he didn't want to see anything. Wished he didn't have to feel! 'Forty whacks with a hard-backed slipper,' Mrs Merringrew said. She placed the cool sole on his exposed hot arse, as if practising where she'd land it. Colin tautened every muscle in his bum.

'Please . . .' he whimpered.

'Say "Pretty please",' his tormentor said. Colin pursed his lips together. He had to keep some pride, damn her! The first blow from the hard plastic sole landed across the centre of his arse, and he let go of the table top and yelled.

'Lucky I didn't order you to keep quiet,' his mistress said in a cool, detached voice. 'Now say what I told you.'

'Pretty please,' Colin muttered.

'You can say it louder than that!' She laid the slipper on with extra zeal, the implement raising its blistering trail across his upper thighs, the main swell of his bum, the crack between his buttocks. Every millimetre felt as if it was being singed.

'Pretty please! Pretty please!' Colin moaned, writhing and bucking. He wanted her to stop the assault on his sore flesh. He wanted to put his cool hands over his arse. Instead, here he was, his helpless bottom exposed to the gaze of any man or woman who cared to walk into the room. What if his boss turned up? What if her husband appeared? They'd see his upturned bare cheeks, all red and raw and squirming. He'd never been so ashamed in his life.

'No more!' he begged. Mrs Merringrew continued to lay on the slipper from left to right. She struck from above, from below, from different angles. Colin jerked his hips and cried out and put his hands round to protect his bottom, only to have the backs of his hands slippered out of the way.

'I'll do anything!' he moaned, between the tormenting yet strangely arousing slaps.

'Let's put that to the test right now,' his mistress said.

She paused, obviously contemplating his well-warmed bum. Colin kept his eyes tightly shut. He ran his fingers nervously over the dressing-table side, and waited. What test did she have in mind for him? Hadn't he already suffered enough?

'I want to please you,' he muttered, wishing he could look round at her.

'Then move your lazy rear end from that dressing-table and follow me to the bathroom right now.'

He reached for his pants and jeans, but she slapped his hands away.

'Butt naked, please! You don't deserve the dignity of clothes. You're nothing, you know, a nonentity.'

'I'm nothing, Mistress.' he repeated fawningly, feeling less than nothing with his stripped legs and scrotum and sore hot bum.

'Crawl,' she added. 'Hands and knees. That's it!'

Head dipped towards the carpet, he made his way on all fours down the hall.

The bathroom was unlike any he'd ever seen, long and wide and black-tiled, with a sunken round bath, above which was positioned a sturdy shower faucet. 'Stand in the bath. Stretch up your hands.' He did as she ordered, and watched, open-mouthed, as she reached under her skirt and undid her fine dark stockings, slipped them off.

'We want the bad boy's hands out of the way so that he doesn't touch his dirty bits. He has to learn to be a *clean* boy.' So saying, she wound one nylon round his wrist several times, then tied it in a complex knot to the shower faucet, binding him securely in place. Then she did the same with the other stocking, his other wrist.

'Promise to behave?'

With his arms stretched high above his head and firmly tethered, he didn't have much option. 'Yes, Mistress,' he whimpered, feeling inately vulnerable – she now had total access on all sides to his cock, his balls, his burning backside. He dared a look at her hands – they were empty. She must have left the slipper in the bedroom. Did that mean he was going to get spanked once more?

'Now – not putting papers down right away was bad.'

'It was bad, Mistress,' he repeated humbly.

'It showed a lack of control, don't you think?'

Colin hesitated. Oh Christ, what did he say next? If he agreed he'd done wrong he was doubtless setting himself

138

up for further correction. But if he disagreed with his betters that was also a thrashable offence!

'I was a bad boy, but I'm now going to be a very good boy, Mistress,' he said beseechingly.

'We'll see about that when we have our little test.'

She rolled the fingers of her right hand round his flaccid cock, so that her hand formed a warm silky sheath of erotic promise. Colin gasped, his manhood immediately lengthening and thickening and becoming stiff.

'Didn't I tell you earlier not to get hard?'

She ran her thumb down the main vein in his shaft.

'Yes, but I can't help it!'

'You must learn to help it. I'll have to cool you down.' Pressing a button behind his back she turned on the cold shower. Colin gasped in the cooling jets, and tried hopelessly to get his hands free and begged for her to stop.

When his cock had shrunk to a tiny frozen slug, she did. 'That's better. You're being well-behaved now, and well-behaved boys deserve a pat or two.' She took his shrivelled prick between her thumb and forefinger. Colin started to think of the football results, of how much his bedsit needed tidying – of anything except what her fingers were doing to his horny hunk of flesh!

'It's getting warmer now,' his tormentor teased. Colin's caressed cock twitched between her fingers. 'Oh, dear – I hope it's not starting to be disrespectful again.'

'No, Mistress, it isn't!' He tried to turn his mind to the other painting job he had lined up today, but all his brain could register was the delicious excited stirrings in his cock.

'You're going to have to be disciplined again.' His arse begged for mercy. His prick pleaded for release. He shook his head dumbly. 'You don't have much option, slug – shackled and waiting, with your bare wet arse.' She looked round the room. 'Ah, this'll bring a blush to your cheeks!' She held up the toilet brush with its smooth plastic back and long thin handle. 'Quite apt, really, seeing as you're only fit to clean the loo.'

Taking his now thickened cock in one hand, she brought the brush back across his soaking arse with the other. The wetness made the punishment radiate. Colin cried out and jerked in his bonds. 'Hold it!' She gripped his cock more cruelly until he stopped bucking to and fro. 'If you're too wriggly I'll have to use a spreader to keep your legs apart.'

'I'll keep still, Mistress.'

The shock of the slap had made his cock deflate by half. Mrs Merringrew caressed his craving balls for delicious moments whilst his balls trembled.

'Let's try again, shall we? I won't stand more disobedience.'

'I'm trying, Mistress. Oh, Christ! I can't help ...'

She fondled his dick flesh till he pulsated again, elongated into a purple-headed leaking piston. She was standing so close as she frigged him that he could see the jutting outline of her nipples through the dove-grey dress. His mouth opened of its own accord -- he so wanted to suck them. To lie at her breast like a baby and just be held.

'You dirty little bastard! Haven't you had enough buttock warming?'

'I have ... oh, please. I don't *want* to get excited down there.'

'You mean you don't desire me?'

'No ... and yes!'

'You don't know what you want,' she said, caressing his cock more cruelly. 'But I know what you *need*.'

She picked up the toilet brush again. Used its back against his backside twice in quick succession. 'You can't believe how hot they are now,' she said gloatingly, throwing down the brush at last and running a teasing finger down both cheeks. 'They feel like they're on fire, they look so sore.'

'I know, Mistress!'

His cock had retreated towards his body during the punishment. He felt as if he'd never get hard again.

'Permission to kiss your arse, Mistress,' he moaned. He wanted to appease her, no matter what it took. It was the most obsequious thing he could think of.

'And are you fit to put your lips to my bottom?'

'No, Mistress, but I beg to be allowed to show my gratitude to your fair flesh.'

Staring into his eyes, she ran a hand down his flanks, smiling as he winced at the slightest pressure on his helpless buttocks. 'Beg nicely to be allowed to lick my crack.'

He begged as she asked. Closed his eyes with gratitude as she unbound him. Tremulously Colin stepped out of the bath.

'Hands and knees, you wicked boy! You know you aren't fit to walk upright.'

'Sorry, Mistress. I'll crawl for you, Mistress.' He got down as she commanded and crawled painfully before her down the hall.

When he hesitated outside the first door, she gave him a warning tap with the toilet brush. 'In there, and don't dally!' Colin crawled into a huge lounge with a recliner and a four-seater settee.

Mrs Merringrew tossed off her fur coat, lay face down on the recliner and edged her dress up. As Colin watched, she peeled down tiny black satin panties to reveal an alabaster backside.

'Lick my arsehole, you troublesome pup! Put your tongue right in deep and lick all the shit out.' He put his lips to the puckered pink hole and gave it a reverent kiss.

'Harder!'

He got the tip of his tongue inside and she squirmed. For a second, he almost felt powerful. Then she backed her arse into his face, sending him toppling backwards on to the thick pile rug. She stood over him, eyes and lips cold.

'What else would you like to lick?'

'Your nipples, Mistress.'

He tried to turn on his side, so that his weight wouldn't be lying on his pained buttocks any more.

'Did I tell you to move?'

'I just –'

'Did I tell you to?'

'No.' He got back on to his sore bum.

'Sit up and edge yourself around the room on your arse five times.' Moaning quietly, he obeyed her. Each circuit seemed to take ages, each scrape of buttock against carpet sent further agonies through his bum.

'I'm teaching this silly little apprentice self-control and humility. What else does he need to learn?'

Colin's mind searched for an answer: 'I'll learn whatever you want me to, Mistress. Only don't hurt my bum!'

'Let me look at it.' She drew a footstool into the middle of the floor. 'Bend over that and keep your hands to the front. It's time I examined my handiwork.' She fondled his tortured roundness. 'Mmm, not bad.'

What could he say or do to take her thoughts away from further chastising his rear? It felt so vulnerable.

'Let me pay homage to your nipples, Mistress,' he begged again. 'I'd tongue them ever so gently, for ever so long.'

'What if I wanted them tongued hard and fast?'

'Then I'd do that!'

'Stand up.' With difficulty he complied. 'Walk into the centre of the room. Now bend over and grasp your ankles.' Shuddering at the prospect of her tormenting his bare arse again, he did as she said.

He waited tautly for the lash. Instead, he felt her palm tickling his balls. He squirmed against her hand whilst maintaining his bent position. 'Does the donkey want ridden?' she asked.

'If that's what my Mistress wants the donkey to be,' he whimpered, writhing. She wrapped four fingers round his elongating cock.

'Beg me to mount you.'

'Please mount me, Mistress, then treat me as you wish,' he groaned.

He felt her fingers on his shoulders, pushing him further down. Uncertainly, he got on to his hands and knees. He moaned loudly as she squatted across his back, and slapped firmly at both his bare buttocks. 'Take me round the room, donkey!' she commanded, raking his sides with her knees. Moving pitifully slowly, for she was a strong woman and he was exhausted, he crawled round the room with her on his back.

'Faster! More!' He did as he was bid. His knees scraped against the carpet. His balls craved a climax. Occasionally she slapped his red sore cheeks, commanding that he give a faster ride. Finally she stood up and ordered him to roll on to his back and bum. 'Let's see if you're built like a donkey. My God, boy, is that all you've got?'

She toed his semi-erect shaft with her heel. It stayed the same size as he waited further instruction.

'Touch yourself,' she ordered. 'Frig your cock.'

Blushing, he put hesitant hands to his now-leaking shaft.

'I've never . . . with anyone watching.'

'A secret little wanker? I thought as much.'

He stroked up then down in the familiar beloved way, felt his prick grow longer. 'That's enough now, donkey! This is for my pleasure, not for yours.'

He took his fingers away.

'Now put your hands behind your head and keep them there.'

Now that it was fully exposed to her gaze, to her ministrations, his cock jerked with excitement and anxiety.

'The animal needs ridden,' his mistress said. She hitched her dress up again and positioned her crotch above him. Colin breathed deeply. Bit his lip as she sank all the way down on his swollen shaft, then ground her hips round and round and round.

As he stared up at her with his hands behind his head, she unbuttoned her blouse, giving him a view of creamy full breasts with plump pink pouting nipples. How he longed to feel them, to suck them, to bury his head in between their warm scent!

'Look but don't touch, you dirty animal,' she said.

'Yes, Mistress. Thank you for allowing me to look.'

She fucked him harder. Her quim was like a clutching sheath of silk. He wailed behind his teeth. His bum wanted to lift up from the floor, but she wouldn't let it. 'I'm going to have spurs made for you,' she said conversationally, and Colin groaned.

'Tell me you deserve to be ridden with reins.' He shook his head till she put thumb and forefinger on one ball and started to squeeze lightly.

'Oh Jesus, don't! I deserve to be ridden with reins, Mistress.'

'What else do you deserve?'

'To have a bit in my mouth.' He was thrusting upwards now. She drove down to meet him.

'And I'll use the whip on you for moving without permission, you disobedient wretch!'

'Yes, Mistress – wear the saddle, take the spurs. Anything!' He bucked up into her as he came.

She kept riding him till her own orgasm made her tense in on his prick. Fear and excitement kept him hard for the vital few seconds.

'If you'd gone soft on me ...' she said as she finished and pulled off him. 'You're already for it – I didn't say you could come.'

'But my arse is redder than the paint stain by now, Mistress,' he gasped.

'It is. But will it be as red next week at this time? If not, I'll have to chastise you all over again.'

Colin swallowed hard. 'But I've paid for my mistake!'

'Getting hard without permission? Spurting up me? I don't think so.'

'I didn't mean to –'

'But I mean to spank you once weekly if that's what it takes.'

Colin tried a different tack. 'I've work to do, Mistress!'

'I'll phone your boss, tell him I've found extra painting chores for you.' She smiled. 'Practice self restraint of your nether regions. The second week's training will be more rigorous than the first.'

She smiled as he crawled over to kiss her shoes, her feet, her ankles. Colin knew that he would turn up at her house again and again to take his punishment in the hope of receiving the ultimate pleasure. 'Be a good donkey when you come next time,' his mistress added, 'and bring a riding whip.'

Custom Built

Amsterdam was amazing! Shona was still tingling at the memory as she got off the plane. Back to normality, to the nine to five. And to airport queues, she thought, seeing several stretch ahead.

'Sorry about the delay,' said a thirty-something official in uniform.

Shona grimaced. 'If I'd known it would be like this I'd have stayed away!'

'Holland, was it?' he asked, checking something on a notepad.

'Mm, Holland.'

And it was more than the tulip fields she'd been to see!

Mind you, guys like this gave a girl something to come back to. Those sure brown eyes! That thick black glossy hair! Shona watched him move the pen with long, firm strokes across the paper.

'I suppose you guys get travel discount,' she said.

The man began to tell her about the perks of the job. He sounded cultured; he used his hands as he spoke. They talked, laughed, smiled, told jokes, flirted.

'I'm off in five minutes. Fancy going for a cup of coffee?' he asked at last.

'Mmm. I fancy it!' Shona murmured. After Holland she felt ready for anything, wild!

'Good.' The official's eyes held hers for longer than was necessary. He gripped her hand. I'm Stephen, by the way.'

He looked like one. You could tell no one would dare shorten it to Steve. Shona told him her name, turned towards the baggage carousel.

'I'll just get my suitcase' she said.

This was better than a holiday romance! To meet a man like this on her home turf ... Collecting her case, she walked confidently towards the security checkers, Stephen at her side. She'd never been stopped – never! Her companions often had, but she'd always been waved through.

'Can you open your case, miss?' the customs officer said as she strolled past him. Shona felt herself begin to redden. It could still be all right ...

They might just rifle through the topmost layer of clothes and ... They didn't. Stephen looking over her shoulder, they pulled out bras and panties and dresses, till they came to the magazines. 'Susie Stoops For A Spanking', 'Bad Girls Bare Their Bottoms For A Firm Hand'.

The officer picked up 'Reddened Arse'. He was staring at her quite openly now.

'Robert – you finish the line up. I'll deal with this,' Stephen said.

Reaching over, he put the contents back in the suitcase, and snapped it shut. Then, taking Shona by the wrist, he led her to an empty room and locked the door.

'You realise I'll have to conduct a body search?' His tone was gentle, teasing. Taking a deep breath, Shona looked away. 'You admit to doing wrong?' Stephen continued. She nodded. 'Then take your jacket off, and throw it on the floor.'

Not looking at him, she did so. With a layer of material gone, she felt defenceless, disarmed.

'It's my duty to frisk you,' said Stephen, walking towards her with measured steps.

'Force yourself – why don't you!' she muttered, striving to repeat his mocking tone. But the longing in his face was so strong she had to look away.

Slowly she felt his hands move round, the fingers sliding over her blouse's silky material. Deliciously they weighed her curves, grazed her nipples, till she whimpered and writhed.

'I'll have to conduct a full strip search,' Stephen told her. 'Remove your blouse.'

'Why should I?'

Her voice was hesitant, tremulous. This was unbelievable! This was something new!

'Official strip search,' said Stephen, smiling mockingly. 'You could have anything hidden in these cups!'

Could she? Should she? Shona hesitated. He was gorgeous, she was randy – what the hell! Inhaling hard, she unbuttoned the satiny top and shrugged it off. He walked up behind her, stared impassively till she fumbled with the bra catch. 'That's better. Now remove your skirt and tights.'

Shona looked at him, looked beyond him. Was this really happening? Stephen raised an eyebrow and slapped his palm against his thigh.

Swallowing hard, she let her skirt slide to the floor, unpeeled black tights from legs that suddenly felt weak. 'Pull down your panties,' Stephen ordered. 'It's my duty to conduct an intimate search.'

'Aren't there supposed to be two women present for that bit?' she asked, determined not to make things easy for him.

Stephen turned towards the door. 'If you want to be watched by my female colleagues, I'll just call –'

'No – please!' Breathing quickly, she hooked her thumbs in the elastic, pushed down, close peach cotton sliding free of firm tanned skin. Like this it was an incredibly erotic game. But for others to see . . .?

'Spread your legs,' Stephen ordered. Noting how his breathing escalated, Shona splayed them athletically apart.

She looked over her shoulder as he crossed to the cupboard and returned with membrane thin gloves and a bottle of baby oil. Standing before her, he warmed the oil in his hands before moving to her rear.

'Bend over and touch your toes.'

She bent, arse hugely vulnerable. Felt his slick palms stroke down her thighs then slide up to her labia, fingers temptingly rimming her rectum with practised ease.

'Too much!' she gasped, 'too . . .'

After a few seconds, she felt one of his fingers slide into her arsehole, and move in and out.

'Aaah!' She cried out at the sensations, and pushed back to increase them. The movement stopped, withdrew.

'I think you're beginning to enjoy yourself,' Stephen whispered, 'and you've been very bad.'

God, but this was embarrassing! Shona stared at the grey expanse of carpet, the locked door.

'How do you think we should punish girls who're bad?' Stephen murmured.

'I . . . it was just a few magazines.'

'Dirty magazines which could deprave and corrupt,' Stephen continued. He walked round and round, gazing at her nakedness, then stopped in front of her. 'What used to happen to you when you were bad at home?'

'I'd get spanked,' Shona whispered miserably.

'You're not too old,' Stephen said, pulling up a chair.

Taking his time, he settled himself on it, patted his knee. 'Come over here, and take your punishment like a good little girl.'

'Or what?' Shona said shakily.

'Or I'll come and get you,' Stephen said.

'Go on then!' Shona made a dash for the door, not really meaning it. She was already dripping fluid, and had no clothes and nowhere to go! Within seconds, Stephen had jumped up and bounded over to her.

'You get double now,' he said, dragging her back to the chair.

'Double what?' she murmured, playing for time.

'A double spanking. A double caning. I haven't decided what to do with you yet!'

'How about a fine?' Shona asked breathlessly.

The first hard slap ricocheted down.

'Say you've been bad,' Stephen murmured.

Shona kept silent. Stephen spanked and spanked and spanked. Thrusting her body forward, Shona found her clit beginning to rub against his trouser crotch. Looking up at his uniform, she began to build.

'Wicked!' said Stephen, slapping. Shona's sex lips pulsed and swelled.

'Disobedient! Dirty! Sluttish!' Stephen added.

His palm continued to flare its tingling torment across her arse.

Finally he gave a particularly heavy swipe at the top of her thighs, which drove her against his erection. Coming, she cried out, and gripped his thigh.

For a long time he just held her across his knee, murmuring gently. Outside the usual noises of the airport went on and on. Then: 'I didn't give you permission to orgasm,' he said quietly. 'That's another breaking of a Customs rule.'

'How can I show you how sorry I am?' Shona whispered. Stephen's hand stroked her warmed, pink cheeks.

'In lots of ways,' he told her. 'You can start by bringing over those magazines.'

'What?' For a second she'd almost forgotten the circumstances which brought her here!

'Your sex mags,' said Stephen. 'Don't play the innocent with me.'

'Do I have to?' She'd feel silly looking at them with him. She'd never been in a situation quite like this before!

'I'm prepared to call in another officer to assist me,' Stephen said mildly. 'I'm sure Robert wouldn't mind holding you down whilst I taught you to behave.'

'All right! You win. I'll get them!' Sullenly Shona walked over to her suitcase, and brought out the most innocuous of the magazines.

'Bring all of them. Put them in your mouth, and crawl back on your hands and knees,' Stephen said in a quiet, compelling voice.

Her sex sap dripping on the carpet, Shona crossed the room on all fours, then crouched at his feet.

'Start reading that one to me,' he said.

Worse and worse!

'The slave girl had been disobedient,' she whispered, 'so her owners had to tie her up and administer the lash ...'

'What do you think they tied her to?' Stephen asked hoarsely.

'To the coathook,' said Shona, looking round the room. It didn't take long – he was good with knots. Soon she

heard his zip go down, felt his hardness probing her in its
rubber sheath.

'An even more intimate body search,' he whispered. 'We
double-check to make sure we get it right.'

'Feels right to me,' Shona whimpered, as he pushed forward and she felt him engorge her. 'Feels brilliant!' she
added breathlessly as he began to thrust.

'You're not supposed to enjoy it!' Stephen mocked, half
pulling out of her.

'I hate it, Master,' she moaned, and he began to fuck her
again.

And then some! There was fluid everywhere – her juices
and perspiration, his sweat. For a long time after he came,
they both rested. Then Stephen led her to the showers and
they soaped each other clean.

Incredible! In the taxi going home, Shona's mind went
into overdrive. Had she really given him her address? It
would be madness to see him again!

And yet ... She smiled to herself, and shifted carefully
on the seat. Her entire sex still felt stimulated, ready for
take two. She'd never had sex like that before! She thought
back over the past three years, its many changes. She
hadn't had sex with a man since her divorce.

Pity Stephen had confiscated her magazines. He'd said
there were one or two features it was his duty as her guard-
ian to read. He intended to come to her flat on Saturday
to conduct what he called a 'house search'. He'd warned
he'd have to punish her again if he found something lasciv-
ious or crude.

Back home, Shona flicked through a paperback. By now
Stephen would be reading 'Reddened Arse'. She smiled, remembering the magazine's photographs. Funny how he'd
just assumed from them that she was sub ...

She walked round the room, suddenly restless. Was that
a speck of dust she saw on the arm of the settee? The phone
rang, and, glad of the diversion, she answered it. 'Tonight.
Eight p.m. And don't be late,' she snapped. Setting down
the receiver, she wrote the man's initials in her diary. He
came round to do the cleaning at least once a week.

It was nice getting back into her routine, she thought contentedly. Back to the known rituals of everyday life. Flicking through her appointments book, she perused the forthcoming entries. Not the best choice of word, really, given that entering her was strictly taboo . . .

Enjoying the irony. she walked down the hall, stopping momentarily at the locked door which led to the basement. It looked exciting, forbidden; Stephen would doubtless descend these steps in his search for the magazines. Smiling, she undid the padlock. This weekend her customs officer might find that she had a few customs of her own . . .

Marking Time

Her tits. He loved her tits. He only wished he could see more of them. More than even the clinging promise of her shirt would allow. The way she walked, the way she stopped, the way she licked her full wide lips. He looked at her sideways as she strolled casually past.

'Hey, Mark – get a grip, man. Concentrate on the game!' one of his mates shouted. He sighed. The only game he wanted to play was in bed.

'Sorry – just thinking,' he muttered, half heartedly kicking the ball towards them. He risked a quick grin at the woman, but she just quirked an eyebrow and walked by.

In a moment she'd disappear inside the park-keeper's cottage, and he'd have to settle for fantasising about her until he played football next Saturday. It had been that way for the past five weeks. He'd initially taken a short cut through the cottage's back garden, seen glossy latex briefs and bras on the washing line, wondered who wore such cock-hardening gear. Later he'd seen this woman – his ideal woman! – entering the cottage. He'd wanted to enter her ever since . . .

Mark sighed and quickly passed the football on again. He knew so little about her, only – from the nameplate on the door – that her surname was Stark. He knew she was the park-keeper, that she looked thirty-something. That he had yet to find the nerve to ask her out.

Damn it! Suddenly enraged, he took a long run at the ball which Jake of the opposition was laconically dribbling. Sent it flying through the air. Up and up and along and starting to come down and . . . 'Oh Christ. Now you've done it!' said Jake as the ball went crashing through the attic window of Miss Stark's house.

'Fuck it!' said Mark. He had to act uncaring: the guys were watching. A moment ago they'd all been enjoying the weekend release after earning their first few pay cheques: macho working men. Now they stood and stared at each other then looked away, toeing the ground, unsure as schoolkids. 'Can I have me ball back, missus?' Jake said in a fair imitation of a six-year-old. Mark laughed along with the rest, but his heart beat fast.

'Guess I'll better face the music!' he said as a familiar face appeared at the cottage's decimated attic window. Tucking his polo shirt carefully into his jeans, he walked unsteadily to her door.

He knocked once. Waited. Started to wonder if she wasn't going to answer. What if the ball had hit some much-loved heirloom? What if she'd been cut by spraying glass?

When the door swung open he wanted to kiss her. Well, he'd wanted to do that anyway. He put on his most apologetic smile. 'My ball . . . I'm really sorry. I'll pay for any damage.'

'Yes, you will.'

Up close she was even more attractive, her dark chignon held in place by an African comb. She'd changed, he noted distractedly, into a mid-calf-length black cloak. What was she wearing underneath it? All he could see was sheer black nylon and black stiletto shoes.

'You'll pay for any damage,' she repeated.

He gulped, tore his gaze away from her long lean body. 'Yes, I . . .' He fumbled in his jeans for his wallet, knowing it only contained eight or nine quid. 'I don't have enough with me, but I could give you a deposit, come back with my chequebook.'

'You don't have enough?'

If only she'd smile. That cool appraising gaze was making him feel really uncomfortable. It was exactly like being back at school. 'No. I didn't plan to break a window!'

'I'm glad to hear it.' That set mouth, those unyielding eyes looked anything but glad.

'So, what should I do?' He looked at her with his big brown eyes. Girls his own age had often fallen for these same eyes – and for the rest of him!

'Fetch the ball and take it back to your little friends. Tell them you'll be staying behind to show how sorry you are.'

Mark gulped, ran his tongue over his lips. He felt like a tongue had been run over his balls, and then some. He felt – desperate. Throbbing with need. Wordlessly he followed her up the stairs to the attic, picked his way over the many glass shards to the ball.

'Just be a mo.' He felt gormless. He felt handless. Almost lost his footing on the first step. Walked out of the door, down the path into the park again, already wishing he could close himself off with her from the outside world.

When he was three feet from his mates, he threw the ball to Lennie. 'Place is in a right state! I've told her I'll help clear up – maybe patch the window,' he yelled. 'Phone me tomorrow to see if we're on for the pub, all right?' A chorus of all rights.

He walked back through the gate, hesitated at the cottage. She'd left the door open. He let himself in cautiously, jumped to find her standing behind the door. She closed it, stood looking at him coldly. 'I told you to tell them that you were staying behind to prove how sorry you were.'

He gulped. 'I'd ... I'd feel silly.'

'But you are silly. A big boy like you smashing up a fine lady's house.'

He said nothing. He felt as if he were blushing. When he dipped his head he found he could see her nipples outlined through the black material. His fingers itched to touch them. His cock just itched. He'd never been sexually humiliated before. He'd never thought of it. He'd been too busy playing at being a man of the world. And yet ...

'You've been bad, haven't you?' she murmured.

He nodded. This only happened in films.

'I used to be a teacher before I took over the running of this park. I often had to deal with naughty little boys.'

Hesitatingly, he glanced up. He licked his dry lips. She still wasn't smiling. 'What's your name, boy?'

'Mark.'

'How appropriate.' She looked him up and down. 'Have you left school, Mark?'

'Yes. Six months ago. I'm eighteen.'

'I didn't ask for your age!' He'd obviously irritated her again.

'Did you ever misbehave there?'

'Y-e-s.'

He wanted to lie. He wanted to make a joke out of it, but somehow he couldn't. 'And what happened when you were bad?'

'I got punished, miss.' He sounded vulnerable, felt disarmed. His prick was pulsing.

Taking hold of his left earlobe she pulled him closer to her. 'How?'

'Caned. I got caned.' He'd mainly been given lines, but he wanted to keep the conversation interesting.

'Caned, Mark? Caned hard?'

'Yes.'

'Yes, miss.' she corrected.

'Yes, miss.'

'And where were you caned, boy?'

He pushed back the reality of a couple of mild palm-canings.

'On my arse.'

Her open palm snaked across his cheek. 'Don't be crude, boy. Say on my bottom.'

'On my bottom,' he whimpered. He could feel the imprint of her fingers in his flesh. Tears came swiftly to his eyes. He wanted her to abuse him, then hold him. He wanted her to take charge of the situation. He just wanted her, full stop.

What he didn't want was to be standing, fully clothed, behind her cottage door. 'The attic – can we go there?' he muttered, turning his body as far as her grip on him allowed. 'I could make amends.'

'Make amends by doing what you're told,' Miss Stark said, taking some heavy-looking leather gloves from the coat stand.

'Yes – I will!' He'd do what she wanted in the hope that she'd then do what he wanted. Though his treacherous hard-on told him they were fast becoming one and the same thing.

'Turn your wicked bottom towards me,' said Miss Stark. Mark faced the wall obediently. 'Now pull your jeans slowly down.' His hands shook as he accessed his button, his zip. When his jeans reached his ankles he made to untie his shoelaces.

'Don't,' Miss Stark said sharply. 'Do exactly as you're instructed each time.'

'Yes, miss. Sorry, miss.' His words echoed in his head, sounding nervous, yet eager. Imagine someone as classy as her wanting to see him undressed!

'Now edge your underpants down to the crease where your bottom meets your thigh – no further.'

'Yes, miss,' he whispered, wincing as his rock-steady rod bounced free.

Maybe she'd ask him to turn round now, and she'd like what she saw and she'd want it inside her. Maybe she'd order him to lick her, then she'd be nice to him after she came. He wanted to come so much. He needed . . . Moaned as her leather-gloved palm lashed hard at least a dozen times over the naked globes of his buttock cheeks.

'You said that you'd do what you were told,' she murmured.

'Yes, miss,' he stammered, wondering what he'd done to earn the sudden spanking. 'Good boy. Then shuffle out there and show your macho mates your sore bum.'

He turned round, forgetting he wasn't supposed to, and she slapped him across the face again.

'I can't! You must be joking.'

'I never joke.'

'But they'd laugh.'

'Of course they'd laugh.'

He shuddered. 'I can't do it.'

'You're disobeying the first order I set you, then?'

He closed his eyes as lust and uncertainty coursed through him. 'Yes.'

'Oh dear, that's bad. That's very bad. Reprimandable.' Reaching out she took hold of his erection, gripping it tightly about an inch from the end. 'We'll have to take you to the school room for some discipline,' she murmured, pulling on his cock so that he had no option but to follow. 'Teach your little posterior some respect.'

He turned towards the stairs, but she gripped his hardness more insistently. 'Follow me, boy. Teacher knows best.' Whimpering at the pleasure-pain in his loins, he was led along a short hallway to a locked door, which she opened. Peering over her shoulder he saw a teacher's desk and chair, a small stool and smaller desk, a blackboard, some chalk.

Looking closer, he saw a cane lying across the teacher's desk – a long, thick, smooth cane. 'You're going to feel the full weight of that in a moment,' said Miss Stark as he shuffled along behind her, his cock in her tweaking, teasing hand. His jeans were still at his feet, his underpants just above his knees. He stared at the implement.

'Yes, miss. Thank you, miss.'

For a second her right hand strayed to her own left breast, and she fingered its fullness through the dark material. Mark let his breath out in a long, lust-crazed sigh and took a step closer to her tits.

'Bend over your stool. Raise your backside up high. Part your legs, boy.' He did as she required. He didn't want to displease her. He didn't want more than the tiniest taste of the cane.

Just a stroke or two – something different, something daring to fantasise about when this weird session was finally over. Nothing that would leave a painful weal that might be seen in the rugby shower. Nothing that would really hurt at the time.

'Grip the lower legs of the stool. That's right. Now count each stroke aloud, and thank me for it.'

There was a long, long pause.

'Yes, miss,' he said eventually, wondering if that's what she was waiting for. The silence continued. All he could think about was his exposed already-spanked rear end.

Then he felt the first stroke. Hard, sharp, its lesson being learned by both buttocks. 'Aaaah!' he yelled, letting go of the wooden legs.

'Get into position. Thank me,' said the unchanging cool voice of the teacher.

'One, thank you, miss,' muttered Mark, fighting a strong urge to protect his hindquarters with his hands.

Two was harder, higher up. He yelled and drummed his feet on the floor. He jerked his head up. 'I can't . . .'

'You can. You will.'

He felt the silky promise of her cloak against his thighs as she walked over to stand behind him. Took his full balls in her empty palm and teased them, titillating the testes till he writhed and squealed.

'Please, let me come!'

'Does a boy who's been disobedient deserve to come?'

'No, miss. But I'll be good from now on.'

'You'll take your punishment like a man?'

He *was* a man. He had to hold on to the fact that he was a man!

'Can't we –' He was going to add 'negotiate' but she rimmed his arsehole with a firm wet pinkie and he was lost.

'Punish me, miss,' he whimpered. 'Please, punish me.'

'Oh yes, I'll punish you. Ask me to use my cane on your disobedient little bum.'

He said it. She told him to speak more loudly, and again he said it. He'd say – do – almost anything if only she'd let him squirt his seed.

'Now, where were we?'

'I'd had two strokes, thank you, miss.' He tensed his arse in anticipation of the third one. She laid it on hard. And the fourth.

Both times he got out of position but she played with his prick, his semen-full sac, his arsehole, till – obediently wriggling against her palm – he got back into place across the hard top of the stool. 'Please don't . . .' he whimpered, putting his hands over his stinging cheeks after the fifth one. God knows why anyone called it six of the best!

At last he thanked her for the sixth stroke.

'Stay there. Think about your naughtiness,' she said briskly. He did so, feeling the cool air against his warmed backside. What must he look like? What would the guys think? He felt his cock start to deflate. Then her fingertips skimmed it again, sliding slowly up from column foot to crown, provoking *frissons*, causing renewed fervour to leak from the juicy tip.

'Go and stand before the window,' she said. He hesitated. 'It's a net curtain. You can see out but no one can see in.' Knowing better than to try and pull up his jeans or underpants, he shuffled over, staring out through white net into the busy park.

'Teacher will now give a biology lesson. It may take a bad boy's mind off his correction.'

He felt her fingers trace the parallel paths that the cane had taken before she started to slick her palm up and down his pulsing length.

'Teacher, please – kiss it better,' he pleaded, and received a sharp slap on both buttocks for his presumptuousness. Thereafter he kept facing the window and didn't move. Only his balls moved, spasming, fluttering. And his cock, which grew and grew.

Jake and the boys were packing up to go – he could see them gathering their sweatshirts and sports bags. Lennie seemed to look over at the window, and his heart almost stopped. 'I'd only have to pull this net aside and they'd be able to see you,' whispered Miss Stark. 'See you display your reddened arse. See me teasing your dick.'

'Is that all you're going to do – tease it?' Mark asked gutturally. A few moments before he wouldn't have dared to answer back, but desire had made him strong.

'What would you like to do?'

'Make love to you, miss. I'd be ever so respectful.'

He could see her nipples jutting out, see how flushed and wide-eyed she was: he suspected that she wanted him too.

'You realise you're not fit to come inside me?'

'I know, miss, but you could just use me in whatever way you saw fit.'

Miss Stark looked at him thoughtfully. 'I suppose I could use your inferior member as a scratching post.'

Mark nodded as she pulled open her headmistress's cloak. She had no bra or panties on underneath. He reached out to touch the smooth triangle of flesh between her stockings, but she slapped his hand away. Took his little finger and bit very lightly at its tip.

'Lie down on your back. Keep your arms by your sides.' He stretched out, his prick bobbing up expectantly. Miss Stark placed her knees at either side of his and lifted her body until her sex lips were pressing against the head of his shaft. 'Say pretty please,' she murmured mockingly.

'Pretty please,' Mark begged.

He thought she might tease him some more, but she half closed her eyes and swallowed hard and slid down on his grateful manhood. 'Jesus!' he muttered, as nirvana grew close.

'Don't speak unless spoken to!' she ordered, reaching forward to grip his hair, 'or I'll put my spurs on before I ride you hard.'

'Yes, miss. Anything, miss.'

'Don't move your loins, boy.'

He tried to keep his hips from bucking upwards, but he wanted to be buried deeper inside her. He wanted his very root to enter her quim. She was so wet, so hot. She was so beautiful. He twitched and groaned as she rode him, and stared at her swollen bouncing breasts.

Sensing his interest, she smiled tauntingly. 'You can look but not touch, Mark.' She sat back on his cock, using both hands to cup her mammaries, thumbs tracing round the full pink nipples till they stood out extra hard.

God, he wanted to suck these tits, to stroke and cup the heavy smoothness that surrounded them! He raised his hips without realising it and earned another slap. She was fucking him. She'd already punished him. She could do anything to him. She was mistress of his prick.

'Miss, please. I need to come.' His scrotum was like a cyclone. Every sinew was whimpering for mercy.

'Beg more nicely, boy.'

'I don't know what to say, miss. Oh, please!'

He came, pushing up into her, cried out again and again.

160

Cried out some more as she ground down on his tender tumescence to bring about her own climax, her face and body somehow staying in control.

An hour later Mark left the cottage and started to walk dazedly through the parkland. Thank God the guys had gone home. He didn't want them to see him this wide-eyed and legless – or this marked and milked.

Marked and milked. The second bit had gone to plan at least – he'd been desperate to get to know her better. As such, he'd deliberately aimed the ball at her window, knowing it would give him an excuse to ask her out. After a chat about broken glass he'd planned to turn the conversation towards a possible dinner date. He'd thought he could worm his way into her good books – not crawl out of the bad!

Mark shivered, remembering the delicate thrill of her fingers on his most sensitive places. And the less delicate thrill of correction caused by more than her hands! He'd learned his lesson for today, of course, but he was such an accident-prone little hooligan. He had a feeling that over the new few days his Frisbee might become entangled in her prize cherry tree, and a miss-thrown rugby ball would well flatten some of her plants.

Fashion Victim

Calfskin tunics lay in uneven heaps on Ailsa's sewing desk, on the arm of her chair, on the workshop floor. Hastily she ran the needle of her machine over a red leather skirt, wincing as she bunched the material, causing the hem to jerk to an uneven line. Hendon would have a fit if he saw this! Which was why she'd sneaked in here after hours.

Stopping to rub the grit from her inner eyes, Ailsa glanced at her watch. God, was it midnight already? She'd been here since 8 p.m., and she still had masses to do. Masses of work that she'd better not make a mistake on if she wanted to work for the exacting but bounteous Mr Hendon again.

And she did! She did! Being a freelance designer sounded very grand, but it had become hard to get commissions in the recession. The thirty-somethings who'd once treated themselves to one of her made-to-measure specials now settled for off-the-pegs from the boutique. Ailsa sighed. She still designed individual outfits, of course, but the work was sporadic. She needed orders like this from small manufacturers in order to pay her rent, in order to eat.

Talking of eating, she'd had nothing since that pizza in the late afternoon. It was time to munch that filled roll she'd bought at the late-night convenience store. Time for a short rest and a large mug of tea. Hendon didn't let his seamstresses snack in the workshop, of course. But then Hendon wasn't here.

Determined to forget for a moment the pressures of work, Ailsa went to the electric kettle, prepared her drink and fetched her snack, then sprawled in the workshop's one comfy armchair, putting her feet on the mini skirts which covered the nearest stool. This was more like it! This was –

'*What the hell?*'

The door flew open. Ailsa dropped her tea. Yelped as it heated her denimed thighs, yelped some more as the hot milky liquid spread over several of the newly made skirts, turning pretty fawn softness to ugly brown patchiness. She jumped up, footstool crashing to the ground. Hendon stood in the doorway gazing at the strewn garments. Ailsa did the same.

It looked bad. It looked – reprehensible.

'You've just soaked two hundred pounds' worth of merchandise,' Hendon said.

Ailsa gulped. 'I didn't mean –'

'I don't suppose you *meant* to sneak in after hours either? Your contract clearly states from nine to five.'

'I . . .' Licking her lips, she took a deep breath. She'd have to admit her transgression. 'Some private work ate into my days, sir. With the deadline due at the end of the week I thought –'

'You obviously *didn't* think. If you had, you'd have worked out a timetable, paced yourself.'

Worse and worse!

He paused, staring at her for long, long moments. Ailsa looked at the ground. She had to say – or do – something to salvage the situation, couldn't afford to lose this big a job.

'We'll have to take the cost of the material from your pay cheque,' Hendon said.

'No, please!'

Looking up in panic, Ailsa took an entreating step towards him. The disdain in his eyes made her falter, stand still.

'How do you suggest you recompense me?'

'I could work longer hours, sir.'

Hendon looked around his garment-strewn workshop.

'And do yet *more* damage?'

Ailsa swallowed hard, and pulled at her tea-soaked jeans.

'You'll better get out of these before you catch a cold,' Hendon said coolly.

The twenty-year-old looked around for some furniture she could hide behind.

'I suggest that you take them off here,' he added, his mouth firm, unsmiling. 'We're both over eighteen.'

Ah! So that was it! She'd strip, and they'd have sex, and she'd retain her contract. Hendon was attractive in a dark and distant sort of a way. And Ailsa had been too busy to date for several weeks, had been aware of a rising hunger, a growing pelvic ache. Once she'd pleased him with her hands or mouth, he'd do anything she wanted. He'd be nice to her again!

Still, it was humiliating to have to undress before a man who kept sizing you up as if you were a piece of property.

'Jeans coming down!' she half-joked, aiming for a light, easy tone. Her voice cracked. Her fingers shook slightly – with nerves and with anticipation – as she unknotted her shoelaces and pulled her trainers off. Unrolled her jeans inch by inch to reveal panties and ankle socks. Kicked free of the denim. Straightened up.

'Come here.'

Hendon walked to a low table and sat down on the edge of it, his feet on the floor, well braced. Feeling silly in her T-shirt and pants, Ailsa walked over to him. Stood. When he didn't reach out to pull her closer, she stretched a tentative hand out towards his suited crotch.

'Hands by your sides!' snapped Hendon. 'Do as you're told!'

Ailsa flinched, looked away, obeyed him. She felt at a loss, uncertain, and increasingly aroused.

'How do you explain your actions in leaving garments all over the floor when we have strict storage procedures?'

Ailsa swallowed. 'It was thoughtless of me.'

'Indeed it was.' The silence stretched on. 'And explain eating in the work room.'

'I . . . broke the rules, sir.'

'Indeed you did. And what do you think we should do with naughty girls who break the rules?'

164

Ailsa blushed. This was awful!

'I ... That's for the boss to decide.'

'Mmm, it should be, shouldn't it?'

Now he'd take her to bed, and life would return to normal.

'Yes, sir!'

'So we have to punish you severely for being bad.'

Ailsa felt the heat rush to her crotch, to her face. This couldn't be happening! Previous staff had hinted that Hendon was a strict disciplinarian but she'd never believed ...

'Get your lazy disobedient young arse over my knee,' her boss continued conversationally.

Her voice quavered: 'And if I don't?'

'Then get out of this workshop and don't ever approach me for a contract again.'

Ailsa hesitated. She'd been in the wrong – and he'd been good to her, both in setting fair deadlines and in the financial pay-off. She'd been lax for taking in too many private commissions, not leaving herself enough time to do the promised work. A spanking would be embarrassing, of course, but she'd just have to humour him.

'I deserve to have my bottom smacked, sir,' she said.

Hendon patted his lap again. Taking a deep breath, Ailsa lowered herself over it. His knees felt hard against her belly, against her crotch.

'Legs stretched out fully. That's it! Put your palms flat on the floor.'

The carpet felt rough against her hands.

'Don't speak unless spoken to. Push your wicked little posterior right back.'

'Yes, sir.'

Blushing further, she obeyed him. Hendon began to stroke her rounded buttocks through the thin white cotton of her pants.

'How many spanks do you deserve for the tea-staining?'

'Twenty?'

'Forty would waken that pretty arse a lot more.'

Glad that he couldn't see her flushed shamed face, Ailsa closed her eyes more tightly.

'Forty, sir. Whatever you say, sir.'

'Count them out loud.' Hendon added, 'You'll need extra maths tuition if you lose the place.'

He slapped robustly at one taut waiting globe and Ailsa shrieked and kicked her legs back.

'Ouch! That was really sore! It –'

'You didn't count the stroke,' Hendon said sadly. 'You'll have to experience that roasting hard spank again.'

He repeated the hard palm on soft flesh.

'One!' Ailsa gasped, tightening her thighs as she prepared for a second. 'Two! Three! Four!'

The spanks came down with a steadfast experienced rhythm on first one cheek then the other, so that she jerked her hips and drummed her helpless toes against the floor. She bucked, whimpered, yelled as his hand heated her rotundities again and again and again and again and again.

'. . . Twenty-five! Twenty-six!'

The end seemed a sore-bummed eternity away.

'Couldn't I . . . ?' she started to bargain, but forgot to count, and had the next three spanks repeated with especial glee.

'You could learn not to take advantage of good employers. You could learn to fulfil your obligations,' said Hendon, slapping down, down, down.

'Forty!' Ailsa gasped, eventually. Her arse felt like two large glowing chestnuts. Her sex felt soaked with excitement or sweat.

'You recognise the error of your ways?' Hendon murmured, beginning to caress her heated bottom.

'Yes, sir.'

'You want to continue to make amends?'

'I . . .' Ailsa opened her eyes and stared at the ground. She'd been thoroughly chastised for her errors. What else did he have in mind?

'The spanking was for eating in the workshop and for spilling your tea,' Hendon explained. 'There's still the matter of these calfskin garments left on the stool. I believe you were resting your feet on them when I walked in?'

Ailsa winced and, for answer, wriggled tremulously on his lap, anticipating further correction.

'So in a few moments I'm going to suggest you put your *belly* over that stool instead.'

Ailsa writhed some more. The heat caused by his hand must have brought the blood rushing to her sex. Her labia felt as if it was opening, entreating. She was very glad that her arousal was hidden by her briefs.

'I'll be a good girl, sir,' she promised.

'I'm going to *make* you good. *Very* good.'

That sounded ominous. She wondered how much longer she was to remain over his lap.

Hendon began to stroke her chastened rear again.

'Bad girls don't get to keep their pants on, do they, Ailsa?'

'Oh, sir – I beg!'

'Do they, Ailsa?'

'No, sir.'

'Edge them down by degrees, then. I want to see a slow striptease of well-warmed flesh.'

He obviously wasn't going to spare her. Gritting her teeth, and flexing her fingers, she did as she was bid.

How on earth must she look, upended like this, her briefs now bunched at her thighs, her bum a fiery red, her pubis visible?

'Should I take them off completely, sir?'

'No. Leave them there, but put your arms to the front.'

Reluctantly, Ailsa removed her hands from the vicinity of her toasted hindquarters. She wanted to cup the tender globes, to protect them from whatever Hendon planned next.

But she didn't *deserve* to guard her rear yet, she reminded herself. She'd been badly behaved, she'd been wilful.

'Such a feverish young *derrière*,' Hendon murmured, his cool palm stroking its warmth. 'Such a troublesome little minx.'

Ailsa slithered against his suit with sexual shame. She wanted him to enter her hard. She wanted to climax.

'How many strokes of the cane should you get for putting your feet on my fashionwear, girl?'

A caning sounded hard, impersonal, merciless.

Ailsa cleared her throat. She sounded breathless. 'Three?'

'Three warming cracks,' Hendon said. 'You're getting off lightly.'

'Yes, sir. Thank you sir.'

She wriggled about some more as he continued to lazily fondle her stripped sore bum.

'Go over to the stool. Put your belly against it. Grip the legs. Count the three strokes.'

He pushed her from his lap and she got up shakily and looked around until she saw the piece of wooden furniture he meant. She walked to it slowly, aware of how vulnerable her hot flesh must look, naked beneath the T-shirt which only came down to her waist.

Going, going . . . She bent over the stool. Her bum stuck out obscenely, made a perfect target. What would the cane feel like? Would she have to count the strokes? Would she fail?

'Shout each stroke out loud then say "Thank you, sir",' Hendon instructed. Ailsa tensed.

She raised her head a little to see him walk slowly into his office. She heard a drawer open, close. He walked back into view carrying a thick bamboo-type implement. It was around three feet long. It looked painful. She could imagine how it felt.

'Arse up higher! Good girl. Show your gratitude of this much-needed lesson.'

He drew his arm back and brought the rod down across the waiting globes. Ailsa cried out, and scrambled from the stool, holding her punished bottom and staring around wildly for the nearest exit.

'Are you leaving us?' asked Hendon.

Reality returned to her.

'No, sir! I'm sorry, sir!'

It would be worse if she left. Rubbing her caned cheeks for just a moment, she got meekly back into position. She had to make up for her wrong-doing. She had to please!

'Thank you for that hard stroke of the cane, sir,' she said belatedly.

'I should really liven your bottom with a repeat stroke,' said Hendon, 'but I sense that you really are trying to make amends, and I'm feeling merciful today.'

'Yes, sir. Thank you, sir.'

She wanted to kiss his feet. She wanted to lubricate her willing tongue and . . . Hendon laid a second searing stroke across the crease where arse met thigh and she squealed. She hadn't known anything could sting so much, could feel so focused. Hadn't known she could feel this exposed, this defenceless, this depraved.

'Aaah! Thank you, sir.' She tensed, waiting for the third. Hendon teased her for long, long moments. Laid the cane against her punished contours, and stroked it up and down, talking about what he was going to do to her next.

'You have to learn to fulfil your obligations. You have to learn to respect your betters.'

'I know, sir. I know! I'll be obedient.'

When the final stroke came it was almost a relief.

'Inspection time,' Hendon said. He put his cool palm on her aching rear and traced the well-disciplined contours. 'You've been thrashed for spilling your tea and for general untidiness. Is there anything else you'd like to admit to whilst we're teaching you manners?'

'But it hurts . . .'

'It hurts at the time, of course – I make sure it hurts! But confession and punishment are really the most honourable way.'

Ailsa thought of the hem she'd bunched. She might have made further errors.

'Everything else is perfect,' she lied.

'So I can inspect any garment, find it exactly made to my requirements?'

Wincing inside, she tried to make her voice strong and certain.

'Yes.'

'Stay there.' Leaving her lying over the stool, he walked over to a heap of fuchsia silk blouses. Looked at the edging round the collars, the buttons on the cuffs, the scalloped pocket. 'OK. These'll do.'

Ailsa relaxed as much as she could against the hard wood. Thank goodness he'd checked the work she'd done at 8 p.m.! If he was to find some of the rushed batch she'd finished off after eleven, he'd probably re-introduce her to the cane.

'What's this?' His expressionless voice broke into her momentary calm. She looked up. He was holding one of the mini skirts. He was holding it by the waist. The skirt stuck out like an umbrella, looked tartish, cheap. 'This is all wrong – horribly wrong. The order was for five straight calfskin skirts that upper-income bracket women would purchase,' Hendon said.

Ailsa felt her tummy flip over inside, Oh-oh! How was she to explain this error? 'I ran out of calfskin for the last one. I used this stiff material I had left over from making ra-ra skirts instead.'

'Ra-ra skirts went out years ago – if they were ever really *in*,' Hendon replied, shaking his head, his mouth going into a firm line that she felt boded ill for her. 'I'm running a commercial outlet here. My customers demand craftsmanship at all times.'

'It'll look nice when it's on,' Ailsa blurted, trying to salvage the situation.

'Prove it,' Hendon said.

She forced her gaze up to meet his.

'Can't I just . . .'

'Just what? Repay me?'

She couldn't afford to do that.

'No.'

'Admit you can't fulfil your obligations? Call it quits and walk out of here without your commission?'

'Please – no!'

'It's really up to you what happens next,' Hendon said, tapping the cane tauntingly against his thigh.

Ailsa looked back at the floor. She seemed to spend a lot of time looking down there now. Uncertainty gnawed at her. On the one hand, her backside really hurt – she didn't want to parade it around in a short skirt. On the other hand, she knew that she deserved to be punished for her wrongdoing, that Hendon was a fair and considerate man.

Why, when she'd been putting in the hours she was meant to, he'd made sure she got luncheon vouchers and cost-price materials. And on the one evening he'd asked her to work late he'd also given her the cash to take a taxi home.

'If I put on the skirt will you promise not to discipline me again?'

Hendon smiled a mirthless smile.

'I'll only discipline you if you agree that your backside warrants it. As I've said, you can go home right now if you like.'

And lose a lucrative contract, her reputation in the industry?

'I'll stay,' Ailsa murmured.

'Then put on that skirt and walk into the middle of the room, then stand still.'

Glad to push herself free of the stool, Ailsa stood up and took the skirt from her impassive employer.

'New staff uniform?' she quipped.

He stared, didn't smile. Licking her lips, she stepped into the scratchy garment. The waistline fitted snugly. She tucked her T-shirt in, did up the zip and button. Wondered how she managed to feel *more* exposed instead of less.

The skirt stuck out at a ridiculous angle. Material that should have draped down to cover the tops of her thighs instead jutted out, making her reddened arse hugely visible, like an apple crowned with a white paper frill.

'Turn round slowly,' said Hendon.

Quivering, Ailsa obeyed him.

'Explain,' Hendon said.

She started to turn back towards him, but his voice went on. 'No. Keep facing the wall. I don't have to see your lips move in order to hear you.'

'I must have cut the material at a slight angle.'

'*Slight?*'

Her punishment wouldn't be slight. She could tell! Heard the control in his voice, felt her exposed bottom trembling.

'Not content with wiping your feet on my materials and spilling your tea on them, you now cut them the way a five-year-old would. What have you to say for yourself?'

Ailsa took a deep breath: 'I ... nothing, sir.' She bit back a sob. 'Except that I deserve to be spanked.'

'Spanked? But you've *been* spanked, my dear, then you lied to me afterwards. You must have known you'd botched part of this work.'

'I'm sorry,' Ailsa muttered, feeling more and more guilty.

'You will be,' Hendon said.

She heard his voice drop an ominous note.

'Now all we have to do is determine *how* sorry.'

'I could please you so much ...'

'I may let you later. But for now we're talking chastisement for carelessness and undue expense and deceit.'

Put like that it sounded like a major misdemeanour. Ailsa stared at the wall, waiting for him to come up behind her, to punish her raging rump.

'Get that recalcitrant little rear over to the main window,' Hendon said.

'But, sir ...'

She turned to look at him.

'Did I tell you to look around?'

'No. I –'

'What did I tell you?'

'To get my recalcitrant little rear over to the window,' she stammered, feeling the prickle of humiliated tears.

There were other prickles as well, of course. The tenderness between her thighs was pulsing, sensuously slicked. Could she really be excited by the palm, the cane, the orders? Or was it just because he was a debonair desirable man who had stripped her semi-naked, stroked her rear? Trembling with lust and uncertainty, Ailsa followed his edict and walked over to the window, stood facing the uncurtained glass.

They were on the second floor, but she could clearly see the pavement which was well lit by street lamps. A man wandered slowly along, accompanied by a tail-wagging springer spaniel. Ailsa drew back.

'Turn so that your bottom is towards the window, very visible. Now touch your toes. Shuffle forward until your buttocks are a foot away from the glass.'

Ailsa straightened, stared at him. 'But if someone looks up they'll see –'

'See me using a ruler on your undisciplined arse? Yes, they'll see that.'

'A *ruler?*'

'Mmmm. Gives accurate measurements. Very appropriate, don't you think?'

But all Ailsa could think about was how the hard plastic would feel as it lashed against her extremities.

'What if I can't bear it?'

'I've already bared it for you,' said Hendon with a mirthless grin. He walked over to her and put an encouraging firm hand on her waist till she bowed to his will and bent over. 'Just four more strokes, then you'll have paid your dues, and your ordeal will be at an end.'

Ailsa wondered if it was really just beginning, for how could life go back to normal after tonight?

'Such an unscrupulous curvy butt. It looks so pretty, too – so fresh and innocent.'

'It'll be innocent from now on, sir,' she moaned. 'I promise!'

'You know I'm tempted to believe you, Ailsa. I think you're basically honest, that for a couple of days you just let things get out of control, got carried away.'

'Yes, sir. I've repented, sir!'

Ailsa shivered as he fondled her nether cheeks. He must know how wet and anxious she was, must know how it felt to be displayed like a piece of meat in a butcher's window.

'Can I be forgiven my last misdeed, then, sir?'

Hendon continued to cruelly caress her scorching globes. 'I suppose if I was feeling compassionate I might . . .'

He broke off. Ailsa tensed hopefully. She wished she could see his face, wished she could please him with her mouth, take his mind off her painful lesson.

'Problem is, there's part of me that wants to see you wriggle and plead a little,' Hendon said.

'Fight it!' Ailsa muttered, and earned a stinging stroke of the ruler for her impudence. She hadn't actually realised he was holding it in his hand.

'That was an extra wallop for being disrespectful,' Hendon confirmed. 'Four whacks with the ruler to go.'

Wishing that she'd been given permission to rub her sore bum, but knowing that it would invite further punishment to do so, Ailsa touched her toes again.

'You can't imagine how this will look to strangers – your welted arse sticking out beneath this silly skirt,' Hendon said. He cradled her contours. 'I might open the window a little so that they can hear your voice pleading nicely for the next ruler stroke, and telling me how much it hurts.'

Ailsa closed her eyes at the image. She *could* imagine! That was the problem. She'd never felt this aroused or exposed.

'Let me –' she started sexily.

'Stroke one coming up,' said Hendon.

Coming down, thought Ailsa, then cried out as the implement scored its memo across both bared cheeks.

'I won't lie from now on! I'll do good work! I'll keep to deadlines!' she gasped, contorting.

Crack two caught her unawares and she lifted her hands from her ankles, then quickly got back into place. She didn't want to be accused of yet more disobedience, earn further chastisement for breaking another rule!

'There's a man staring up at your well-warmed arse,' said Hendon. Facing away from the window, Ailsa had no way of knowing if he was telling the truth or not, 'He's about to see you ask nicely for the third whack of the ruler,' her boss continued.

'Oh, please!'

'You'll get double if you don't say it,' he warned.

'Please use the ruler on my rebellious little posterior,' Ailsa moaned.

'*Louder*. More obsequiously. So that our friend outside can hear. So that he can tell his friends.'

He ran the ruler from the top of her cheeks to her taut stretched legs, as if threatening to lay on an extra stroke or two if she didn't obey him. Ailsa shouted the words out loud, then cried out even more loudly as the third stroke hit the crease where arse met thigh.

'Only one to go,' murmured Hendon, fondling her sore flesh. 'Should we make it an extra hard one, do you think?'

'Yes, sir,' whispered Ailsa, ready to volunteer any begging words that would get her buttocks away from a stranger's appraising gaze.

'As you wish,' Hendon said.

She felt the air currents twitch as he swung the ruler back, felt the jarring impact as he brought his arm forward.

'Aaaah!'

'Punishment completed,' Hendon said calmly, letting the ruler drop.

'Sir, let me make amends properly,' begged Ailsa, turning round to face him and dropping to her knees, her lips parting. She put a tentative hand near his crotch. He nodded. Cells flooding with need, desire, near fulfilment, she tugged the zipper down . . .

'I'm going to walk you home, now,' Hendon said much, much later. 'You can't get through the night on a mere sandwich, so I'll have turkey slices and baby vegetables delivered to your flat from the all-night bistro bar.'

Ailsa nodded. Sleepily, she pulled her pants on, wincing as they clung to her chastened rear.

'Quite swollen and sore,' said Hendon, as if he was a vet talking about a dog with a sore paw. 'Hope you can still get your jeans on, bear their weight.' *Why not keep me in that stick-out skirt without the panties?* Ailsa thought with a flash of spirit – but she knew better than to say the words out loud.

'After you've eaten, I'll put some cooling ointment on that punished posterior, put you to bed,' Hendon continued.

Ailsa shrugged into her jacket. 'Thank you. Yes.'

'Then I suggest that you sleep on your tummy all night to give your bottom a chance to recuperate.'

She blushed, looked away.

Hendon studied the garment-strewn workshop. 'I'll arrange for another employee to tidy up first thing tomorrow.

But I want you here at ten a.m., want you to pace yourself throughout the day.'

'Yes, sir. I won't let you down again, sir.'

'You might,' Hendon murmured, putting a warning hand on her denim clad soreness. 'You might.'

He smiled. 'I'm giving you an extra week to complete the order. Your weals should heal quite nicely in that time – especially if you work standing up, my dear. After that, I'm giving you another commission. Crocheted waistcoats. Sounds ancient, but my market research tells me they're all the rage.'

'That's right – a return to the Seventies look, a hit with teenagers,' Ailsa confirmed, following him towards the door. 'But I've never quite mastered crochet, sir.'

'Really? How unfortunate for your hindquarters! I suggest you learn fast, then,' Hendon said.

Ailsa looked around at the workshop, at the desks and chairs that she had yet to be bent over. At the long silk ties that could be used to bind wilful female hands.

Hendon smiled. 'I hope you don't let me down. I hear the fashion amongst weary bosses these days is for wearing slippers.' He looked meaningfully at her tenderised young bottom. 'I've got a pair of hard-heeled ones at home that I've yet to try out.'

Talking Heads

'Ms Ross is here to see you, Mr Beaumont-Smythe.'

At the receptionist's words, the psychiatrist nodded. He adjusted an already immaculately knotted tie as the last patient of the day was ushered in.

Alicia Ross, twenty-six-year-old magazine journalist and novelist, made her hesitant way into the hospital side-room that served as Psychiatric Outpatients, the depression on her face less manifest than it had been for several days.

'Well?' Dr Beaumont-Smythe began encouragingly. 'How have you been feeling since I saw you last? As I recall you were feeling increasingly perturbed about your employer and were considering leaving him.'

'Yes, sir.' A little sigh.

'You'd been having dreams about him that made you feel uncomfortable, dreams in which he was the more dominant party.'

'Yes.'

A Pinteresque silence followed, which Beaumont-Smythe, conscious of his patient's impulsivity patterns, knew she would soon break.

'We – the office had a night out and I had rather a lot to drink.' She looked at him through long dark lashes.

'Bill, the editor, brought me home afterwards and we ended up in bed. We did all the things I told you about during my last appointment: prolonged punishing things.'

'Your fantasies – you acted them out?'

This was new.

'Uh huh.'

'And was it fulfilling?'

A good doctor had to remain impassive, not assume.

'Not initially, no.' Alicia dipped her head.

'Go on.'

'I was afraid when he tied me down.' She flushed, stared at her small pink fingernails. 'He rolled me on to my tummy on the bed, then scissored my legs and arms apart. Used my stockings to bind my wrists, used scarves to tie my feet.' She looked up, then away. 'I started to think what if he's a psychopath or something?' She grimaced. 'But later, when he started stroking my bare bum and telling me what he was going to do to me, I started to build and build.'

'And what exactly was it that excited you?'

Alicia looked into the middle distance as if it contained the answers. 'The helplessness, the slight pain, the loss of control . . .'

Unconsciously Beaumont-Smythe smoothed back his perfectly arranged hair and recrossed his legs at the ankles. The session ended some time past the appointed hour and Ms Ross was hurriedly dispatched with instructions to reflect upon how her masochism related to her everyday persona, and whether she wanted behaviour modification or not.

Driving home, Beaumont-Smythe went through a red light and forgot to collect his evening suit from the cleaners. His wife, *en route* to the theatre, resolved to obtain a biofeedback machine for him and buy the man a vitamin supplement. He was, after all, reaching that dangerous age.

'Try to explain exactly what happens when you and Bill are together.' He was, the psychiatrist told himself, anxious to assess whether irreparable conditioning had already taken place.

With studied casualness (he had obviously begun to win her trust) Alicia began to describe the previous night's events. 'After the last escapade with Bill he made no arrangements to see me again. I couldn't face working with him after what had happened, so I sent in a letter of resignation – I can live off my book royalties by now, you understand? But he came round to the flat that evening to return my office things.'

A pause. 'It was awkward at first, so I made coffee and put on some music. I was talking nineteen to the dozen out of sheer nerves! Then he put his arms round me and pulled me down on the settee.'

'You didn't initiate anything?'

'I responded. After a moment he clasped my wrists above my head with one hand and unbuttoned my blouse with the other. My breathing started to quicken, especially after he put his mouth to my breasts. At the same time I felt ... well, wanton, as if I ought to put up more of a fight.'

A pause.

'Go on.'

'I said *don't* a couple of times, that we shouldn't go any further, that I wasn't on the pill or anything. He said, whispering now, that I just needed warming up a bit. Then he pushed me over his knee and pulled down my briefs and ... well, you can imagine the rest.'

'And was it the spanking that excited you, or the fact that he was in charge?'

'Both, I think. I felt so open to him, so wet, like every cell in my body was electric. And when he did bring me to a climax, I mean ... wow!' A slight smile. 'I slept for twelve hours afterwards.' Then, more soberly, 'When I woke up, he'd gone.'

The doctor regarded her steadily. 'You said you weren't using a contraceptive. Was the risk element perhaps part of the stimulus, with the maternal part of you hoping to conceive?'

Alicia hesitated, pinkening. Then she smiled. 'He didn't fuck me in the traditional way. He took me from behind.'

'And did you feel violated or invaded or ...?' For the first time in fifteen years of psychiatric practice, Dr Beaumont-Smythe loosened his tie.

Ms Ross had cancelled her appointment by phone that morning claiming flu and now the consultant psychiatrist decided to put the time to good use, compiling a paper on aspects of the case for a medical journal. He wrote of the patient's history, her general neurosis, stopping only to search for a more evocative word or phrase. At the section on masochism he faltered and began to feel increasingly exhausted, almost ill.

That night he dreamt of his work, watching with detachment as huge surrealistic fountain pens dipped erratically into flowing inkwells. He awoke as the ink splattered the dream canvas to find his manhood was pulsing especially hard.

'. . . And this has interfered with your psychosexual development,' the doctor finished. He was aware that they had not discussed her social shyness or her latent hostility towards her father for several weeks in succession, and Beaumont-Smythe now searched for a natural way to return to it. 'Exactly how do you react to a man in a new social context?' he asked. 'Say an encyclopaedia salesman who knocks on your door?'

Alicia thought for a moment. 'Well, I'd probably invite him in – if nothing else I'm always on the look-out for new characters to put in my novels. And as a salesman he'd be commanding, you know, master of his subject and all that.'

A pause as she obviously pictured the scene. 'After a while I might find myself looking at his hands – imagining them coming down on my arse, making me squirm. Or his belt. It's worse if he's wearing a belt.'

'Such fetishism is very common.'

'I know, but sometimes it's like a drug. I crave the pain . . .'

Crave, need. He cleared his throat. 'Most of your sexuality has been repressed till recently when you started to explore your dreams in psychotherapy. Now we have to coax your sexuality back into the mainstream. It might take a year or more.'

'And at the end – will I really be cured?'

The doctor swallowed and picked at a splinter on his desk. 'Your urges would be reduced somewhat. Such predilections are seldom completely cured.'

Alicia licked her lips. 'I suppose . . . I think I can live like this, as a submissive. At the end of the day, I don't really want to be in control.'

Control, he thought, was what it all came down to – the power politics of the hospital ward, the committee, even of the couple. And then its antithesis, the loss of power, of decision-making, of being a man. To wait in delicious anticipation for the cane to fall, creating a release beyond measure. To be tied down, stripped of all responsibility, crying out in a void of semi-conscious bliss.

He went as one dazed to the rooming house and peeled notes from his wallet into a waiting hand, then stood, with eyes downcast, waiting for further instruction.

Motivator

'Discipline – that's what you need.'

Arlene looked at her new coach and gulped audibly. Prior to meeting him she'd thought joggers' nipple was the worst thing she'd have to worry about. Now she stared incredulously at the man and at the fifteen-page training schedule he'd just pushed into her hand.

'Oliver, this is far too –'

'Call me Mr Cartwright.'

'But my last coach –'

'Is no longer here.'

'More's the pity,' Arlene muttered as she set off on a thirty-minute run round a nearby housing scheme. Her old coach had been just that – of a biddable age. This bastard looked like something from a fitness video and wanted her to get into similar shape.

Which was the whole point really, she admitted to herself sulkily. Two years ago she'd been Arlene the Actress and Athlete, a small star with big potential for the silver screen. She'd won several marathons which had led to TV advertising work for fitness foods. She'd been in the shadow of fortune and fame. Then she'd fallen in love with a fellow actor and followed him all the way to the Big Apple. Was back now having been ditched for a debutante, feeling as squashed as rotten fruit.

Hard pavement below. Sighing, Arlene moved on to soft grass and decided on some off-road running. Detoured along a heavily wooded track. This was pine-centred sensation. This was back to nature. This was . . . agony. She yelped as her shoe slid into a muddy puddle and one ankle gave.

'Oh dear,' said Oliver when she limped back. 'We've done something silly, haven't we?'

'There was this muddy puddle . . .'

'You use a higher knee lift for off-road hikes or it leads to ankle problems,' he explained. He shook his head sadly. 'What are we going to do with you? You should have worn higher ankle-line shoes.'

She'd known all this once. Now she just knew that her legs ached.

'Let's get you to physio,' Oliver Cartwright sighed.

He pressed one hand down on her shoulder, scooped another behind her knees and lifted her effortlessly. Arlene decided to hate him just a little bit more.

Only he smelt enticingly of woodland scents and his sensuous lips were all too close to her face, and his fingers would touch her thighs if they cared to slide up a few inches.

'A casualty,' he said, setting her down on the physiotherapist's couch.

The woman smiled. 'We see a lot of them!'

Oliver Cartwright looked unsmilingly down at Arlene.

'Once I teach this one some self-restraint you won't see her again.'

What did he plan to do – accompany her on every race, get her a minder? Even professional runners got careless and made mistakes.

'Next time wear thin socks – soaks up less water,' said her coach as he exited the room. He looked back, taking in her baggy shirt and knee-length shorts. 'Means you take on less weight – you're carrying enough as it is.'

Damn him! Fuck him! Well, no – just damn him. That night Arlene undressed before the mirror and stared at her naked breasts. Still large and high with the cutest pouting pink nipples which cried out for attention. A great cleavage in a low-cut dress. OK, so her waist was a little fuller than it once had been, the belly slightly more rounded, but it still looked sexily strokable, led down to a cropped coffee-coloured mons. Her hips were smooth and shapely, desire in denims, even if her thighs were a little plumper than before.

'Train don't strain,' Oliver said the next day.

'Maybe I should just jog to the Pizza Parlour!'

'Shake the attitude, Arlene. You lose this race, you lose the Jumping Juice advertisement contract and I lose my reputation with the Creating Champions Club.'

'Yeah OK.' She was really mad at herself rather than him. 'Spare me the lectures!'

'I'll spare you nothing if you carry on like this.'

'I'm quaking in my shock absorbers!' Arlene said, looking down at her assisted-propulsion running shoes. Which is probably why she didn't see what was coming, couldn't dodge out of the way. Because before she could add 'only joking', Oliver Cartwright had thrown himself down on the work-out bench and hauled her over his athletic knees.

'You can't do this!'

'I already have.'

He'd somehow got both her arms behind her back and was pinioning them at the wrists with five strong fingers.

'I'll tell the club!'

'You can – but you won't.' He used his free hand to trace the contours of her shorts-clad bottom. 'I'm the best in the business. If you lose me as trainer you'll lose the race and you'll probably never get an acting contract again.'

It was true. Even the fact that Jumping Juice had hired Oliver Cartwright to arrange her pre-race drill had given her a certain amount of good publicity. Without him . . .

'What are you going to do to me?' Arlene squeaked.

'I'm going to give you the spanking of your life, then I'm going to drive you home and put you to bed for a good sleep. You'll come back tomorrow ready to do what I say.'

'I'll bet you say that to all the girls!' Arlene muttered, determined not to show the macho pig she was embarrassed. In answer, her trainer drew back his hand and slapped smartly down.

'Ouch!'

She'd no sooner gasped the word when his large palm again warmed her posterior. And again and again and again and again and again.

He seemed to find a hard hot rhythm, slapping first one helpless buttock then the other.

'Ah! Uh! Oh, you bastard!' Arlene gasped and writhed.

'You must show respect. You must listen to your trainer. You must try harder.'

After every second word, Cartwright's hand whacked down. Her blue shorts must be showing through red by now!

'All right! I'll do what you want!' Arlene muttered.

Oliver continued to berate her upended cheeks. 'It has to be what you want too.'

'I . . .' Arlene moaned and whimpered as he continued spanking her hard. 'I want to win the race! I want to be a star again! I'll train properly.'

'Glad to hear it,' said Oliver Cartwright, and half-lifted and half-pushed her from his lap.

Was that it? On her knees on the floor, Arlene stared up at him. Didn't he want to see the colour he'd turned her arse? She'd half expected him to peel off her T-shirt. Expected him to want to stroke her and kiss her. Not that she'd let him, of course!

'Get your tracksuit on. I'll drive you home,' said Oliver as if nothing had happened.

'If you like.'

A hot bum and a cold flat.

'Get into bed. I'll bring you through a cool glass of water.'

'Why . . .?' She choked back the words, decided not to argue.

'After a session like that girls tend to feel rather sleepy.'

Now that he mentioned it, her lids did feel heavy, dull.

He disappeared into her kitchen and Arlene undressed and slipped hurriedly into bed. Her rump was smarting, the top of her thighs fingerprint hot. She lay on her tummy. After a moment she heard Oliver's footsteps approach the bedside cabinet, watched him set down a drink.

'Sleep now.'

He laid a firm hand on her nearest buttock and stroked it and its neighbour through the quilt, over and over. As sensation swept through her, Arlene moaned softly and closed her eyes.

'I'll see you at nine a.m. prompt tomorrow,' her coach said evenly – and promptly left.

Damn the man! He was insufferable! He was ... words failed her. But gestures didn't. Arlene turned over, planning to raise two rude digits towards the window, then whimpered and rolled on to her belly again after her backside scraped the bed. God, her rear felt hot – very *stimulated*. Somehow the hateful heat had moved round to between her legs.

Settling on to her tummy, Arlene slid a hand between her thighs. Her sex lips were slicked with need, her clitoris peeking out of its prison. Suddenly stifling, she kicked the duvet away. Looked round at her bum: the globes two fiery rounds demanding to be noticed. Caressed her clit ever so lightly. Remembered Cartwright's palm coming down.

He'd been hard – she remembered her tummy registering just how hard. The sight of her arse wriggling about in those tight frayed denim shorts must have been exciting. He'd have felt her mons pushing against his muscular thighs. Arlene brought the lubrication from her labia up to her love bud, started stroking herself more strongly. He'd probably been as desperate for a fuck as she.

She was glad he'd gone away frustrated! He didn't deserve to see her naked like this, her nipples taut against the bed, her belly quickening. Didn't deserve to fondle her fleshy female parts. Not after he'd thrashed her for so long, ignored her desperate whimpering, turning her cheeks first pink, then puce, then red. Arlene touched, teased, her breathing deepening. Not when he'd held her down and watched her plead and beg.

She'd said ... Arlene pleasured herself some more. She'd done ... Nearly, nearly. Awful being across his knee like some overgrown schoolgirl, her bum a helpless target under his hard male palms. He'd held her down so firmly she couldn't kick. She'd promised all sorts of things if he'd show mercy. She made one last circuit of her craving clitoris, and she came. Arlene slept then, though she'd promised herself she wouldn't give that know-all Cartwright the satisfaction. And the next day she turned up at Creating Champions before 9 a.m.

'We'll do interval training for the next three weeks. Ensures your heart strength increases.'

Arlene felt her clit's size increasing. Pity the know-all was so alluringly attractive, so self-controlled!

'Endurance rather than speed for a marathon, right?'

Last night she'd reread some of her old training notes, committed them to memory.

Cartwright nodded watchfully. 'Right.'

For a second Arlene felt absurdly pleased, then she reminded herself she wasn't supposed to be sleeping with the enemy.

'I got you those reflective tabs for evening running,' he added. 'Arranged for you to have a running sister for your night-time jaunts.'

Aren't you coming with me?' She felt ridiculously hollow.

'No, I've made plans.'

Probably screwing some bimbo in a lycra leotard, Arlene thought, setting off on a short run with Oliver keeping pace beside her.

'Talk,' he said. 'Means I can check your breathing.'

'Fuck you,' said Arlene, 'I'd rather sing.'

A month later he made her sing like a bird. It had been a weird month – twenty-eight days of strange dreams and wordless dark yearnings. Arlene paced the flat when she wasn't running. Each short jog somehow produced a cavernous crotch.

'Circuit training today,' Cartwright said when she turned up one Monday.

Arlene shook the rain from her Reeboks.

'Couldn't we go out?' She felt closed in, restless.

'No, the weather's unconducive. I've set up your equipment in the gym.'

He'd set up the smallest gym. He was a large man. Arlene felt hugely aware of his athletic male presence. He was wearing a close-fitting black tracksuit. Knowing that her own figure had lifted and tightened in all the right places, she peeled off her joggers and sweatshirt to reveal silky micro-shorts. Her lycra vest top clung to her rounded bosom. She put her hands on her hips.

'March on the spot for five minutes to warm up.'

Arlene did as he asked. She felt stupid. Cartwright walked round and round her. 'Mmm, not bad.'

'Thanks.'

'Lift your knees higher, though. You don't want to strain a hamstring.'

For a moment she'd thought he was complimenting her curves!

'Now what?'

'Run from one wall to the next ten times.'

'Gosh! How exciting!' She was in a foul mood, hadn't been sleeping.

'Just do it,' Oliver said.

'And if I don't?'

'You'll get a red hot arse again.'

'Yeah, from you and whose army?'

Squealed as he grabbed hold of her and pinned her arms to her sides.

'You wouldn't dare!' But he was marching over to the low gym horse. 'You haven't locked the door, idiot!'

'Calling your trainer an idiot earns you extra strokes.'

Strokes not spanks. Arlene swallowed hard. She'd gone too far this time. Now that he was tying her wrists to the gym horse with the plastic bands they used for resistance work, she felt a little scared.

'Not as hard as last time,' she pleaded, as he fastened her legs.

'Much, much harder.'

'But these shorts are thinner!'

'I'm going to thrash you on the bare.'

'You wouldn't . . .' She felt his hands on her shorts. 'Oh please, the embarrassment!'

'You should have thought of that before you were so rude.'

Arlene remembered all the insults she'd thrown at him these past few days, and her buttocks trembled. She shivered with fear and pleasure as he edged her shorts down, cried out as he tugged off the panties beneath. She could feel the garments bunching at her knees – knees that were spreadeagled.

'Right, you bastard – get it over with!' she said.

'Oh, I like to take my time.' Oliver stroked her bare bum over and over. 'It's going to be very sore in a moment, isn't it, my dear?'

Damn him! She gritted her teeth. Stared straight ahead – not that she had much option! Felt the vulnerability of every fibre of her naked rear.

'We have to teach this bottom manners.' Her trainer went over to the equipment cupboard and came back with a small hard ping-pong bat. 'A spanking obviously wasn't enough,' he added.

'It was! Please – spank me again. Hard as you like!'

'Spanking's for minor indiscretions. You'd been committing major crimes. I'll teach you a lesson with this little beauty instead.'

The first whack was measured, as was the second. Arlene started to relax in her bonds a little. The third stroke struck harder, increased the warmth in the helpless cheek.

'Ouch! That really hurt, Cartwright!'

'It wasn't meant to tickle.'

'I'll be good!'

He punished on. 'By the time I'm finished with you, you'll be perfect.'

'I'll be perfect now! Oliver . . . Mr Cartwright . . . please!'

Her coach set down the bat and put a palm to her posterior, stroking alternate stripped sore buttocks. 'So this is the proud lady who was going to do her own thing, now showing off her bottom to whoever walks in.'

'Mr Cartwright – I'll do anything!'

'Anything?'

'I could fuck you so good.'

'I'm not sure that's grammatical,' Oliver Cartwright said. 'You've probably neglected your elementary as well as your athletic education.'

'You could educate me with your cock, sir,' Arlene said. She wanted to get rid of the ache between her thighs. She wanted him to stop paddling her. She wanted to be untied.

'Ask nicely,' her cool coach said.

'Fuck off,' Arlene muttered – then yelped as the bat came down again.

'Please fuck me,' she muttered, wishing she could push her fingers up herself and be done with it.

'I'll think about it,' Cartwright said.

She felt his fingers on her fervent slit.

'What's this? Such a pretty pussy!'

She moaned as he caressed her leaking love-lips as her bonds held her in place.

'Can you keep still, my dear? An athlete needs durability and stability.'

He started to coax out her clit with a rhythm she could rely on, and she wriggled some more.

'I need . . . I need your cock.'

'I think you do,' said her trainer, stroking, stroking. 'The question is, is he coming out to play?'

His fingers took her to the edge.

'When I say jump, what'll you say?'

'How high, sir!'

She heard him pull off his tracksuit trousers – but he kept her waiting still.

'What else will you say, my wilful charge?'

'Everything . . . Anything! Want you inside me.'

'I suppose I ought to put your covetous crotch through its paces,' Cartwright said. He slid into her, slow yet hard: she could feel his sure stiff prick against the top of her cervix.

'Oh, yes!'

Her taut nipples rubbed through her training bra and vest against the horse's hard top.

'It's more than you deserve.' He started to thrust in and out.

'I know, sir.'

'After you've come, we'll start the circuit training again.' Arlene whimpered.

'I'm going to take off your bra and vest set so you're totally naked. Then I'll handcuff your hands above your head.'

Christ, he knew how to fuck! Every thrillable cell in her body seemed to have rushed to her crotch and was liquefying, yearning.

'Handcuffed!' she moaned, clit twitching and projecting.

'And I'll make you do twenty or thirty squats.' He sighed. 'Of course, if your knees give out you'll have to go across my lap again and I'll take my palm to your arse – I won't have any slacking.'

'No, sir!'

Arlene whimpered as his pleasure pole hit a most sensitive place.

'Then I'll have you doing The Step,' Cartwright added. 'Same rules apply, you naked with your little red arse like a beacon. Me standing behind ready to spur you on.'

'Spurs?' Arlene gasped. Her clit was rubbing against the horse. Her contours were full of him, close to coming.

'Just a figure of speech, my dear. I'll be standing behind you with my riding whip.'

'Your whip?'

'Mmm. I've heard it's particularly impressive on the press-ups. Imagine how quickly you'll lower your little bum down to escape that leathery lash!'

Arlene groaned loudly and pushed her quim back as best she could. Cartwright ground into her, probing, pushing, pleasing.

'Uh . . . ah,' she gasped. 'Ah . . . aaah.'

'Your quim will be dripping, but your hands will be cuffed to stop you touching yourself as you do the jumping jacks,' her trainer added, and the wild bliss flowed through her orifice and took her over the edge.

'Your bum's cooling down again,' Cartwright muttered. She could feel his balls banging against her thigh tops. 'It'll sting all the more when I pick up that bat again.'

'But I thought –'

'Don't think. Just obey. Learn.' He squeezed her bared cheeks in both hands as he thrust into her, and his breathing increased.

'Want me to keep to a tight schedule, sir?' Arlene gasped, tensing in her internal muscles to pleasure his prick further.

'That's . . .' the coach started. But she never found out exactly what that was. For he let out a half-strangled grunt, a sound between ecstasy and anger, and pushed forwards rapturously, his head against her back.

Six weeks later, Arlene was back on form.

'Did it!' she gasped, breaking through the ribbon. Looked up with relief as they wrapped her in a warming blanket, looked down with pride as the Jumping Juice Queen sash was slipped on from shoulder to waist.

'. . . series of six different ads. Programme to encourage kids to train.' In her ears there were offers, offers, offers. She looked for her coach, saw him slipping away into the refreshments tent.

Ten minutes later she shook off her entourage and walked in.

'Thought you'd be there to congratulate me!'

'No need – I knew you'd do it.'

She looked down at his broad belt. 'I knew I had to pass – or else!' Oliver Cartwright smiled an enigmatic smile.

'Oh, he may be in use yet. We've got the Super Snacks Swimathon coming up.' He sighed. 'I've seen you in the water, and though you're fast, your technique is sad.' His thumb stroked his buckle over and over. 'I wonder how long it will take for you to learn some style?'

The Punishment Chamber

'You will speak only when spoken to,' Rachel instructed.

Chernon tugged at his tied ankles and wrists. 'Christ, what do you think this is – *The Story of O*?' But despite his attempts at levity he recognised the fear in his voice, a fear which intensified as Rachel dealt him a stinging slap across the face.

'Speak only when spoken to,' she reiterated, 'or I'll have to take it out on your arse.'

Shocked into silence, Chernon stared at the quilt underneath his naked flesh. In truth he was still dazed at the way events had turned, deposing him from his position of fly-by-night lover to prisoner, even slave.

'I hear you're leaving town tomorrow,' Rachel had said to him on the phone earlier that day. 'How about having a good fuck tonight for old times' sake?' Excited by the crudity of her suggestion, by memories of how good she had been in the sack, he'd agreed, responding with his balls and not his brains.

'Let's play some games,' she had said after he'd arrived at her cottage and partaken of several drinks. 'I've become quite experimental recently – even bought a four-poster bed for the basement.' She'd been in a good mood, he'd noted appreciatively, different from the somewhat remote brunette he'd dated in the past.

Happily he had followed her to the previously unused basement room with its thick white carpet, impressed at the mirrored décor and king-size bed. There they had made love, and he'd tied her up for a while, then she'd done the same thing to him. Which was where the fun stopped and the seriousness began.

As Chernon mulled over the past two hours a score of questions ran through his head. Realising this, Rachel gave him permission to speak. 'How long do you intend to keep me here?' he asked quietly.

Rachel shrugged. 'Till it no longer suits my purpose. Till your bottom's been heated enough.'

'I see.' Chernon ran a tongue over lips suddenly dry. 'But why?'

'To teach you a lesson, to show that you can't pick women up and discard them on a whim.'

Chernon cleared his throat. 'Yet when we were together you were often dismissive.'

'Only because I knew of your other women.' Rachel smiled mirthlessly as Chernon flinched – he'd thought he'd been so discreet!

'Enough talk!' So saying, she rolled him over on to his stomach, walked to the cupboard and extracted a table-tennis bat that looked made for severe spankings. Noting his approaching fate in the mirror, Chernon cowered helplessly on the bed.

Carefully Rachel weighed the bat in her right hand then sat on his back, facing his small firm buttocks. 'Let's see how red this turns a bum.' She slapped down and he jerked up, but her weight kept him captive in place. 'Does it hurt most here or here or here?' She spanked his inner and outer thighs and helpless cheeks till he moaned for mercy. When at last she stopped, his reflection showed two writhing buttocks covered in angry scarlet prints.

'That really hurt,' he whispered confusedly.

'It was meant to.' Smiling, she rolled him over to lie on his newly tormented flesh.

Don't speak without being told. Be obsequious when making an enquiry. Ask for permission to urinate. Moments after the first chastisement ended, Rachel gave him his instructions as her slave. Numbly, Chernon stared around the underground room. 'You'll never get away with this!' he blurted. 'My landlady will find my suitcases still in my room. She'll know something is wrong.'

Rachel shook her head. 'I've been planning this for a

194

long time, my dear. The landlady won't be at all surprised if she sees me collect them. After all, I'm one of your many obliging girlfriends!' She paused. 'And I've already phoned your hotel down south to cancel your reservation.' To Chernon's dismay she picked up the table-tennis bat.

'Meanwhile you spoke without permission so I'll have to heat that bad bottom all over again!'

The next morning before breakfast Chernon obeyed Rachel to the letter, saying the correct words, asking for permission to use the basement commode, then kneeling to kiss and lick her feet with fervour. 'Good boy,' she said slowly, looking at him with chilling narrowed eyes. 'Now we're ready to move on to the next stage.' Chernon swallowed hard and she indicated that he could speak.

'The next stage, Mistress?'

'Mmm. I teach you not to ejaculate without permission.'

Chernon's heart sank: he'd always been easily aroused and she knew it! She was obviously looking for excuses to chastise him some more. 'We'll start immediately,' Rachel determined, producing the ropes and fastening him to the bed on his back. 'You don't come unless I tell you to – is that understood?'

'Yes. Yes, Mistress.' A mere whisper now.

With silky suggestiveness Rachel began to finger Chernon's puckering arsehole and flick her tongue against his fast-growing shaft. Face taut with effort he tried desperately to concentrate on politics, war, *anything*, but her sure knowing touch broke through his reserve, took him beyond the limits of his endurance. All too soon he cried out and spurted over her arm.

'You filthy little boy! You disgusting untrained little wretch!' Meticulously Rachel wiped his semen from her suit, staring at him contemptuously. 'Looks like I'll have to correct you again,' she murmured. 'Teach the bad little boy to do what he's told.' She lit a cigarette and deliberately blew the smoke into his face, her eyes daring him to turn his head away.

The telephone, ringing as it seldom did through the

house, startled them both. 'I'm going to answer that, then I'm off to work,' she said, looking at her watch. 'Whilst I'm gone you may urinate where you lie and when I return at lunchtime you may use the commode.' She paused. 'I think that we'll play with your cock again when I come back, see if you've learnt a little control. If not ...' She jerked her head in the direction of a leather tawse displayed on the wall.

Wearily, Chernon endeavoured to change position, wincing at the pain of the ropes as they chafed against his bound ankles and wrists. She'd been in such a hurry to answer the phone, he realised, she'd forgotten to give him food and water. Oh, well, he'd best try to sleep till she returned.

With effort he turned slowly on to his side. And then he saw the lighter. It was lying to the left of his head on the duvet, sparkling, beckoning. His passport to a life beyond fear if he could only reach.

Carefully, his heart beating fast, Chernon stretched his head along the bed, grabbed the silvery rectangle in his teeth and transferred it to his hands which were bound together in front of him. Several attempts later he succeeded in igniting it and positioning it against the ropes. And suddenly his hands were free and he went on to untie his ankles and unbuckle the loose leather thong that secured him by his waist to the bed.

Shakily, Chernon stood up and flexed and stretched each liberated limb and muscle. His first thought was to find his clothes and immediately flee the house. But as he searched for his shirt and jeans he had time to reconsider. Time to plot his revenge. Chernon ate, bathed and dressed, then spent the rest of the morning making an inventory of the Punishment Chamber and its various devices. No longer did he wish to search for work down south – there was a major task he had to take care of here!

That lunchtime he was waiting for Rachel behind the door of the Punishment Chamber and the second she entered he grabbed her round the waist. 'I hope you're going to be a good girl for your master!' Moments later he stripped her almost naked and bound her securely over the punishment stool he'd found.

'Excuse me one moment. I just have to make a phone call.' Calmly, Chernon walked to the telephone and dialled the temping agency Rachel worked for. 'I'm phoning on behalf of Rachel Lewis,' he said smoothly. 'She's flying out to Australia this afternoon due to family illness and may not be back for some time.'

'I understand, sir,' the clerk said indifferently.

Savouring the sensation, Chernon walked back to where Rachel lay.

'You won't get away with this,' she said faintly, struggling a little against the ropes that bound her extremities.

'Don't speak without permission,' Chernon murmured, pulling down her pants to unveil her as yet lily-white rear. 'And it's *Master* to you,' he added, stroking the taut waiting hemispheres with cruel deliberation before picking up the martinet.

He watched as she shuddered, spoke: 'Master, please. I'll do anything!'

Teasing her with the leather thongs, he slid a cushion under her belly to raise her arse still further, then calculatingly struck the first blow.

'Cut!' the director enveloped the room with his relieved cry. 'That's it, kiddoes! It's in the bag!' He treated the actors to his most rewarding smile.

Shakily, Chernon put down the martinet and untied Rachel. Then, with equal unsteadiness, he lit a cigarette.

'Jesus, Don, I don't know where you get your scripts from, but that one gives me the creeps!' Turning to search for an ashtray, he missed the look that passed between Rachel and Don. 'God knows how much of it'll get past the censors,' he continued, aware of how querulous he sounded. He dragged deeply on his cigarette and the rush of nicotine to his brain made him suddenly calm. 'Well, I'm for home, folks. Anyone going my way?' He looked in the cameraman's direction first.

'Sorry, Chernon – you're on your own tonight,' the man said. 'I'm stopping off for a few.' Chernon thought longingly of the pub. He'd like a skinful himself after a production like this, only he was meeting Gilly and he never performed so well after a few. And Gilly was worth staying dry for: she was wet, wet, wet.

'Coming back to my place, then?' Rachel teased, pulling on the pants that Chernon had pulled from her during the final punishment scene. Again he felt that uneasiness, that fear.

'Not tonight, love. I really need to get my flat in order.'

'You can do that later – I'd run you home for about ten p.m.'

'No, really.' He felt a rising irritation. God, just because he'd been screwing the silly bitch for a few weeks didn't mean she owned his every hour!

'Well, I'll drive you home anyway,' Rachel said, with a smile.

The drive home was all shadowy trees and nocturnal sounds, surrealistically invading. Once Rachel touched his arm and he jumped so violently that he hit his head against the roof of the car, and when her keys jangled against her belt his heart leapt like a frog.

'Any work lined up after this?' he asked, trying to inject a note of calm into the conversation. 'Or do you think you'll be resting for a while?'

'Oh, I never rest.' Again that slight sinister inference. Moments later they reached the vicinity of his flat.

'Sure you don't want to come round for even a couple of hours?' Rachel pressed. Hastily, Chernon exited the car. He had never felt so glad to be free of someone. 'Hope the next role you land is a bit more mainstream,' he added as she wound the window down.

'Oh, I liked my role in *The Punishment Chamber*,' Rachel said. She switched on the radio and added, 'That DJ always reminds me of the one in the film *Play Misty For Me*. I'd have liked a part in that too!' He could hear her laughing as he started to hurry towards his flat.

* * *

Driving home, Rachel continued to laugh. So what if things hadn't gone to plan? It was of no consequence. That was one of the nice things about being the scriptwriter: when things went wrong you simply changed the script.

Reaching her house she went straight to the telephone and dialled. 'Gilly, there's been a slight change of plan about Chernon – he's coming direct to your flat tonight.'

She listened to Gilly's surprised low whistle: 'You mean he wouldn't come home with you first? I didn't think he'd have been able to resist the prospect of screwing two women in the same evening.'

'Oh, he resisted! I think the similarity between the part he plays in this film and the philanderer he is in real life is getting to him. He was jumpy as hell when I drove him home!'

'Serves him right.' She paused. 'So what do we do now?'

Rachel grinned. 'Well, the cameraman knows of the change of arrangements so he'll be bringing the film props round to you at any moment. He'll set them up as close to the way they were on the set, then leave. After that it's down to you – just follow your copy of the script and put that bat into action on those two-timing little buttocks! It'll be enough to give the bastard the shock of his life!'

Happily, Chernon prepared for an evening in Gilly's arms. Lengthy shower. Short underpants. A wide smile. An intermediate application of *Pour Homme* applied to his pulse spots. Then a bottle of wine and a scarlet-foiled chocolate heart. In truth, Rachel had given him the heart some weeks before, but Gilly wouldn't know that. The two actresses had never met.

Chernon smiled, thinking of how salty Rachel's pubis was compared to Gilly's more neutral taste. Rachel was the more fiery of the two, the more inventive and demanding. But for the last few days he'd found himself preferring Gilly's more girlish small-nippled charms.

His groin tingled as he completed the ten-minute walk to Gilly's house, imagining just how he would fondle these same nipples before taking her roughly against the wall, his

cock grinding up against her cervix. Wine, chocolates . . .
he wondered what delights were in store for his flesh.
Would she concentrate on his prick, balls or buttocks? He
was still wondering when she opened the door.

The Deal

Laura blushed as the boutique owner searched her bag.

'Sir – I didn't mean to steal them!'

'Going to bring them back, were you?'

He deposited the unpaid-for leather belt and velvet choker on the counter top.

'I'd pay if I could, but I'm between jobs,' Laura added, trying to keep the mortified tears from spilling over.

'Oh, you'll pay.'

He reached for the phone.

'No – don't call the police!'

'But you have to be punished.'

'You can punish me yourself!' she blurted, her self-serving streak working overtime, not realising the implications of what she said. Maybe he'd ask her to work unpaid hours in the shop amongst these wonderful leather skirts and calfskin jackets. Maybe he'd ask her to clean his car for him or . . .

'If that's what you prefer,' said the man, staring at her dispassionately. 'You'd better follow me into the back.'

Laura walked through to a flat which held a double bed and a dining table. After a moment the boutique owner joined her there. 'I've just locked the door so that no one comes in and sees you taking your thrashing.'

'You mean . . .?' She looked at his large hands imagining them coming down on her tender backside. It was a powerful image.

'That's right, I'm going to punish you for your transgressions – though I'll deliver you into police custody if you prefer, the shop owner said.

Their eyes met, his determined, hers fiery. Should she tell him where to get off? Flee? Hand herself in? Yet that meant a police record, a court case, her name in the papers. Everyone would know she was nothing but a common thief!

Laura licked her lips. 'How . . . how do you want me?'

'Over my knee.'

He sat down on the edge of the bed, and she inhaled hard and lowered herself across his lap. This couldn't be happening! She whimpered with anxiety and desire as she felt him push her gypsy skirt up, and peel her underskirt away.

'Little thiefs don't get to keep their pants on, do they, my foolish beauty?'

'No, sir,' she whispered, and felt him edge her pretty pink knickers down.

'So that's what a shoplifter's bum looks like.' She felt the strength in his hands as he fondled her rear, imagined him staring down at her small smooth bottom. Felt him shift position slightly, then the first spank lashed down.

'Uh!' She grunted half in surprise, half in pain. Repeated the sound as he warmed her other cheek.

'Thou shalt not steal,' he said grimly, and toasted both helpless globes again.

Her face was glowing with shame, her bottom was glowing with heat. To her chagrin, she found her sex was glowing with excitement. Anticipation filled every cell in her body when the boutique owner deposited her on the double bed. Uncertainly she smoothed her skirt down. Was he going to enter her? She wanted him inside her. Wanted him to ride her hard.

'Now that you're nicely warmed up your real punishment can begin.'

Laura sat up and licked her lips. 'I thought . . .?'

'My dear, we've hardly started. You plunder my stock, you try to deny the charges. Now I've had to shut up shop early and am losing valuable customer time.'

Put like that it sounded really heinous. Laura hung her head. 'I've never stolen before. I swear it! Only my sister's

202

birthday is next week and I wanted to get her something really special.'

'One of my handstitched belts,' said the man, shaking his head sadly. 'It's only fitting that I try it out on your arse.'

She'd never been beaten before, but the spanking had left her with a not-unpleasant tingling. Maybe a taste of the belt wouldn't hurt too much? Laura held her breath.

'Lie on your tummy, then raise your skirts again,' said the boutique owner, flicking the belt down experimentally on the bed.

This time there were no panties to come down.

'How many?' Laura asked tremulously, once again pushing away her skirt to bare her helpless bottom.

'How many do you think you deserve?'

'Six,' she said, burying her face in her hands.

'Six on the bare – that seems fitting.'

'Yes, sir. Thank you, sir.' She tensed her naked posterior as she waited for the first blazing brand. Instead the man palmed her spanked sore hindquarters round and round till she moaned with desire and rubbed her Mount of Venus against the quilt top.

'Easy,' he said. 'Exercise some control, my little beauty. You haven't earned an orgasm yet.'

'No, sir.' She felt the weight of him leave the bed, then the strap whistled down across the centre of her rear end.

'Aaaah!' She started to rise. Her stunned tearful eyes met his.

'Do you want to leave? I left the key in the lock in case you wanted to opt for a different sentence.'

'No.' She got back on her belly on the bed, determined to have a punished bottom rather than a police record. 'I deserve this. I wasn't brought up to steal. I have to learn.'

'I think you do.' He traced the first welt over and over. 'Would you like to ask nicely for the second?'

Laura hesitated, then she cleared her throat twice. 'Please use the belt on my wicked little bottom a second time.'

The boutique owner obliged. The lash fell over both buttocks, felt like it marked it into quartets. Laura writhed and groaned, but kept obediently in place.

'That's it, sweetheart – almost halfway there. Your bum can take it.'

Again the man talked to her and fondled her till she acquiesced to the third. This fell above the previous two, forming a wide band that must have looked as red as it felt to the bottom's owner. Laura yelped.

'Good girl!' The fourth taste of the belt landed at the tender fold. She took the fifth high up, just below the place where back meets buttocks. 'I'll do the sixth one specially hard so that you always remember that it doesn't pay to steal.'

'Please, sir,' Laura whispered, her entire being concentrated on her chastened *derrière*, 'I'll never forget!'

She curled her fingers into the duvet and waited for the lash. As if keeping her in suspense, he teased her bottom with his fingers for long, long moments. 'Kiss the belt before I use it on you.' One tear dripping on to the expensive leather, she did.

He brought the punishment implement down across the middle of her backside.

'Uh!'

Laura felt as if her breath had all been expelled, as if all the heat in her body had rushed to her bottom. Reaching fervent hands back, she rubbed her corrected reddened orbs. 'I'll be good from now on, sir,' she whispered tearfully as he lay down beside her and took her in his arms.

'How good?' he asked moments later, positioning her on her hands and knees before sliding into her. And, tightening her internal muscles for his pleasure, Laura showed him that she was very good indeed.

A Boy's Own Story

'Haven't I got enough to do as it is, Lillith?'

Anthony Ledear glared at his live-in girlfriend before slumping into a chair in their lounge.

'All I said was that the Sports Club membership's due to be renewed.'

'Meaning I've to fill in the forms? Write the cheque? Thanks to Ruccat, I've already brought work home with me.'

'For the fifth night in a row,' Lillith sighed.

'Are you complaining? You like the perks my salary brings.'

'Tony – you know damn well I do my bit to support us!'

For a second, Anthony's cock stirred at the angry glint in Lillith's eye. She grabbed her purse from her bag. 'Forget I asked – *I'll* pay the bloody Sports Club! Oh, don't leave the room. I haven't finished with you yet.'

'Madam has spoken!' he jeered, wrung out with overwork and underhand rivals. But something compelled him to stay.

With controlled short movements, Lillith walked up to him then paced round him. 'If you value our relationship you'll be home at six p.m. on Friday night.'

He was there at the appointed hour – if only because she was a special sexy lady.

'I know I've been neglecting you,' he murmured, hurrying into the lounge. He stopped when he saw the teddy bear and white crocheted blanket on the settee. 'What on earth . . .?'

'Come along, darling,' said Lillith, holding out her arms to him.

'Time my baby had a little nap.'

'Oh, very droll!' His voice seemed to be coming from very far away.

'Mummy's serious,' said Lillith. 'Baby's been trying too hard for too long to please the nasty Mr Ruccat. He just needs to gurgle in his carry-cot for a while and relax.' She took the exhausted Anthony by the hand and led him towards the soft talcum-scented cover. 'Let's get this tired boy out of his day clothes right away.'

Anthony started to unknot his tie, but Lillith pulled his hands to his side.

'Mummy will do it!'

Anthony fought back a strong urge to cry. He hoped Lillith's game wouldn't go on for too long, because Ruccat, his boss, wanted a last-minute report and Anthony had hoped to put it together this evening. He could hardly do that with Lillith coddling him naked on the settee!

Well, not naked exactly. She'd gone into the plastic baby bath behind the chaise which he now saw was full of pretty blue romper suits and turquoise bonnets.

'Hands up! Good boy – let's get these pearly buttons done. There!' She kissed his nose chastely. 'Baby's ready to have a nice long sleep.'

'But I haven't eaten!' He usually dined at home before going to his study for extra work sessions.

'Does baby wants a bottle of milk?'

Anthony saw an opportunity for some mammary-mouthing and mischief. 'Baby gets breast-fed,' he said.

Lillith smiled as she unbuttoned her blouse. Her tits, unhampered by a bra, swung free to meet him.

'Don't be too greedy!'

Anthony knelt in his romper suit on the settee. He put his tongue to one hard nipple and licked it lasciviously, did the same to the other, then started to suck.

He nipped with even greater glee.

'Ouch!' Lillith moved his head to her other breast. 'Remember Mummy has two udders.'

Anthony guzzled at the second nipple, teeth grazing it, and Lillith winced again.

'That's it – you're deliberately making Mum mad! I'll have to spank you.'

Was she serious? Anthony wondered how much the terry-towelling romper suit would protect his arse.

'Over my knee. This'll hurt me more than it's going to hurt you.'

Somehow he doubted it. He was still musing on the subject when she pulled him over her lap.

She spanked him for a long long time. His bum grew warm under her palms, then fiery, baking, scalding. His cock grew larger, rubbed and begged against her thighs. He slid a frenzied finger towards her clit, but she pushed it away firmly.

'A baby must be respectful to its Mum.'

'Yes, Mummy,' Anthony whispered, revering her ruling, wi-hing he wasn't so desperately hard.

At last she stopp∿d spanking him and tucked him under his coverlet.

'Oh, almost forgot – some little boys get their hands all dirty by touching their secret places.' She put a wollen mitten on each of his hands, tied the little ribbon straps round the wrists, then knotted them together above the quilt.

'Mummy's going to make up baby's milk bottle and chicken soup whilst baby has his sleepy time. Mummy knows baby's going to be good.'

Baby was going to be excellent! When she'd gone, Anthony turned with difficulty on to his tummy, so that his substantial shaft was against the underside of the crochet. Then, using his elbows to prop himself up slightly, he rubbed his fountain of fulfilment forward and back.

Thought of Lillith's tits – and felt some more juice work its way through to his balls and to his excitement centre. Thought of his well-warmed buttocks and felt more erotic enjoyment spread from erection to arse. His bum was well taught, his wrists well tied – but he was coming, coming. He thrust his prick especially vigorously against the romper suit and tremulously came.

A surfeit of pleasure, then a short, needed sleep. When he woke up, Lillith was smiling down at him. 'Time for baby's dinner.' She helped him into a sitting position, then dipped a spoon into his soup and held it to his lips. Anthony allowed himself to be fed. He felt a little silly, a little excited – and very peaceful. Then the clock struck nine.

'Lillith – I've a report to do. Ruccat wants it for tomorrow.'

'He'll have to write it himself then, won't he?'

'But –'

'No buts!' She held the bottle to his eager mouth. 'Do what Mummy tells you. Or do you want to be spanked again?'

Not if she'd stay in the room afterwards so that he couldn't come! He shook his head mutely.

'Good. Let's get you in the playpen now.'

Clutching his snuggly blanket and crawling at her bidding, Anthony followed his Mama into the warm spare room. There she'd set up a pen with building bricks and a truck, crayons and a drawing pad. Anthony reached for the bricks, intending to see how many he could pile into a tower. Looked up at her for maternal approval, then looked down as he saw her staring at him and shaking her head.

'Oh dear – baby's had an accident! I'll have to get the potty.'

He stared down at the sperm stains on his romper suit.

'No, I . . . well, yes.'

'Never mind. It's a difficult thing for baby to control. Let's get you out of your wet clothes, you poor little mite.'

His cock twitched again as she stripped him. She left the room then came back with a large cotton nappy over her arm.

'Let's potty train you first.' She made him squat over the pot till he produced four drops of urine. 'Good boy! Oh dear, you've gone all excited – must be pleased with yourself.' Anthony reached for her delectable rear in its sensible skirt, but she pulled smartly away from him. 'Let's get these rubber training pants on.'

By the Sunday night he'd rubbed himself off using most of the furniture in the house, but was desperate to be inside her.

'Have a bath, love, then put your usual clothes on,' she said at last.

'You mean . . .?'

She nodded and smiled.

'I'd rather leave all my clothes off!' He grinned.

'You randy bastard.' She looked pleased: he really had been neglecting her. He must try harder.

'See you in the bedroom in twenty minutes, all right?'

She was there. She was bare. She lay on the top of the duvet reading a Mothercare manual. He smiled and threw it on the floor.

'Forget that – I'm all man again!'

'Mmm, so I can feel.' She used thumb and first finger to circle his priapic piston, placed a coaxing palm beneath his fluid-filled balls.

'What way do you want me?' she whispered, pupils wide with the knowledge that she'd soon climax.

'Monkey-fucking style,' he muttered, helping her on to her hands and knees. 'You've done enough work this weekend! Now I'll take charge.'

'I'm not arguing.'

Her voice had gone its familiar turned-on husky. He rimmed her entrance to find it already desire-drenched. She was asking for it, facial lips open and fanny lips fevered. So dressing him up and talking him down had excited her too.

'Would you like a little cock?' he teased, entering her by an insinuating inch, then holding his body in position.

'A *lot* of cock!' she muttered, trying to push her urgent cave against him, trying to suck him in.

'Whoa!' He held her by the shoulders, just the head of his hardness inspiring her. 'As you said, we've got all night. Let's take it s-l-o-w . . .'

He fondled her front rounds and rounded backside. He slid in another leisured length, backed out a little.

'God!' said Lillith. 'Just do it now!'

'I'm not sure . . .' He smiled into her back. 'I mean, this shouldn't be like work – you don't want to pressure me!'

'All right! Just go at your own pace. But caress my clit.'

'Too worried about Ruccat's unfinished report to remember where it is!'

Lillith howled in frustration, and the vibrations went thrillingly through his semi-disappeared dick, his desire deepening: he wanted more of that warm wet hold. Anthony plunged forward, watching his shaft slide into the darkness inside her. Felt his balls getting closer to seeing the light.

A hot woman, a fired-up man. A prick-tease to Paradise. 'Harder!' Lillith urged as she always urged, and Anthony was happy to oblige. He shafted firmly, one hand round her waist, the other locating her love bud. Let her rub against his fingers in the special way only she knew how.

A primed prick-length, well-practised hands. He thrust his dick in and out, moved his digits up and down. Looked along at her smooth back, down at her small firm bum, and felt his heartbeat quicken. Read the note-giving splendour of her super-hardening nipples, mammaries elongating and expanding as they did when she was almost at the edge.

'Up a bit, lover – Oh Christ!'

Caressing her craving clit, hands so soaked with her juice he could hardly retain the connection. Free hand moving down to her soft round stomach, the muscles hard beneath his palm as she used the leverage to thrust back.

'Oh . . . ah! Oh yes!'

Bum banging against his belly, hands gripping the pillow. He treated her blossoming bud to a little more fingertip foreplay and she moaned long and loud, pushed back hard on his spout. 'Got to . . . uh.'

He felt her thighs tensing against his thighs. Kept the speed, kept the friction, hearing her breath catch in her throat, a momentary stillness, then the rasping wildness that preceded the wordless wail.

'Aaaaaaaaaaaah!'

Groaning alongside her with pleasure as she shocked half the neighbourhood by her shuddered screamed release.

'Tony! Tone!'

'I know, sweetheart, I know!'

Her after-orgasm contractions clenched congenially round his cock.

Thrusting forward, pulling back now: the testes rhythm. That teasing tension – harder! harder! harder! – that wild *nearly* spiralling through his balls. No need to hold back, just a pulsing prick in the pursuit of pleasure.

'Lil . . . Lillith. Ah, ah, ah!'

Going, going . . . the moment when his head went blank and his firing rod went frenzied, then he strained into his girlfriend, ecstatically offloading his sexual sap.

'That was unreal! I was so relaxed after . . .'

They collapsed on to the bed, lay face to face in each other's arms, breastbone to breast tips. The mere-babe-in-arms weekend seemed like a wondrous wet dream, felt a lifetime away. For a few blissful hours he'd forgotten about work demands, the executive nightmare, the nine-to-much-later-than-five.

'If only I could get Ruccat off my back.' He sighed. 'Doesn't the man ever think of anything other than work, ever rest?'

'He does as of last week.' Lillith cuddled up to him and reached for something under the bed. 'I've been having boozy nights out with Cindy, his girlfriend. She's passed on quite a few secrets. Obviously you're not supposed to know!' She smiled. 'Think of this every time Mr Ronald Ruccat Senior is ranting and raving, and you'll realise he's not so big and brave.'

Anthony stared at the Polaroid of Ruccat with his briefcase.

'Jeez, he's definitely not taking work home with him!' he said. For the briefcase was of yellow shiny plastic, and the man was dressed in rubber training pants and had a big blue dummy between his orgasm-stretched lips.

Repentance

Tunisia's splendid ruins were genuine. But the so-called ancient coin the street-seller held out to her was pre-naturally aged. 'They make them in a factory along the road,' said a helpful passing stranger. Things in this country were rarely as they seemed . . .

Gemma turned away from the seller, murmuring, '*La shukran.*' (No thank you.) She felt his dark eyes assessing the curve of her hips beneath the full-length dress.

'Neckle, then?' he said, going into his leather bag and bringing out a fish-shaped medallion.

'*La shukran.*'

She'd been saying no a lot since coming here – since before coming here. Had said no to the idea of continuing to be Adam's mistress two weeks before. Had fled from Britain on this last-minute package, exploring the mosques and markets by day so that she would be too tired to miss Adam's cock by night.

Gemma sighed, and skirted round yet another stretching pillar. So thick, so hard, so certain. She touched the rigid stem. Earlier her pubis had throbbed as she rode a camel, bra-less nipples deepening in colour like the huge red buds on the roadside prickly pears.

Pricks. Pairs. She had to get used to being single again, start to masturbate. Adam hadn't let her masturbate. Adam had said . . .

Forget the man! Remember his wife! She trekked back towards the coach that had brought her here. Ignored the chewing-gum sellers who were known to give counterfeit change.

The next day, after a restless night, she set off alone for Sousse's Medina. Men shouted comments at her, made kissing sounds. She hurried by. Stopped to buy a coke, hugely aware of the strong fingers holding hers as they handed over her change in millimes. Moved on again, the sparkling coolness slipping over her tongue and teasing her throat.

The heat had made her hungry: she left the stalls and made her way to a row of cafés near the beach front. Went inside and ordered lemon sole, a ridiculously early lunch. Ate, finished reading her paper, waited for the waiter to bring her the bill. He seemed to have disappeared somewhere. Bored, she looked with peripheral vision at the only other person in the café.

He was elderly. He smiled beneath his hooded cloak. She rubbed several dinars between her fingers and made a shy, quizzical gesture. He pointed to the table before her.

She blushed a little: 'Leave it there?'

He nodded encouragingly.

Awkwardly, she set down more coins than the bill could possibly be.

She'd reached the pavement when she felt the hand on her arm.

'You. Stealing.'

'No, I . . .' She turned round and faced the young waiter, tried to smile. 'I left the money. It's there . . . on the table.'

'You come with me.'

Somehow the dinars had gone and she found herself in the manager's office. It held a coffee table, a footstool, a settee. She paced and paced. Waited for ten, twenty minutes. Jumped when the door opened, when a man strode in.

Thirty or so, with the classic brown eyes, thick black hair and smooth olive complexion of the Tunisian. His impossibly white shirt, well-cut black suit and leather shoes spoke of style, confidence, wealth.

'There's been a misunderstanding,' Gemma began, rising quickly.

'You mean you were caught trying not to pay,' the

owner said. Beneath the accent, his English was perfect. 'I own six restaurants in Tunisia. I see this all the time.'

'I *did* pay,' said Gemma, nervously licking her lips. 'Your waiter wasn't around. I left the money.'

'Invisible money?'

She felt her helplessness increasing. 'Someone must have taken it!'

'Oh? Who?' asked the man. He walked towards her slowly, methodically.

'This man!'

A cold stare. 'My waiter saw no man.'

'He came in after your boy left. He must have slipped out in front of me!'

'That's a lie,' the man said evenly. 'Admit your crimes.'

'Crimes! What crimes? He wore a cloak with a hood.'

'A holy man!' said the restaurateur, mouth tightening.

'I don't – I didn't mean . . .'

My God, had she really just accused a holy man? Could she go to prison for this? Or worse? Gemma swallowed hard. She felt vulnerable – very, very vulnerable. 'What do you want of me?' she asked in a faltering voice.

'That's better,' said the man. 'Repentance can be very cleansing.' He sounded like Adam, Gemma thought, swaying on her feet. 'Come here' he added firmly.

Stepping awkwardly over the coffee table, she went to him.

'Stop there.' She stopped. He reached a hand round thoughtfully and took her hair. Pulled her head back a little so that her eyes looked into his, held his.

'What do you think we should do with you?' he said.

'I . . . I don't know.'

The area around each nipple pulsed, making its own suggestion.

'You obviously need to be punished,' the stranger said.

Gemma felt her lids close of their own accord. She couldn't look at him. Was very relieved when he let go of her head.

'Our own women wear such modest skirts,' the man murmured, putting his hand to her rump. 'But then our own women aren't criminals. Should a criminal be allowed to dress so demurely?' Gemma shook her head.

'What is your name?'

'Gemma.'

'Gemma. I can't hear you.'

She forced the words out through vocal chords fast closing in: 'No. Criminals shouldn't be allowed to dress demurely,' she said.

'Then we'll have to strip this from the criminal. Show her in her true colours.'

No, shouted Gemma's brain. But her clit said yes . . .

She felt his fingers undo the single button, heard the zip go down. Shivered as he edged the thin cotton over her hips. Stood before him in ankle socks and shoes and tiny panties, wishing she'd worn a bra that day despite the heat.

'Nice,' he murmured, 'very nice.'

She stared at the carpet, lacing her fingers before her.

'But criminals don't get to keep those on,' he added, sliding a knowing palm over her brief-clad cheeks.

'Can't we talk?' asked Gemma wildly, 'I could pay again.'

'Oh, you'll pay all right. Either myself or the police will decide how you pay.'

Didn't the police carry guns – or was that just the gendarmerie, the military? She didn't want to see them. She was out of her depth.

'Do you want me to pull my pants down?' Gemma whispered.

'Of course. Arse facing me. Slowly, if you please.'

She turned her back on him, stared unseeingly towards the settee, put her fingers to the waistband. Edged the scrap of silk down to unveil the previously covered portion of her backside. Pushed the garment down to the top of her thighs, hands trembling.

'Leave them there!' he barked.

She took her hands away again, left them hanging by her sides, waiting further instruction.

'Now socks and shoes,' he added coolly. She could feel her buttocks jutting out as she bent.

Would he make love to her now? Something in his voice told her it wouldn't be that simple. She stood, naked save her half-mast panties, waiting for him to tell her what to do.

'Pick up your nearest shoe.'

She bent again and did so.

'Hand it to me.'

Turning round, she dared a glance at him, saw the erection tenting his trousers. His eyes followed her gaze. 'You want to please?' he asked, unzipping himself.

As she had hundreds of times with Adam, Gemma sank to her knees.

She felt him take the back of her head in a gesture already becoming familiar. He pulled her forward. She took his thick dark stem deep into her mouth. He tasted of soap and salt and a fast-forming perspiration. She sucked him hard and then harder and he spurted over her tongue.

So that was all right. Gemma sat back on her haunches and ran the back of her hand across lips which felt stretched and sperm-smeared.

'Did I tell you to do that?' an angry voice said.

'But I thought . . .'

'You're not here to think. You're here to pay for your sins. You've yet to do so.'

'But I thought . . .' she said again.

'Oh dear. You dirty girl. You mean you wanted to bribe away your crimes with sexual services?' His tone was mocking.

Gemma raised her hands in a half shrug.

'Now where were we when your greedy mouth got the better of you? Ah, I know.' He zipped up his trousers. 'You were about to hand me your shoe.'

Gemma did, aware of the hard flat sole's possibilities.

'Good. Now lie across that coffee table, your rump towards me.' Could she . . .? Stretching out seemed to take a long time. The marble felt cold against her belly. She was intensely aware of the line of her rolled-down knickers, emphasising the bare curved target of her cheeks. 'Stretch your arms out so that one hand grips each corner. Spread your legs.'

She obeyed again. It was easier like this, not looking at him. Adam would have positioned a mirror at her face, made her stare into it so that they both could see. As she mused, she felt the sole of the shoe come down, asterisks of anguish exploding behind each eyelid. Again and again.

'Tell me you've been bad.'

He used the shoe some more and she told him.

'Tell me you deserve lots more of this.'

'No! Please!'

'I've hardly started,' he added, tracing a large cool palm over her fast-heating bottom. 'I'll know when you genuinely repent.'

He stood up and walked over to the settee. 'Come here.'

She stood up shakily to find him already seated. Walked over to him, eyes unable to meet his face.

'Lie over my knee. No, this way.' He indicated her position. She did as she was told, tummy now rubbing against his trousers as she wriggled with shame.

His erection had returned. She could feel it pulsing against her belly button. Her own hardened bud swelled and tingled. She rubbed it greedily against his leg.

'Bad . . . bad. You know wicked girls can't have pleasure until the pain's been dealt them.'

Gemma swallowed and blushed again. Felt him pinion her wrists, reposition himself so that her bottom was further raised, awaiting attention.

'How many spanks,' he asked, 'for trying to bribe me with your tongue?'

Gemma licked dry lips, tried to think of a reasonable number. Enough to satisfy him justice had been done. Not enough to overheat her already warmed arse.

'Ten?' she asked, knowing that Adam would never have let her away with that.

'Ten it is.'

She thought she'd won till the first spank came crashing down on the buttock nearest to him. He had a palm like a paddle. She cried out into the settee. Felt his grip tighten as he applied the second spank to her other cheek, heat radiating out towards her back, towards the crease where *derrière* met thigh. 'I can't take eight more!' she yelled, feet drumming a tattoo.

Now he turned his ministrations to her labia. She whimpered as he slid a finger round her clit. 'Ask for the other eight spanks, Gemma,' he murmured, fondling lightly away.

'No. I can't!'

The hand withdrew. 'You mean you *won't*, and that's different.'

'It's too much!'

'Concentrate on your clit instead.' He teased at her sex some more. She pushed her mons hard against him. Her canal felt cavernous. 'Beg,' he said, taking his fingers away.

'Please! I *beg*!' She was breathless.

'Beg for eight more hard spanks.'

Her bottom said no, but her sex was crying out for her to do as he wanted.

'Please spank me, sir,' she begged.

'You can do better than that.' His palm scoured round and round her already reddened arse cheeks. 'Tell me that your bottom needs to be taught.'

She gulped. 'My bottom needs to be taught a lesson, sir.'

'Mmmm,' whispered the Tunisian. 'Doesn't it just?'

He raised his hand again. She tensed. Took the slap on her right cheek. Felt the next spank warm its neighbour.

'Let's hear you,' he ordered. 'Count the final six.'

Writhing against his cock, she shouted the numbers.

'Now thank me, my dear, for giving you six of the best.'

Gemma muttered her thanks into the settee cover. Her hindquarters felt scalded, sore. Then his fingers touched her mons again and she forgot all about the stinging.

'Want fucked?' he asked.

She nodded.

'Don't be shy. *Say it!*'

'Please fuck me, sir.'

'It'll be a mercy fuck,' he said softly. 'Get your arse over that footstool on your hands and knees.'

She bent over as he wished. Felt him kneel on a cushion behind her and unzip himself. Felt his sheathed cock taunt her slick swollen labia, entering the first centimetre of the rim. *'Fuck me!'* she begged again. 'Let me come against your shaft, sir.'

He pushed his thickness into her. His hands came round to cup her tits. 'Do you deserve this?' he whispered into her hair, thrusting harder and harder.

'No, sir.'

'Should you pay for your lewdness later?'

'Yes! Yes!'

'I should take off my belt . . .' He played with her clit. He played exquisitely. She came against his hand, lust dripping down her love canal, soaking her thighs. He grunted as his own surge overtook him, fingers gripping the soft spherical splendour of her breasts.

She'd got off lightly, Gemma told herself, as he lay down and gave her permission to put her clothes back on. Those lost few dinars could have resulted in her being taken to court, even imprisoned, for in Tunisia things were rarely as they seemed.

As she walked dazedly down the road, the restaurateur stared out of the window after her. Adjusting his well-milked balls, he walked into the adjacent room.

'Good work, Karthia,' he said, handing the man in the hooded cloak ten dinars. 'You were right about that one too.' He paused. 'I won't need you again now until Thursday lunchtime.' He smiled thoughtfully. 'If there's a choice available I'd prefer a blonde this time.'

Male Order

Reindeer pranced over snow-clad rooftops and anorexic angels perched on Christmas trees. Emma threw down the sticky-backed page with a cynical smile. She'd recently spent her nights putting Christmas stickers like this into charity appeal envelopes. Now a firm had delivered some of the adhesive squares to her home.

It was 5 p.m. – two hours till her evening shift at the charity office started. Not that she was doing it for free! She'd get paid tonight – the nineteen-year-old student hugged herself at the prospect. She'd buy a large bottle of cider and book a taxi to take her to a party across town. She'd shower long and hot, change into that slash-necked crimson dress, matching high-gloss shoes and black-seamed stockings. She'd dance, tease, drink!

But her part-time job came first. As usual, she raced breathlessly into Homes For Horses headquarters.

'Cutting it fine again, Miss Smart?' murmured Vincent Mearns, the chief administrator, as she unbuttoned her jacket in the hall. He'd cut her a few times already with his tongue when he'd caught her taking extended coffee breaks.

'Casuals like you are ten a penny. You're on your last warning,' he'd said.

Emma looked at him now, tried to smile, muttered something about the icy pavements making walking difficult. He was tall and well built, with thick black hair and a thin pale smile. Most of the female staff found him distractingly delectable. Emma did, too, and yet he also made her feel afraid.

'You don't want to get behind with your quota,' he said now, referring to the fact that the casual workers had to fill a certain number of envelopes per shift in order to be asked back again. Emma swallowed nervously. If only he knew!

'Yes, sir. I'll work late if you like, sir.'

'Fire regulations – everyone must be out of the building for nine p.m.'

'Maybe I could take some work home and –'

'No. Don't think about infringing the rules.'

Unable to meet his gaze any longer, Emma slunk into the main work area. Karen, Shona and Leanne were already enveloping the latest Foster A Foal By Mail campaign.

'Vincent was having a go at me there – it's like being back at school!' she called, aiming for levity.

'Don't get on the wrong side of him, love,' Shona said.

'He doesn't scare –' Emma started. Froze as the man himself walked in. He looked even taller, stronger, harsher.

'Emma Smart – wait behind tonight after the others have gone.'

For the next two hours Emma's tummy trembled inside and her hands shook a little on the outside. Which of her many minor transgressions had he found out about now? She couldn't afford to lose this job – it would pay for her train fare home for the Christmas holiday, help pay off at least part of her substantial flat rental debt.

Eight-thirty p.m. The others left. She was almost relieved when he strode up to her workstation.

'In my office now, Miss Smart!'

Those same appraising eyes, that ungiving mouth. She slunk past him, went through his doorway. Stood scuffing her black patent heels on the matt-grey wool carpet, wishing she'd been provided with a chair.

'This was waiting for me tonight,' Mr Mearns said, taking a seat behind his desk and staring up at her.

It was the charity's telephone bill. She looked at the Amount Due column. Four hundred pounds.

'It's high,' she said confusedly. 'But you phone lots of businesses asking for private donations. You phone –'

'I didn't phone this private address in Scotland six times.'

Emma stood before the desk and felt the panic trill from belly to breast to voicebox. So he knew about Steve, her boyfriend! She hadn't seen much of him since he went to the University of Aberdeen. She didn't have a phone in her student flat, so the opportunity of using the Homes For Horses one had been too good to miss.

'How did you know?' she asked faintly.

'We have an itemised phone bill. Helps stamp out fraud.'

'Fraud?' It sounded awesome.

'You've effectively stolen from our funds,' Vincent added. He rubbed his palms together. 'We'll have to inform the police.'

Emma trembled. 'No – please!'

'Then how do you suggest we punish you?'

Her mind conjured up penalties, dismissed them. What could she do to make amends? She had no cash! 'If I wasn't so broke –' she began.

'You presumably had no collateral at school,' Vincent Mearns said. 'How were you corrected?'

'We –' Oh Christ! Emma gulped, remembering. 'We were caned.'

'A short sharp shock. That seems fair,' said Vincent Mearns. 'If you'll just bend over the desk and raise your skirt . . .'

He stared at her as she shuddered, reddened, mouth opening, closing.

'I can't!' Licked lips that had long gone dry.

'Fine.' He reached for the telephone. 'Operator, can you connect me with the local pol–'

'All right! I'll do it,' Emma said.

She watched and listened as he told the operator he'd changed his mind. He was a smooth talker, quick-witted, slow to anger. She thought of how controlled he looked. Thought of her about-to-be-humiliated backside.

'Now all we need is something hard to connect with your wilful little posterior,' he said dispassionately. Emma followed his gaze as he looked round the room.

'Mmm, this has potential.' He walked over to the five-foot cane that was tethered to the ceiling-high rubber plant. 'It's too long, of course,' he added, pulling it from the soil. 'Wait there.'

Emma stood in place, recalling the thrashings her headmistress had meted out to her, the feel of that stinging stick on her panty-clad teenage rear. She'd had to touch her toes in the woman's study, had to keep them there as she received six of the best. She'd been fourteen or so at the time, immediately felt reduced to a more junior level. Now, five years later, she was to be caned by this dreadful man!

'Lucky I keep a toolbox in the store cupboard – saves calling in professionals for minor repair work,' said her boss, coming back with a small saw. 'But then you wouldn't know about prudence and foresight, would you, Miss Smart? That's why you're here.'

'I'm sorry, sir,' Emma whispered, lacing her hands behind her back as she watched him remove and discard the half of the stick that had been buried in the plant pot. Incredible to watch the implement that would chastise you being fashioned before your very eyes!

'The plant no longer needs the cane – you obviously do. The lesson will be over by nine,' Vincent said conversationally. That gave him twenty minutes with her buttocks, a painful length of time.

Emma cleared her throat. 'How many strokes, sir?'

'One for each illicit phone call,' the administrator said. He stood up. 'Bend over my desk. Edge your skirt up. Oh, what a shame – you're wearing such thin briefs, my dear. So brutally *unprotecting* of your tender cheeks.'

Closing her eyes and her mouth and her fists, Emma stuck her bottom in the air and waited for the first corrective strike.

It didn't immediately arrive.

'We must learn to be honest,' Mr Mearns said. 'We mustn't cheat our betters.' He fondled her buttocks as he spoke. Emma longed to squirm away, to lash out at him. 'We must give generously of our time, think of the common good.'

'I'm basically trustworthy, sir. I simply –'

The cane suddenly scorched her brief-clad bottom, and she squealed. Its successor singed her waiting bum with equal zeal.

'I'm sorry!' Emma cried. 'I'm so sorry!'

'Sorry for phone calls three and four . . .?'

He laid them on hard rather than fast. It took all her willpower not to rise from the desk, to run away and conceal her tempting target.

'. . . and five and six.'

Coming soon after, they seemed to heat the tramlines where the cane had already been. Emma skulked against the polished wood. When she opened her eyes she could see piles of the now dated Christmas stickers. Mearns must never know that she'd . . .

'Are you going to be a good girl now?'

Emma felt him step closer and palm the soft rotundities that he'd so recently welted. 'I'll be good,' she muttered, standing up and putting her hands to her punished extremities.

He went out into the hallway and came back with her jacket and bag. 'Then put this on and go home to think about the error of your ways.'

That was it? Emma felt ridiculously cast-off, almost disappointed. The heat of the cane must have brought the life-force rushing to her labia. It felt swollen, stirred. And she hadn't seen Steven – far less slept with him! – for weeks. And a good emptying of Mearns' balls would stop him being such a supercilious and despotic little toad.

'I was in such a rush to get here, I may have left my house keys at home,' she lied. She started to rummage through her bag, a pretend frown on her fringed brow. This would earn her an Oscar! She'd fib that the keys were missing, and he'd ask her back to his house to eat and rest. Watching TV, or listening to a CD, she'd somehow find her fingers on his inner thigh, and they'd fuck like bunnies under the Christmas tree. When it came to teasing his cock, she'd be merciless!

'Have you no organisational skills whatsoever?' snapped

the administrator, tipping the entire contents of the bag over his desk. Soft brown eyeliner and hard block mascara. Pastel tissues and a parched-looking pigskin purse.

'What's this?' he said, pushing aside an individual bag of strawberry chews. Emma winced. It was her keys – plus a Homes For Horses pen and notepad set! 'Stealing company property now? You were told that temps don't get the same perks as regulars.'

'I . . . er, must have forgotten to hand them back after writing something down.'

'I know what'll be coming down soon!' Vincent Mearns cast his gaze over her from foot to fringe. Emma played with the strap of her shoulder bag. God, she mustn't think about straps!

'I'll drive you home, though the journey may prove daunting for your posterior. You can always sit on the side of your hip, or lie on your tummy in the back of the car.'

The bastard was obviously enjoying this! Emma followed him to his Escort, and wriggled about beside him as he nosed through the snow-softened December streets. She stared at the tinsel trees in the windows, heard Chris Isaak crooning 'Wicked Game', her brain tuning in and out to the radio's beat.

'Just here is fine!' she exclaimed with relief as he edged the car into the pavement two doors along from her own.

She reached for the handle. 'Thanks! See you on –'

'Employee Premises Inspection,' he said. 'I'm coming in.'

'I don't think –'

'No, you don't. That's the problem. Your silly young head is full of parties, your life filled with unplanned-for debts. You're disorganised and dishonest and invariably late. You need to be taught.'

'But you've already punished me for –'

'For illicit phone calls. Now there's the matter of stolen company property. I just want to check that the problem isn't any larger. We did a follow-up survey on our clients' response to the Christmas stickers mailshot, you see.'

Oh shit! Emma suddenly knew what was coming next.

'Don't run on ahead,' Mearns continued, taking her upper arm in a firm grip and marching her towards her front door.

'I just want to . . .' She hadn't realised he'd kept hold of her keys, but now he produced them as she rummaged in her bag.

'Are there any flatmates around to watch you receive a thorough spanking?'

'No, but I haven't done anything to –'

'You're already guaranteed four spanks for the theft of that notebook and pen.'

'I didn't mean –'

'You *never* mean. Maybe after today you'll become more logical. A painful lesson on the seat often makes its way to the brain.'

Still being held by the arm, Emma walked nervously into her rented flat. Could she steer him towards the bedroom?

'Where's your lounge?'

'It's a lounge-cum-kitchen, really. The place only has the two rooms.'

'Where's your . . .?' he started again.

'That door,' she confirmed, nodding at the one on their right.

As they walked in, she prayed that a cold wind would have miraculously blown the contents of the kitchen surface out of the window. Prayed that . . . Mearns switched on the light.

'Oh dear,' he said, 'Oh dear, oh dear. It looks like I haven't finished with you yet.'

Homes For Horses yellow appeals letters and rainbow-coloured Christmas sticker sheets and manila envelopes littered the breakfast bar.

'These should have been sent in November! We've been mailing the Foster A Foal For February campaign for the last few weeks.'

'I . . . got behind.'

'Mmm, didn't you? What an appropriate expression!' the merciless Mearns said.

Emma went hot, then cold. He looked around. 'There's

not enough room for you to go over my knee in here. Lead the way to the bedroom now and stand beside the bed.'

She would die of embarrassment! 'Oh, please, sir, not again, sir.' Going over his knee seemed so much more *personal*, so much more shameful.

'Would you rather go to court? Have your name in the paper? Lose any chance of a reference?'

'No.'

'I thought not.'

Mearns went into the bedroom. Emma stood cannibalising her nails for a moment, then slowly followed him. Sitting down on the side of the bed, he patted his lap. Wincing, the nineteen-year-old went over it, her palms and toes on the ground, her middle supported across his thighs.

'Four for the pen and pad theft,' the administrator said casually. 'And then . . .?'

She wouldn't let herself think about that. It was just a spanking. She could take it! Emma opened her mouth in silent surprise as the first slap ricocheted down.

It seemed to set the cane stripes on fire again. She could feel each individual line warmly protesting. Mearns spanked her other buttock, then repeated the twin gesture as hard as he could.

'Just to warm you up on this cold night,' he said silkily, 'I'll start in earnest in a little while.'

'How many?' Emma quavered.

'That depends on how many appeals you've failed to process.'

'I sneaked them home planning to send them out from the flat, but I forgot about the November deadline.'

'Then we're going to send a sore reminder to your little backside.'

She wanted to spit on the man. She wanted to shag the man. She wanted her mother.

'Ten for breaking the rules, for starters,' her boss said. 'Pull down your pants.'

Oh Christ, no. Was she to be totally bereft of her dignity?

'Couldn't I just –'

'And another ten for procrastination,' Mearns said.

Blushing for what felt like the twentieth time that night, Emma put her fingers back to her briefs, aware that his grip on her waist had increased to ensure she didn't topple over. Awkwardly she edged down the well-fitting pink panties. Steven had sent them as a little extra pre-Christmas present for her to wear when she met him later that month. They covered every inch of her cheeks, but their almost-see-through thinness made them sexy. A fine first showing this was turning out to be!

'Good. Just leave them at your knees,' Vincent said. Emma wondered how her backside must look. It felt completely helpless. Why didn't he caress her, correct her – *something*? The silence went on and on. He must be eyeing her exposed sex, assessing her aching arse.

'Yes, it's a disobedient little bum,' he said eventually. 'It'll benefit from twenty hard spanks.'

'Yes, sir! I'll deliver the festive appeals tomorrow by hand, sir!' she gasped, trying to reduce her correction.

'Too late. Everyone will have written their Christmas cards by now.' He stroked her bare globes of flesh. 'They'll have used the stickers from rival charities. I'm beginning to think twenty spanks isn't really enough.'

'It is – I swear! The caning really hurt, and –'

'It was meant to.'

'I'll be the perfect employee!'

'You'll have to be numerate as well for the next hour, my dear. Now count!'

He delivered the first arm-extended slap. Emma yelped, then belatedly shouted, 'One, sir!'

'Respond faster next time.'

'Two! Three! Four! Five! Six!'

'Now a little rest, because I'm annoyed with you, and I know that it'll hurt more when I start again.' He fondled her raised extremities whilst she wriggled and whimpered over his trousered lap. The fact that he was still fully dressed made her feel even more vulnerable. Made her want to unzip him and unbutton him, and slide her warm hands along his chest ...

'Seven!' she howled, a few minutes later. Something hard was digging into the softness of her belly. The swine was getting off on this! But then so was she . . .

'Eight! Nine!'

If she could just get her crotch a little further over so that the tip of his suit-clad cock went into her crevice. She pushed herself up a little, slithered along, pushed down.

'Ten!' she yelled, the cry part-triumphant as she felt him nudge against the entrance to her sex.

Vincent Mearns shuddered. Emma took a deep breath. Put shy slow fingers over his concealed erection.

'Sir, I've caused you cost and inconvenience. If I could make amends?'

'Such as?'

Did she have to spell it out? The man sure knew how to shame a girl!

'I could . . . take you inside me. I'd go on top, do all the work. I swear!'

'I suppose I could amuse myself . . .' He hitched her further over his knee. 'But given that the *horses* are the ones you've really wronged, I've got a better sexual position,' he said.

He pulled himself back, and hauled her fully on to the bed.

'Get on your hands and knees. I think they usually call it doggy style or monkey-fucking, but you look as much like a mare as anything else.'

Wincing, and unable to make eye contact again, Emma did as he ordered. At least he's stopped chastising her! If she became the boss's favourite, she could get some perks out of this yet.

'Like this?' she asked obsequiously, aiming for innocence.

'Don't play the shy virgin. Get that arse raised further. Push it back.'

Staring at the headboard, she did as he demanded. Felt the heat of his belly move against her own heated arse. Felt his palms cupping her tits, thumbing the nipples into renewed lilt of life, into rigour.

'The horse has a nice pair of reins, though she lacks a saddle and bridle,' he said.

She was oiled and open. He seemed to know. He slid in and in and in until he reached the crown of her.

'God, you feel brilliant!' Emma gasped.

'The animal enjoyed being mated,' Mearns said in a cool voice. He edged his cock out a little way, until she desperately squirmed back against it. 'And didn't have to be tethered to the stall.'

He ran an experienced hand over her flanks and underneath to her tummy. Thrust at a steady rhythm as he moulded his palm to her pubic patch, kept the pressure there.

'Push against my hand.'

Her arms and thighs taut as they were, the command was too awkward.

'I can't . . .'

Her elbows couldn't stay straight any longer and the front half of her body sagged, so that she put her head down on her now-folded arms, her backside still hugely raised, thighs tautening.

'The animal lacks a strong skeletal structure or hasn't learned to follow all instructions yet,' continued her seasonal boss, thrusting, thrusting. 'A session with the riding crop may be required.'

'Please. I want . . .'

It was becoming hard to think about anything other than the quivering sensitive bliss intensifying in her crotch.

'Its genitals showed normal response.'

He put a finger tip on her slippery slit and she cried out, rubbed hungrily against the contact.

'Oh yes, sir! Like that, sir!'

'If the mare gets too excited the trainer will pull back.'

The very uncertainty of the situation was making her more aroused, more clit-craving, urgent. Sex on the back seat of Steve's car had never been like this! She'd never felt so taken over, so depraved, so open. Cried out in disappointment as Vincent Mearns grunted into her shoulder, and palpated her pleasured bust, and shudderingly came.

Would he stop now? She was so close . . .

'I need it!'

He kept driving forward. Brushed his fingertips over her clit till she thought she'd drown his prick, she felt so wet.

'Oh yes! Oh yes! Oh . . .'

Teased and taunted and almost, almost, almost.

'Oh, uh, ah. Aaaaaaaaah!'

Her nipples tingled, her clit twitched. She shoved her pudenda against his probing fingers, and after a build-up that was almost as charged as the actual orgasm, her body convulsed into erotic ecstasy.

'Donation complete!' she whispered, collapsing flat out on her belly and taking the administrator with her. After a few moments, she edged her way out from under him, turned on her side so that she was facing his still-suited body, touched his hair. She wanted to kiss his lips, wondered if she dared make the first move. He was still so much more powerful than she, so ruthlessly effective at mastering each new situation. Ruthless in mastering her pleasure too, the teasing pig!

But he'd shot from the hip, and a man with well-milked balls was often an amicable man.

'Forgiven?' she murmured, smiling.

'Let's just say I never forget.'

'But I've done penance for –'

'Done *partial* penance for. You're still due ten spanks that I didn't get round to earlier.'

'But I thought . . .' She tailed off.

'You thought what?'

He'd accuse her of blackmail, prostitution, if he thought she'd been bargaining sexual favours.

'Nothing.'

'Nothing, *sir*.' He sighed. 'Your thoughts are still far too disjointed. Time you learned some lucid reflection over my knee.'

He zipped up his pants. He looked calm, assured. Her face was flushed, her thighs were soaked, her bum was hectic. He swung his legs easily over the side of the bed, and looked pointedly at her, then at his lap.

231

'Leanne, Shona and Karen kept to their quotas, so I should really thrash you in front of them, show what happens to slackers.'

'No! Please!'

'Won't you ever learn? You've just earned five more spanks for your second bout of procrastination,' Mearns said.

'But it's Christmas!'

She laid her belly over his knees. Resistance was useless.

'Think of this as your Christmas cracker!'

Mearns' hand cracked down.

Emma squealed, 'The boss usually gives the staff a present!'

'Hang up these long black stockings on the floor over there and I'll fill each with a whip.'

'What about my festive bonus?' she wailed, determined to have the last word.

'It'll be yours in the next twenty minutes, my dear,' said Vincent Mearns, his cock hardening again.

A Taste for Pain

Aha! Kay Reid sat up straighter in her chair as she heard
the floorboards on the stairway creaking. Someone was obviously sneaking downstairs. Experience told her they had
to be making their surreptitious way towards the kitchen.
A kitchen which was out of bounds to everyone except the
dishwasher and the chef. For days now he'd been complaining that ingredients were going missing. She'd been
right to stay awake and on guard.

Leisurely, Kay stretched out her tennis-toned arms, then
tiptoed towards her bedroom door, the mirror showing her
five-foot-eight frame in the khaki shirt and matching army
surplus trousers. Heart starting to beat harder, she flexed
her firm right spanking palm.

As owner of Trim Camp, she'd found that keeping discipline sometimes involved more than an inspirational
lecture. A couple of stinging slaps to the back of some
eighteen-year-old's thighs was usually enough to take the
over-eater's mind off food. A shaming spank to a jean-clad
rump usually shocked the girl into more sensible snacking,
the option being going to college in the autumn still looking fat.

She, Kay, was there to see that they got slim. That's why
they had enrolled at Trim Camp. Why they or their parents
had paid sizeable numbers of dollars to base them here
near Los Angeles for twelve whole weeks. Kay talked to
them and watched over them and weighed them. She was
the British slimming leader who'd got first-class results
here in the States.

And would continue to do so! Kicking open the kitchen

door and turning on the light in one co-ordinated move, she took in a breath and got ready to shout at her failing teenage slimmer. Felt her mouth slacken as she saw who the culprit was. '*Lynnette!*' Lynnette, a fellow Brit, was her recently appointed junior diet lecturer. She had already ticked the girl off for weighing more than she should have on Weigh-In Day.

Kay stared at her trainee, who stood clutching three centimetre-thick slices of cheddar. The large multi-grain loaf, pound of butter and jar of pickles on the kitchen worktop told of her plans. 'Sorry – sudden snack attack!' she muttered, reddening.

'According to the chef, you've been having them every night.'

'I've . . .' The girl rubbed one bare foot behind an equally bare suntanned leg. Her thigh-length white lace nightie rose even further at the awkward movement, showing her naked cheeks. 'Well, the dinners have been small recently . . .'

'And I've told you to make a second trip to the salad bar,' Kay interrupted, 'What am I always telling the girls? Choose fibre over fat!'

'Sorry, Miss Reid. I am – really.' The girl turned to put the cheddar and butter away.

'No – leave them out. I want you to look at them while you're being punished.' She let the younger woman dwell on the humiliating words. Would she acquiesce? She, Kay, doled out sly slaps and spanks whenever the situation merited it, but this would be the first time she'd given a sound thrashing to a staff member aged twenty-two.

She stared at the blonde girl's slightly rounded tummy and made her voice unimpeachable, hard. 'What happens if you get plump?'

The younger woman swallowed. 'I . . . get sent home, miss.'

'Yes, you do.'

'Don't want to go home!'

'Then what do you think we should do with you?'

'You could . . .' The girl spread out her palms helplessly. 'I won't do it again!'

'But stealing and stealth still deserve chastisement.'

'Please forgive me!' The diet lecturer dipped her head.

'What you need is a good spanking,' Kay added. She glared at her employee and held her breath. Watched the hot shame redden the girl's face and neck and stay there. It was time to go for it!

Kay took hold of the wooden armless chair and pulled it out into the centre of the room. She sat down and patted her lap with obvious inference. 'Now get that over-indulgent little bum over my knee!'

'You can't mean . . .'

The junior lecturer took a step back, stopped, stared at Kay's hands, her lap, met her eyes for a panicked second.

'Or go home tomorrow morning, if you prefer.'

'But I love it here!'

'Then accept due penalty for breaking a Camp Trim rule.'

'It was only a sandwich.'

'A nightly diet-breaking sandwich. Leave now without a reference if you prefer.'

'For a moment's weakness?'

'A sore bottom will encourage you to be stronger.'

'But no one's ever spanked me before!'

'Mm, it shows.'

The girl hadn't yet fled. Now Kay had to make her approach. 'Get over here now before I phone the airport and book a seat for you.'

Lynnette put her hands behind her back, then brought them forward, moved from the ball of one bare foot to another. 'What if another camp member comes in?'

'The kitchen's out of bounds, so they'd be transgressing too. I suppose I'd have to spank you both one after the other.'

'You mean you've done this before?' Lynnette's eyes were wide and fixed and slightly glassy.

'Mm, frequently. More often than I'd have liked.'

That last sentence was a lie. She loved to feel a young firm female bottom under her hands, adored making the flesh jerk and redden. Ached with desire as she found her rhythm and caused the owner of the bum to emit little squeals and louder cries. Enjoyed everything from the first moment when she pulled down their panties and told them what she was going to do to their helpless buttocks, to the last seconds when she let them slide, whimpering, from her knee.

'I'm going to use the wooden spoon on you for being slow. That's after your spanking for breaking our kitchen rules, of course. If you don't come over here now I'll have to fetch you, and that equals an ever sorer bum.'

'If you'd lock the door –'

'No, bad girls have to take their chances.' She patted her lap again. 'All this procrastination's earning you the hottest time.'

Lynnette glanced at the door. She stared at the food she'd removed from the fridge. She looked at the big notice on the wall which warned slimmers that they'd lose privileges for dietary transgressions. Slowly she approached her superior, her bare feet dragging on the warm floor.

'There!' Kay took hold of the girl's nerveless wrists. 'That wasn't so difficult.' She started the controlling sideways pull that would win her this pouting blonde victim, get her positioned and held defencelessly in place.

'Now get that disobedient young arse across my lap.'

She hauled the junior lecturer down and manoeuvred her till she was fully stretched out across her knees. Caught sight of them both in the chrome panel of the cooker door. She, Kay, looked strong and slightly sturdy, her short auburn hair and large dark eyes giving her a look of control, of especial presence. The girl over her lap had a fair-haired slender prettiness of a more traditional kind.

'Right, let's get that arse warmed,' Kay said, looking down at the bum curves outlined by the nightdress.

'You won't do it too hard?' The words were a half gasp, half whisper, a frightened plea. A plea that was going to be ignored, wasted.

'Oh, I'll do it very hard indeed.'

Kay slid a roving palm beneath the lacy garment and stroked the girl's twitching rear until she trembled. 'How

236

fortuitous – you aren't wearing any knickers! Maybe you secretly wanted to be caught and given a thorough thrashing. Do you think that's true?' She squeezed more strongly at the still-hidden prize, watching the back of the blonde girl's neck pinken with embarrassment.

'I . . . no!'

'You mean you wanted to eat forbidden food? To put on weight? To ruin my reputation? Dear me, I do have a lot to flog out of this betraying backside!'

She raised her hand and laid on a firm left cheek spank over the nightdress. 'Ouch!' Lynnette exhaled hard, and reached both hands back to cover both her chastened and not-yet-chastened nether orbs.

'Bad girl. I didn't give you permission to touch your bum,' Kay murmured, glad of the excuse to discipline her young charge further. 'You've left me no option but to tie these wicked little hands out of the way.'

Slowly she leaned back, enjoying the girl's nervous squirming, and unbuckled the calfskin belt from her waist. 'Right, let's get these protective fingers held in front of you.' She used the belt to bind the girl's wrists together. 'You have to learn to take your punishment without complaint.'

Lynnette gave an experimental tug at her bonds. 'But it stung! You did it so hard!'

'Of course it stung – that's my intention. And it's going to make your arse ache much much more. We'll start by baring this wicked rear.' Kay pulled the thin nightdress up her victim's back and tucked it under her armpits. Then she contemplated the bottom she'd just bared – a bottom that was small and taut and frenzied. The handprint she'd made on one sunlamp-goldened cheek was already fading. Kay flexed her fingers then slapped smartly down on the other helpless orb.

'Ow!' Lynnette was halfway through another squeal when the older woman doled out five full force spanks on alternate buttocks. Buttocks which writhed and pushed forward and arched backwards and moved sideways and jerked.

'Save your histrionics till you feel the wooden spoon on your backside,' Kay said, spanking on and on and on, glad that her hours in the gym had lent her right arm such power. She was going to show this bum that she, Kay, was the one in charge!

After a few spank-intensive moments she stopped to fondle the glowing trophy and to tell its wriggling owner what she was going to do to her next.

'Is your bottom hot now, Lynnette?'

A humiliated whimper: 'Yes, miss!'

'And I'll bet you're not hungry any more.'

'No, Miss Reid!' The girl sounded small and eager to please and breathless.

'Which shows that spanking you is good therapy, don't you think?'

There was a pause. Kay stroked the hot pink globes some more. 'Answer me, girl, or you'll make my right arm even angrier.'

'I . . .' Each syllable sounded dragged from her. 'Suppose you were right to spank me, Miss Reid.'

Kay ran her left thumbpad over the backs of the girl's thighs. '*Were* right to spank you? That's past tense, suggests that I've finished. Believe me, my dear, I've hardly started yet.'

She watched the girl's shoulders tense, heard and felt the shuddering indrawn breath. 'But my bottom's so sore, miss!'

'I can see that it is!'

The camp leader caressed the well-warmed fleshy sphere. 'But I have to teach you discipline, and a few light slaps will hardly do that, dear. I need to know you've learned total obedience and self-respect.'

The fellow-Brit swallowed. 'I won't steal food again! I'll fill up on salad. I'll be obedient, miss.'

'A good walloping will make sure of that, will remind you of the penalty for breaking rank here at Camp Trim.' Kay had been in the army long before she'd made it to the top on Civvy Street. She knew how to re-educate a young recruit, how to mould her into snivelling subservience. 'I have to administer a thrashing that will remain in your memory for ever,' she continued.

'Please, no more spanks!' Lynnette begged.

'Very well, we'll progress to using the spoon on your naughty bum.'

'No! I didn't mean –'

'I'd planned to spank you for, say, twenty minutes, then use the spoon for another ten or so,' the Leader said quietly. She ran a thoughtful hand over the blonde girl's squirming cheeks. 'Now you're telling me that you need harder discipline, that you want things the other way round?'

'That wasn't what – I mean, my rear end's so sore!'

Kay squeezed each scarlet globe. 'You're not welshing on the deal, are you? I thought you agreed to a spanking and a beating with the wooden spoon as an alternative to being sent home?'

'I did! I do! I . . .' The younger girl slumped more heavily over the older woman's knee.

'Then stop complaining and thank me for this spanking.' Kay doled out four ferocious spanks. 'Thank me now!'

'Th . . . thank you for spanking me, Miss Reid.'

'You're very welcome. And tell me you're looking forward to the session with the wooden spoon.'

She fondled the new-heated bum flesh as she said the words, revelling in the warmth she'd just added. The junior slimming leader seemed to be lost for words. Her glowing bottom spoke volumes, though, shouted its message to its tormentor. It tried to flinch away in shame and uncertainty and fear.

'Tell me,' Kay repeated.

'I'm . . . oh, please, miss, I'm sorry I stole food from the Camp, miss!'

'Say it or I may have to fetch my hard-soled slippers. And I have such big feet!'

The punished red posterior trembled. The front half breathed hard and fast. 'I'm looking forward to the session with the wooden spoon, miss.'

'So am I, sweetheart,' Kay said.

She slid her right hand between the girl's labial lips. Her fingers came away coated with gelatinous pleasure. Lynnette moaned with what Kay presumed was uncertainty and lust. 'Your cunt's getting ever so hot,' she said crudely. Let her pussy beg a little. 'But the only part I'm interested in roasting is your arse.'

She smiled to herself as Lynnette hung her head nearer the floor in shame. The girl had given up tugging at her wrist bonds for now and seemed resigned to the remainder of her spanking. Kay laid it on hard, but not as hard as she was capable of. She was pacing herself, pacing the helpless bottom beneath her right palm. She wanted to leave some of the girl's spirit and energy intact for when she tasted the more focused pain of the spoon.

When the junior leader's indrawn breaths grew closer to sobs, Kay stopped. 'Let's have a little talk about your diet. What does eating too much butter do to the female bottom?'

'It makes it bigger, miss.'

'And you want a small high bum, don't you, Lynnette? A bum that both men and women will admire?'

'I . . . yes.'

'So walk over to the table and put the butter back in the fridge.' She untied the girl's wrist bonds and watched Lynnette get up slowly from her lap. Her movements were stiff and uncoordinated. Lynnette stood facing her for a second, then pulled her nightdress down over her punished bottom and turned towards the table top.

'No – keep your nightdress under your arms. I haven't finished with that wilful small *derrière*.'

'But if someone comes in, they'll see!'

'We've covered this ground before. It'll be worse for your backside if we repeat such a boring discussion. You'll just take your chances.' But the nightdress stayed down and Lynnette's hands stayed by her side.

Kay got up and strode purposefully across the room. Grabbing the girl's right arm, she used her other hand to inch the lace right up. 'Now hold it there or I'll have you back in Leeds before you can say the words *sacked for gross misconduct.*' Lynnette obediently tightened her arms around the nightdress and dipped her head.

'Where were we? Ah yes, you were going to put the butter in the fridge.' Lynnette followed the instruction immediately.

Kay looked at the cheddar. 'Any comments about its calorific value?'

'A little goes a long way, miss.'

'If only the same were true of punishing a recalcitrant backside,' Kay said. 'What I've found is that the harder you thrash young women, the more they respect you. The more prolonged the lecture and punishment, the longer it remains in the naughty girl's mind.'

'Yes, miss.' Lynnette stared glassily at the floor.

'That's why I'm going to make this thrashing last a considerable time, with lots of reflection between the strokes to remind you of its object.'

'I understand, Miss Reid.'

Kay looked searchingly round the room. 'So I think we'll have you bent over the fridge, my dear. Don't you think that's fitting?'

'I ...' The blonde girl shrugged nervously and her mouth turned even further down. She stared at the window and the door as if seeking escape. Kay walked round till she was facing the girl's bottom and was pleased to see it jiggling. Lynnette looked nervously over her shoulder at her camp leader, but stayed in place.

'Get that belly on top of the fridge, arms and legs hanging down. No matter how hard the strokes, you mustn't get up without permission.'

Lynnette looked at the smooth white top, then at her superior. 'Oh please!'

'You'd rather go over my knee again first?'

'No, it's not that. It's ... A spoon? Will it sting as much as your hand?' She put both palms tearfully over her punished bottom.

'You'll just have to take your birching and find out,' Kay said.

'I'm never going to overeat again,' Lynnette continued in a small pleading voice.

'Good girl. Now get your belly over that fridge and stick out your bottom.'

'I'll exercise more in the gym. I'll give up sweets completely.'

'Sounds somewhat unbalanced. Now present your naked cheeks for the rest of their punishment, please.'

'I've said I'll be good!'

Kay walked to the far wall and took down the large decorative spoon. 'This will make you better.'

The girl took a step backwards. 'No it won't!'

Kay smiled pitilessly. 'Well, it'll make *me* feel better. And if I feel good I'm less likely to tell the rest of the camp about how you've let us down, my sweet.' She ran the thick spoon through her hands. 'If you're a good girl I'm less likely to dismiss you. Now, what's it to be?'

The girl looked at Kay. She looked at the fridge. After another few seconds she walked over to it and put her hands to the centre of the side surfaces. Then she gave a little jump and let her weight take her forward so that her bum was a perfect target for the wooden spoon.

'There, that wasn't so hard.' Kay fondled the bum, enjoying its new humiliated display. 'Looks very tempting. Looks like it's just begging for this kitchen alternative to the cane.'

Lynnette whimpered. The sound seemed to come from very far away. It was from the head, of course, which was obviously feeling very sorry for itself and dreading what was coming. But Kay just wanted to concentrate on warming the arse.

She lined up the spoon with the underswell of the girl's rump and swung the implement forward. The twenty-two-year-old yelled and started to push herself back and down.

'That's bad. That's very bad.' Kay stepped forward and cupped the girl's buttocks, cradling them like she would a frightened animal. 'You don't want me to have to start all over again?'

'No – not that!' Lynnette looked wildly round, then used her arms to propel herself fully over the fridge again. The camp leader contemplated her handiwork: the lower curve

242

of one spank-reddened cheek showed the first precise lash of the spoon. 'Let's make these cheeks nice and symmetrical,' she murmured gloatingly before laying on a second above-thigh stroke.

'Aaah!' The junior lecturer flinched, and drove her belly closer against the fridge. She drummed her toes against its door. Kay could hear but not see the scrabbling noises made by her fingers. They obviously wanted to propel her away from this torment, to at least cover her punished posterior, whereas her brain was warning her to get the thrashing over with, to stay in place.

Her brain was obviously winning – at least for now. Kay moved the spoon up a centimetre, and got ready to use it like a mini-paddle again. She was more familiar with using her hand or a belt, but was determined to try and make the individual scarlet marks become fairly uniform.

'My friends at the other camp like to make their charges' bottoms as striped as possible,' she told Lynnette. 'They love the distinction between the hot red cane marks and the cool white surrounding flesh.' She smiled as her victim wriggled with shame. 'I'm not adverse to caning a few narrow pink bands on to a naughty girl's bottom myself, but I prefer to create a roasting red arse.'

This particular arse was halfway there. Kay whacked the implement above the previous glowing stroke then immediately added a fourth parallel mark to the other buttock. Lynnette howled and swung her feet around but otherwise stayed in place. 'Now where shall I put marks five and six? Oh, I know, up here where it's feeling neglected.' Kay stepped forward to tauntingly stroke the expanse of spanked-but-not-yet-paddled flesh.

'Oh, it hurts, it hurts!' Lynnette wailed. Her sex lips were wetly swollen, obviously begging for liberation. So was her backside.

'Just a few more to go,' Kay said. Part of her wanted to warm this pert bum for ever, but the girl was more likely to acquiesce to further thrashings if her pain threshold wasn't over-reached.

She added lashes five and six where she'd indicated that

she would, and swiftly followed them up with seven and eight towards the top of the luckless girl's posterior. Lynnette cried out and pushed herself off the fridge. Holding her small crimson cheeks in both palms, face flushed and eyes downcast, she backed away.

'You've done well,' Kay said. Lynnette faltered, then looked over at her. Kay approached very slowly. 'I'd almost finished, dear.'

'I just couldn't bear . . .'

'I know. I know.' She looked over at the sink as if the idea had just occurred to her. 'Look, there's that cold cream the dishwasher uses to soften her hands. I could use some to cool your toasted backside.'

Lynnette's hot face reddened further. 'Please, no. I . . . could do it myself!'

'Are you refusing my generous offer, then?'

The twenty-two-year-old swallowed hard. 'I guess . . . it's just the thought of another woman touching me intimately.'

'Yet you were happy enough for me to spank you!'

'I didn't want to be sent away.'

'Of course you didn't,' Kay said. 'It's cold back in England compared to here. The food isn't as varied. Opportunities for promotion are considerably less.'

The girl nodded.

'Which is why you want to stay here. Want to please your camp leader. Are very grateful when she offers to soothe your punished bum.'

Kay patted the kitchen table. 'Put your tummy over there, my love.' Lynnette looked at the furniture. Looked more quickly at Kay. Moved very slowly towards her bottom's next ordeal as if expecting to be rescued. Was just settling her belly obediently in place when Kay recrossed the room with the cream.

'It's an awfully red rump,' the camp leader murmured, caressing the trembling smooth globes. Lynnette twitched in mute but vociferous agreement. 'So you'll be very grateful to Auntie Kay for massaging in some coolness,' the older woman continued, taking a golfball-sized globule of

244

cream and starting to massage it into the reddened rump. She used slow but firm strokes – *erotic* strokes. Felt her own groin expand as the girl breathed fast and hard.

Kay kept using her right hand to knead the ointment into the girl's bum. She slid her left digits between the girl's parted thighs. 'This is just to hold you steady.' Smiled in power and anticipation as her squirming victim started to rub her clit against Kay's hand just as she'd known she would. 'Such a sore bottom,' she continued, rubbing the emollient between the writhing cheeks. 'So *wriggly*. Especially when I massage this dividing crack.'

'Mmh!' Lynnette muttered. Her voice tone was something alien and hoarse.

'Did you say something?' Kay asked conversationally, feeling the girl move slicker, wilder, harder. 'Say that you were ready to take the rest of that paddling on your arse?'

'Mm. Uh. Aah . . .' Lynnette gasped out.

Kay scooped more cream into the sensitive crease and stroked on and on and on, loving the way the girl's sore bum quivered, exulting in her little desperate moans. Suddenly the clit beneath her fingers was pushed even more frantically forward and its owner cried out long and gutturally:

'*Aaaaaaaaah!*' A minuscule pause till the next rush of rapture obviously took over her desperate body: 'Aaaaaaaaah! Aaaaaaaaaah! Aaaaaaaaah! Aaaaaaaah! Aaaaaaah!'

Screams over, she gave a series of little grunts, pushed her thighs tight together, then lay, prostrate, across the table. 'Oh dear,' Kay murmured, 'I give you a motherly respite from your much-needed rebuke and you repay me by indulging in an unnatural act.'

'I . . . But your fingers were . . .' Lynnette muttered into the table. Kay picked up the spoon and used it four times in quick succession on the girl's anointed rear to bring her flagging energy back. Lynnette wailed and squirmed quickly away. Sex juice leaked on to the area beneath her. Sheepishly she got up and took hold of her hem as if to pull her nightie down.

'No, leave it there so that I have access to your bum whilst you make amends.'

Make amends? I thought I'd . . .'

'It's the least you can do, don't you think?'

'I guess,' Lynnette muttered.

'Good girl. Now get your tongue over here.'

Praying that the girl would bring her satisfaction, Kay undid her army surplus trousers and edged them to her knees. Still staring at Lynnette, she did the same with her crotch thong. Then she sat down in the chair and spread her legs into an expectant V.

'I'm not a lesbian, Miss Reid!' Lynnette stammered.

'Darling, you just came against my fingers.'

'But . . .'

'Would you rather feel that spoon against your cheeks again?'

'God, no!'

'I mean, technically we hadn't finished.'

'It's just . . . I've never . . .'

'Pretend I'm a man, then,' Kay replied.

'And you won't tell anyone?' The girl looked round the room.

'It'll be our little secret. You've taken a licking and now you're going to give a different kind of licking back!'

Lynnette blushed at the older woman's words and stood, clutching her nightie-hem under her armpits. 'Now get that hot little rump across the room.'

She smiled as the girl neared her chair, exulted inwardly as she knelt before her. 'I like a fast light pressure. Put the tip of your tongue directly on my clit.' Groaned as wet tissue met wet tissue: she was almost there already. Doling out that spanking and paddling on such a fair bum had been all the foreplay she needed. Just a few flickering licks . . .

'Up a bit, sweetheart. Make sure you get it right, or I'll have to teach you. Have you ever had a big studded belt lashing down on your poor bare bottom? No? It's not too late.' Tensed her thighs as the pleasure started to peak. 'You'd never be able to bear it without restraint, of course. I'd have to tie your arms and legs over the tallest stool.'

Her groin swelled at the image. 'Have to prepare your

bum first with a sound slippering, then gag you so that you couldn't beg for help or start squealing.' Heard her own half-strangled scream coming from somewhere above her head as the ecstasy flowed through her throbbing pubes. Moaning, she grabbed the blonde girl's head and held it there to make sure she kept licking. Finally slumped back in her chair.

When she opened her eyes a moment later, Lynnette was still crouching on the floor. 'Stand up. Bend over. Let me look at your chastened arse, my fallen angel.'

The girl's lids fluttered down in embarrassment, but she obeyed. Kay stared at the bent cheeks of pain, at the wet trails of pleasure. 'You can go. Your punishment is over. Obviously I'm trusting you not to transgress again.'

'I won't, miss. I swear!'

'Good girl. Then go to bed. Tomorrow, life will go on as normal.'

'Yes, Miss Reid!' Lynnette walked towards the door with unusually stiffenend thighs.

'And you can pull your nightie down.'

The girl gingerly smoothed the pale lace over the crimson hemispheres. 'Yes, miss. And ... thanks.'

The door closed. The stairs creaked. After a moment Kay heard the girl go into her room. Then silence. Slowly she got to her feet and pulled up her crotch thong and army trousers. Thoughtfully she picked up the wooden spoon.

When would she have a chance to use it again? There was this particularly impish twenty-year-old redhead had just started at the camp as games mistress. She must use up lots of calories on the playing fields. Which meant she'd be hungry if the dinners were small and might try to sneak extra rations, midnight treats.

Kay smiled as she buffed the hard punishing oval of the spoon. She'd tell chef to heap lots of meat and veg on Lynnette's plate for a change, but to give the games mistress half rations. She wondered how much of a thrashing a well-exercised bum could bear before it turned scarlet and its owner started to beg.